DEDICATION

As always, this book is dedicated to my Lord and Savior, Jesus Christ. I would also like to dedicate this book to all the people over the last 25 years who have served with me on mission trips to Mexico, Ireland and Guatemala. It has been an honor and privilege. Each of you made those trips a blessing to me even in the midst of the many challenges we endured. I believe there were many more blessings than challenges. Each of you taught me much and loved me well. Most of all, I loved seeing what God did with each of us as we served Him on these trips and how He used us to bless the people we served. I am thankful for each of you.

Angie Pearson loves writing Christian fiction mystery, suspense and romance. The Women of Heart series comes from her heart for women and her desire to see them embrace their faith, find their identity in being daughters of the King of all creation and walk in a manner worthy of that calling living their lives to God's glory in all circumstances. Angie has been blessed to be the wife of John for the past 43 years and the mother of their three wonderful sons. She cherishes a special relationship with each of her three daughters-in-law and revels in being "Gigi" to her four adorable grandchildren. She loves every minute she spends with them! All she can say is "to God be the glory!"

Books by Angela Pearson

Women of Heart
Ellie's Faith
Holly's Heart

Devotional
Knowing My Father, a 30 Day Devotional
on the Character of God

www.hisspringsoflife.wordpress.com

HOLLY'S HEART

ANGELA PEARSON

PROLOGUE

As Miguel sat counting his money with two of his men he wondered how he could stop the "do-gooders" from coming to his streets and trying to help the people by teaching them about this guy Jesus who would supposedly save them. After these "do-gooders" persisted in visiting his streets, the people on the street started giving Miguel trouble until he decided to use some of them as examples of what would happen to those who wouldn't obey him. He especially wanted Gabriel to see that he was the only one who could take care of these people.

"Raoul, someday an opportunity will come when we can get rid of these "church people" once and for all. We have to be patient and wait for the right opportunity." Raoul nodded his head and looked at Julio. They both knew Miguel hated the "church people".

Gabriel peeked around the corner and listened to their conversation. He liked it when the "do-gooders" came to the streets and talked about Jesus. Their stories made him feel good and there wasn't much Gabriel felt good about in his life. Miguel was teaching him all about business on the street so that one day Gabriel would take it over from him. When Gabriel didn't obey or run drugs like Miguel ordered him to do, Miguel would beat him to teach him a lesson. Soon Gabriel learned to obey even if he knew in his heart it was wrong to be doing the things Miguel required.

Miguel gave Julio and Raoul their take of the money as they got up to leave. Gabriel backed up so they wouldn't see him as they walked out the door. He hoped that getting this money from Julio and Raoul would put Miguel in a good mood this evening so that he wouldn't be mean to Gabriel.

"Gabriel," Miguel yelled.

"Si, Miguel", Gabriel said coming from around the corner.

"I am going out with the guys and will not be home this evening." He walked toward Gabriel, grabbed his shirt and said, "You stay put. I do not want you to leave here until I get back tomorrow. Do you understand?" Miguel's face was inches from Gabriel's face.

"Si, Miguel".

Miguel walked out the door and Gabriel breathed a sigh of relief. This would be a night where he could sleep peacefully knowing that Miguel was gone.

CHAPTER 1

"Aunt Howy, can Katie have shomore shookies, pease?" asked Katie all wide eyed while licking her chocolate covered fingers.

Holly lovingly looked at her three year old niece. Katie looked so much like Micah with her dark hair and dimples. It was fun to listen to her as she learned to talk. Many of Katie's words started with the "sh" sound so sometimes she had to figure out what Katie was saying. With a smile in her eyes, Holly walked over to the cookie sheet on the stove, got another cookie and handed it to Katie saying, "That's it or you'll burst if you eat anymore." Holly bent over and gave her a kiss on the cheek.

"But they sho good and brover would like me have his. He too wittle to eat shookies", she replied with her dimples showing.

Holly laughed at Katie's words. She thought of Caleb upstairs in the crib taking a nap. Her brother, Micah, and his wife, Ellie, didn't get time away from the kids often so she took advantage of the opportunities to babysit whenever possible.

"I'm sure he would love for you to have his cookie, but I know he wouldn't want you to burst either. Then he wouldn't have a big sister anymore."

Katie giggled. Aunt Howy, shat no happen. You sho funny." She licked her fingers when Holly snatched her out of the chair and twirled her around showering kisses all over her little face.

"You are so cute, Katie. I could kiss you all day. Let's go wash your hands and face and then you'll be ready for some quiet time in your room. Your mom said you like listening to your tape and looking at the book that goes with it."

"Okay, Katie shisten to Noah and Ark."

"Alright then, let's go."

Holly finished washing Katie, took her up to her room and got her settled in for a rest. She checked on Caleb before going downstairs to clean up the kitchen.

After cleaning the kitchen, Holly grabbed her book and went into the family room. She loved this room because it had a great view of the rolling hills behind her brother's house. Over the years, her favorite thing to do was riding her horse over those hills. There were a couple of long, meandering streams with a waterfall or two where she enjoyed sitting and meditating on life.

She was so glad when Micah and Ellie decided to build their home on the land her mom gave them as a wedding gift. They quickly developed house plans and got started shortly after their marriage a few years ago. She loved that she and her mom lived on the same land just down the hill about a hundred yards from each other.

In designing their house, Micah and Ellie wanted the family room facing the mountains with a large, plate glass window that took up half the wall. It gave you a beautiful view of the mountains. Looking out the large window, Holly thought back to the time five years ago when Ellie entered their lives. She'd lost her parents in a car accident and came to spend the summer with her aunt and uncle, Dave and Maggie Saxton. When Ellie and

Micah met, Holly didn't know if it was love at first sight, but they sure liked each other from the beginning. They started seeing a lot of each other as time went by.

Nobody knew the danger Ellie was in because of her dad's job with the CIA. Fortunately, everything turned out alright and the CIA caught the guys responsible for her parents' death. Sometime later, Micah and Ellie got married; later Katie came along and was named after Ellie's mom, Catherine, and her cousin, Blair, who died a few years ago. Then earlier this year Caleb was born. What a blessing Ellie was to her as a sister-in-law. They really enjoyed each other's company. Her brother, Micah, was a great husband and father. Holly's heart wanted what God wanted for her so she prayed often that God would bless her with a godly man when the time was right.

With a sigh of contentment, Holly went over to the couch to read until Micah and Ellie returned. They had a church meeting and since it was Saturday she didn't have to work. Holly was only too happy to watch the kids. Usually she and her mom wrestled over who would take care of the kids, but her mom had to be a part of the church meeting, so Holly won out this time.

Micah and Ellie came home later that day to find Holly napping on the couch. They quietly tiptoed into the room at the same time Katie came walking down the stairs. Her eyes lit up when she saw her parents. She put her finger to her mouth to let them know they needed to be quiet and then she pointed to her sleeping aunt. Then she softly ran over to her dad and leaped into his arms.

"Hi Daddy, gad you shome," she whispered into Micah's ear. She looked over at her aunt and continued,

"Daddy, Aunt Howy tired," smiling and wrapping her arms tightly around her dad.

"Hi sweetie", her mom said. Katie leaned over for her mom to take her and give her a kiss.

Katie still whispered, "Hi mama, Katie had fun with Aunt Howy. We made shookies and she give Katie two. She said Katie burst. Brover too wittle so Aunt Howy said okay for Katie to eat his. Yummy in my tummy mama," Katie said rubbing her hand over her belly. She giggled and snuggled closer to her mom.

"I can't wait to taste one of your cookies. I bet they are really good! I'm sure glad you didn't have any more than two cookies because we would miss you if you burst," Ellie said with a twinkle in her eye as she looked at her husband. Katie laughed as her mom started tickling her.

Holly stirred as Katie laughed. She stretched out her arms and looked over at them.

"I guess I was more tired than I realized. All the work we've been doing preparing for this Mexico trip is more exhausting than I remember from previous years."

"I'm sorry we woke you, Holly," Ellie said as she snuggled with Katie in the chair. "I couldn't help tickling Katie after she told me about the possibility of her bursting from eating too many cookies. How was Caleb?"

"Great. He should be waking up any time now."

After hanging up their coats in the closet, Micah asked, "How are the preparations for the trip coming? Do you have all the money you need for the trip?"

"We sure do. We reached our goal after last month's fundraiser but we decided to do one more chicken barbecue next week to have some extra money to take with us as a donation to the church in Mexico."

Ellie took Katie into the kitchen for a drink so Micah and Holly followed. Ellie continued the conversation. "How many people are on the team this year?"

Eating a cookie after giving one to Micah, Holly responded, "There are four team leaders and six college kids. Pastor Bill is our leader, Jeff and Becca Paxton, and me. I think it's a great team!" Micah and Ellie saw the excitement in Holly as she told them about the trip.

"I've forgotten when you will be leaving," Micah said as he got some fruit from the refrigerator.

"We leave in two weeks, July 5th and return August 5th. It's a longer trip than what we've taken in the past because there's more construction work that can't be finished within the normal two weeks plus we will work with the Mexican children. We don't want to start something and not finish it, so we hope to get everything done within the month."

After putting Katie down, Ellie got some meat out of the freezer. "It sounds wonderful, Holly. Someday Micah and I hope to be able to go on one of these summer short term mission trips to Mexico. I would love to work with the children doing bible school. Is that what you will be doing with the children?"

Holly nodded as she grabbed her coat off the kitchen chair. "We sure are and we will be working with street people as well. I'm really looking forward to that part of the trip. It's something I've not done before. You know since graduating, I've been waiting to look for a full time job because of this trip. I decided to take the opportunity to participate in this longer mission trip first. Besides, I'm not sure what I want to do, maybe go back and get my counseling degree.

She picked up her book after putting on her coat, kissed Katie on the head and walked to the front door. "Anyway, I decided there was still plenty of time to figure it all out when I get back. I'm looking forward to being a leader this year and getting a different perspective than when I went as a student. We're working with the same church as before and they're supposed to be getting an intern from our country that will be working with us. He will also be leading the street ministry work in Mexico City."

Katie ran up to Holly for a hug and another kiss. Ellie and Micah hugged her. Holly turned at the door and said, "Please continue to pray for us over the next two weeks as we get the final details done. We need to finish up the chicken barbecue next week and I want that to do well financially. Also, it will be a challenge to get everyone to the airport by 5:30 in the morning so we are supposed to meet at the church by 3 am and leave for the airport together by 3:30 am."

Micah replied, "We will be praying and if you need any help with anything, please let me know. Do you still want me to take you to the church that morning?"

"I do if that still works for you. Could you pick me up about 2:45 am?"

"I'll be there."

The three of them waved to Holly as she walked out the door. She blew them a kiss as the door closed behind her.

Micah and Ellie looked at each other and smiled. They were excited for Holly and this new adventure, knowing she loved to serve the Lord on these short term mission trips. She's been participating in them for several years. They looked forward to what God had planned for her on this trip. Micah took Katie into the family room to watch one of her favorite cartoon videos while Ellie went upstairs to get Caleb. She had heard him stirring a few minutes before Holly left.

CHAPTER 2

A week later Sunday morning came with sunshine streaming through Holly's bedroom window. Today their team would be having a lunch meeting after church to discuss the final preparations for the trip. Their chicken barbecue successfully raised $2000 so she silently thanked God for the extra cushion of money. Everyone had been given the items they needed to pack along with the host gifts to take to Mexico. Some were also given tools, some were given paper supplies, pencils, crayons and all the things they would need for bible school. Some were also given soccer balls for when they played with the street people. The thought of working with the street people gave Holly butterflies in her stomach because it was something she hadn't done before. It was hard to imagine people living on the streets.

After her shower, she went down to breakfast. Her mom was fixing eggs and bacon which she could smell as she walked into the kitchen. Holly loved the aroma of breakfast food floating through their home!

She walked over and gave her mom a kiss. "Good morning. Did you sleep well?"

"I sure did. It was wonderful to fall asleep hearing the birds sing. I love this time of year when the evenings are dark and the skies are filled with stars. This is a beautiful place this time of year!" She smiled and hugged her daughter. Abigail Brady loved her home but even after seven years she still missed her husband.

Holly interrupted her mom's thoughts when she asked, "Mom are you going to lunch with Ellie and Micah after church? I don't want you to forget that I have my final Mexico meeting and it's going to be a lunch meeting."

Serving the two of them plates heaped high with bacon and eggs, her mom replied, "Yes I am and I didn't forget about your meeting. We're going to Appleby's. You know how Katie loves their sweet potato fries. What time will you be back from your meeting?"

Holly buttered some toast and put it on a plate as she turned towards her mom and replied, "I will probably be home mid-afternoon. We need to wrap up the final details." She got up from the table to get a cup of coffee. "Can I get you a cup of coffee while I'm up?"

"That would be great. Thanks."

Holly put their cups of coffee down and took her seat. "I'll pray Mom. Father, thank You for this new day which You have given us. Thanks for this food that You have given us. May we honor You this day in all we say and do and may this food strengthen and nourish us to be better servants for You. Help us to focus on worshipping You today at church. In Christ's name I pray, Amen."

"Thanks Holly. We better eat now so we can leave and get to church a little early. I wanted to see Sue Halterman for a few minutes before church starts. We are going to be serving a spaghetti dinner for July 4th and I need to talk to her about something."

They finished their breakfast, cleaned up the kitchen quickly and left. Their church had two pastors, a senior pastor and a youth pastor. Their senior pastor, Jess Lawson had been with their church for ten years and they always enjoyed hearing his sermons. He was a good expositor of God's Word. Bill Nash had been their youth/college pastor for three years. He started taking young people on short term mission trips the first summer he came to the church.

CHAPTER 3

As Holly listened to Pastor Jess's sermon, she thought about how important it was to know the character of God. Pastor Jess said our view of God dictates our view of everything else. Holly contemplated that thought regarding her own life. She knew it was important to study God's character and that it was a lifetime pursuit. She also knew that she had not really studied the character of God or developed an intimate relationship with Him until her dad died several years ago when she was in high school. She still missed him. Over the years as she came to know more about God she recognized and embraced His sovereign control in her life. Though some things were more challenging than others such as accepting God's will over her own desires, she believed God knew exactly what He was doing and that He didn't make mistakes. She was confident because of what she knew of His character now and looked forward to the future. She wanted to trust His promises even when she didn't understand why things happened the way they did.

As she contemplated these truths she zoned out for a few seconds, Pastor Jess started quoting Psalm 16:8, "*I have set the Lord continually before me; because He is at my right hand, I will not be shaken.*" Holly remembered this Scripture because she clung to it a lot over the years. She smiled as she resolved to continue to get to know God even more. In that moment she thought of Mexico and knew God would teach her more about Himself this summer. With that thought, she realized the pastor was finished and they were getting ready to sing their closing hymn.

After church she walked her mom out to Micah's car and waited for her brother and his family to come out. Then she drove to the restaurant where her meeting was being held. She always loved the team meetings. They were always fun because of the excitement of the team and the bonding that took place within the members because of these meetings. She was singing softly to herself as she walked into the restaurant, praying God's will for each of them this summer.

~~~~~~~~~~

At the same time that the American team was meeting in the United States, there was a Mexico team meeting in Mexico City in preparation for the arrival of the U.S. team. The little church called Beth El was getting ready to construct a small building that would house two small bathrooms. The American team was going to help with this project along with painting the inside of their one room church building. They hoped to have the Americans build cabinets in the kitchen area of the building to store kitchen items along with hymnals and whatever else they needed for their church. This job would take every bit of the month the American team would be in Mexico so they wanted to be sure they were as organized as possible.

Abraham Hernandez was the Pastor of Beth El. He enjoyed the help and enthusiasm of their American intern,

Zachary Benson, who had been working with them for a couple of weeks. His home was in San Antonio, Texas. He was attending a seminary in Orlando, Florida and part of his curriculum was to participate in an international internship.

During his interview with Pastor Abraham, Zach told him he wanted to know more about the Mexican people because his mother was Mexican and they were part of his heritage. That's why he chose to participate in Mexico mission trips as a youth. He grew to love the Mexican people during that time. Zach felt God leading him to minister to the Mexican people so he decided to do his internship in Mexico City. Pastor Abraham knew Zach was the right young man for their intern position and hired him shortly after their interview. Zach came to Mexico early in June and planned on staying through the summer.

Pastor Abraham valued Zach's wisdom so he gave him quite a bit of responsibility this summer. Thus far, Zach had proven Abraham correct in his estimation of this young man.

Zach was sorting through some papers on the table when Pastor Abraham started the meeting. Zach enjoyed the time he spent with this godly man and they had accomplished quite a bit together already. God had opened the right doors for him to be here this summer. He was excited to see Beth El adding a couple of bathrooms for the growing number of people attending this little church.

Up to this point the small congregation of Beth El had been sharing a toilet housed in a cement dwelling a few feet from their property. There was a family of five living in this one room dwelling and they were very generous in sharing their toilet.

Zach's real passion, though, was working with the street people. He was anxious for the American team to come and be a part of the work he was doing there.

"Zach, have you finished the housing arrangements and faxed them to Bill Nash?" asked Pastor Abraham.

"Yes, I did that last week and they sent me their room assignments. I gave each of our host families the names of the Americans that will be staying with them. I think it will work out fine." Though the families had very little they were happy to share it with the Americans. The Americans would bless the generosity and kindness of these host families by contributing financially to them for housing and food.

"Have you finished the schedule of what they will be doing each day?"

"I have and if you look at the packet of info that you have you will find a copy of the schedule that I have prepared. I know we will have to be flexible, but at least this gives us a plan. During the first two weeks, Monday through Thursday, a couple of the guys will be helping our men construct the bathroom building. The other guys will be working on building the cabinets in the kitchen area. The ladies will be putting on a bible school in the park next door so that the Mexican children won't be in harm's way here. The following two weeks, the plan is to have everyone join in painting the inside of the building, the cabinets and the bathrooms. Along with painting, a couple of the ladies will make curtains for the windows. On

Friday and Saturday of each week, we will work with the street people.

After pausing for a few minutes to let the men look over the schedule, he continued. "Halfway through their time here we will take them to Taxco for the weekend to souvenir shop and relax as well as see some of the Mexican culture. Also, during their trip we will take them sightseeing. I think they will enjoy Xochimilco and riding on the boats through the canals. The evening of their arrival, we have planned a welcome celebration with Mexican pizza and sodas at the church."

"Thanks Zach. The plans sound great. I am glad God brought you at a time when we needed your help and organizational skills. Okay, is there anything else that anyone can think of before we break up?" asked Pastor Abraham.

He gave them a few minutes to think of anything else they might need to discuss. When no one said anything, they closed with prayer and headed home. Zach's mom had the flu recently and he wanted to see how she was feeling so he looked forward to calling her when he got back to his apartment which was owned by a wealthy family in the church who agreed to let him rent it over the summer for free.

The American team would be here in less than two weeks and he wanted to be sure everything was ready for them. He silently prayed for God's protection over their travel and last minute details. He also prayed that all would go well while they were in Mexico City and that they could finish the projects. Ultimately he would trust God with these plans and the projects.

~~~~~~~~~~

On the streets of Mexico City homeless people lived under cardboard boxes that were hung over lines of rope strung from two trees. It was their only protection against the weather and unsavory people so it was really no protection at all. Young children ran around wearing very little clothing and they didn't have much food to eat. There were babies without diapers and old people with blank stares on their faces drinking themselves into oblivion. There were young boys and girls sniffing glue hoping to drift out of the reality of their lives.

This particular area of the streets was run by a guy who was known only as Miguel. He sold drugs to anyone who had money and put a lot of young girls on these streets as to make money for him. He made plenty of money off the hardship and despair of others. He wasn't very tall, but he was muscular. His face bore a lot of battle scars from his own experiences living on the streets. He had a scar that went down the entire left side of his cheek. His eyes were cold and dark. No one would mess with him. He had a couple of bodyguards that worked for him who were just as mean. Miguel was the one man on the streets that people feared and they did everything they could to stay out of his way.

The only person that Miguel showed any care for was a little boy whose name was Gabriel. Gabriel was only eight years old, but anyone who knew him recognized a maturity way beyond his years. Surviving on the streets did that to people. Sometimes in weak moments Gabriel would let his guard down and exhibit a childlike vulnerability. He was a compassionate little boy but learned quickly enough that if he wanted to survive living on the streets with Miguel, he had to bury that urge quickly. One time when Miguel saw Gabriel being kind to a dog, Miguel shot the dog before beating Gabriel, saying there was no place for kindness in their business. The only time Gabriel let himself be kind was when he knew Miguel was nowhere in the vicinity and then it was only to animals because they couldn't tell Miguel. Gabriel believed Miguel wouldn't hesitate to kill him if it ever happened again. Miguel took great pleasure in mistreating or killing anyone or anything.

No one really knew where Gabriel came from, but you could be sure that Gabriel was not far from Miguel. Miguel used Gabriel to do errands for him and collect money when necessary. Miguel secretly planned that one day Gabriel would take over this territory so he wanted to be sure that Gabriel was tough enough to handle it.

The one thing that continued to be a problem in Miguel's eyes was the "church people" who came down to his area to help people. So, unbeknownst to the Beth El Church, Miguel and his men were planning to get rid of these "church people" who taught about Jesus and provided food for some of the people. The preaching that was done by the American whose name was Zach gave people a small glimmer of hope and there was no place for hope on these streets, not while Miguel was in charge. He wanted his people dependent on him forever. He was just watching and waiting for the right opportunity to get rid of these "church people" for good.

Gabriel stayed out of their way pretending to be occupied with something while listening to their plans. He really enjoyed when the "church people" came down to their streets. He liked to hear about this One named Jesus. The stories of the kindness of Jesus made him feel good. He had to be really careful that Miguel didn't find out he was listening to these stories or he would get a pretty severe beating. Right now, he was shivering as he thought about how Miguel might hurt these people who talked about Jesus. He would have to wait and see what developed, but his hope was that this Jesus would somehow protect the "church people" from Miguel. Maybe this Jesus would also be able to help him as well one day. That thought was comforting to him, but he really didn't know why.

CHAPTER 4

The day finally arrived for Holly and the team to leave for Mexico. The night before was a flurry of activity in the Brady household as they needed to get Holly's suitcase packed with all the things she needed to take to Mexico. Finally, at 2:30 in the morning, Holly finished packing her backpack. Micah was coming over to drive her to the church where the team would meet and leave for the airport. Her mom fixed a quick breakfast and a little snack to take on the plane for the layover they had in Houston.

Drinking a cup of tea, Holly looked out the kitchen window and saw the headlights of Micah's car coming down the driveway. She called to her mom that Micah was here and poured out the remaining tea from her cup into the sink before putting it in the dishwasher.

As her mom walked into the kitchen, she asked, "Holly, do you have everything?"

Holly opened the back door as Micah walked up to the porch. Looking at her mom she said, "Yeah, I think so. It helps that you can check in only one suitcase and the backpack is a carry on so, therefore, it allows me to only take so much stuff. It's much easier when you have to pack light."

Micah gave Holly a kiss and then walked over to his mom and gave her a hug and kiss. He picked up a piece of bacon to chew on and looked at Holly's suitcase while winking at his mom. "It sure is early in the morning. Is our world traveler ready?"

"As ready as I'll ever be. I am so excited! Let's get going. I don't want to be late."

She ran over and gave her mom a kiss and hug. "I love you. Please pray for me and I will be praying for all of you."

Her mom had a few tears in her eyes. They had already prayed together before Micah got there but every time Holly left on one of these mission trips her mom got weepy. Since her husband's death, she was lonely when Holly was gone. It helped that Micah and his family lived close by, but there was also a part of her that worried about Holly being in Mexico. Ultimately she knew she needed to trust God with her children, but sometimes that was easier said than done.

As she wiped her eyes she said, "I love you too, Holly. Take care of yourself and God bless you and your team. I'll look forward to hearing from you. Call if you need anything. You are always in my prayers."

Holly took her backpack and headed out the door while Micah grabbed her other suitcase. He walked over and gently wiped the tear off his mom's face and then kissed her on the forehead. He and his sister talked all the way out to the car while their mom watched from the door. It was still dark but Micah knew Holly was keyed up and ready to be on her way. Abigail waved from the porch as Holly got into the car. She silently thanked God for her two children. Holly waved back and blew her mom a kiss.

As they drove off Abigail asked God to keep His angels around her daughter and that He would reveal His presence to her throughout the time she was in Mexico. Abigail smiled as she shut the door.

Micah unloaded Holly's suitcase at the church while she greeted everybody. There were four guys and two girls on this team. There were also four team leaders which included Holly. Micah knew each of these young people because their families had been members in their church for years. They were a terrific group of college students. As he looked at each of them for a moment he remembered different things about them.

Chris Elliott was the biggest guy on the team with a gentle, sensitive spirit. The Mexicans would call him "grande" meaning large or great because he was 6'5" and had to be around 250 pounds. He was a great football player and hoped to play professional football someday. Seth Matthews was next in line by size and was loaded with personality, always the life of the party. He wasn't much smaller than Chris. When Micah led a guys' bible study a couple of years ago, he could always count on Seth to have solid input and godly wisdom. He hoped to be a doctor one day. Jackson Scott was the playful one of the group. He loved to play jokes on people and had a head full of red hair. He was at least six feet tall and slender. He enjoyed playing soccer and had been the top soccer player in his class. He hoped to go on the mission field one day but wasn't sure where God would lead him. Liam Taylor was the smallest of the guys but still measured about 5'10 in height. Micah knew Liam was extremely strong. While helping a family in the church move into a new house, Liam was one of two guys that helped moved the

27

family's upright piano. During high school, he worked part time on a farm and did a lot of heavy lifting. He was hoping to be a youth pastor in the future. He loved working with kids and the kids loved him. He was the quiet one of the group. God knew what He was doing when He raised up each of these guys for this trip. They all possessed strong character with a strong moral compass. Through this trip Micah was sure God would reveal more of Himself to them and also more about themselves than about the people they served.

Micah then looked over to the girls contemplating each of them. Kylie Evers was an attractive young woman who had a great sense of humor. She had a beautiful head of curly black hair and dark eyes. She always went with the flow. She loved kids and hoped to be a kindergarten teacher one day. Emma Wells was very athletic. She was a brunette and always had her hair in a ponytail. She was a guy's girl because she loved sports and was usually ready to try anything. She hoped to be a physical therapist one day and work with athletes. These two girls would be a real asset to this team. He sighed knowing this would be a life-changing trip for each of them.

Micah looked over at the other leaders as they were loading luggage into the bus and waved to Bill Nash. Bill waved back as he put luggage on the bus. He has been their youth pastor for the past five years and was a strong, godly leader and an all-around great guy. The other two leaders, Jeff and Becca Paxton, haven't been at the church very long. They were newlyweds and were youth leaders in the church. He liked what he knew about them but hadn't much interaction with them.   He knew that Bill would take good care of the team.

Holly came over to Micah with tears shining brightly in her eyes, smiled and then gave him a kiss and hug. Micah hugged her tightly and kissed her cheek. She whispered love you in his ear and walked away waving good-by as she headed over to the group. Micah walked to his car, turned and silently prayed for God's protection and care over each member of this team especially his sister. He drove off watching from his rear view window as Holly blew him a kiss and waved.

CHAPTER 5

As Holly waved to Micah leaving the parking lot she heard Pastor Bill Nash calling everybody together before leaving for the airport. She walked over to the group as Bill gave instructions.

"We will be taking a small bus to the airport. Please keep your carry on with you in the bus. We put your other luggage under the bus in the storage compartment. There will be more space on the bus that way. Once we get to the airport, quickly get your belongings and go into the airport to wait for all of us to get inside. Then we will head over to the United Airlines ticket desk. It will get pretty hectic at the airport so I have given Jeff the envelopes with your passports and travel documents in them. He will distribute them once we get off the bus and into the airport. You will need them when you check in at the ticket counter. Keep them safe until after you get through customs in Mexico and then give them back to me. I will be storing them in a safe place until we return. It should take us about two hours to get to the airport. I know we have covered all of this before but does anybody have any questions?"

He looked around at his team, but no one had any questions or comments. Bill continued, "Remember the schedules are in your folder that I gave you at the last meeting. Now let me pray for us. Father God, thanks for this wonderful opportunity to travel to Mexico and minister in Your name. It is a privilege to be a part of Your kingdom work in Mexico. Help us to be flexible with the traveling today and all the details that we have to handle. I pray that You will enable each of us to keep our eyes fixed on You and that You will continue to equip us for the work You have set before us. We desire to give You praise and glory ahead of time for what You will accomplish. Thanks for desiring to use broken vessels like us to do Your work. We pray that You will speak and serve through each of us. Please give us safe traveling mercies today and protect our families while we are gone. In Christ's Name and for His glory we pray, Amen."

Everybody grabbed their gear and headed for the bus. Holly knew no one would be sleeping on the bus because they were already busy talking and sharing. She had to admit she wasn't ready to sleep either. She loved the last several times she was in Mexico and was excited to see her friends.

Chris settled in his seat while watching Holly make her way to the bus with admiration shining out of his eyes. He thought she was a lovely woman in looks as well as personality. She seemed to be just the kind of girl he hoped to find one day. She was a lot of fun and always showed respect for others. He knew she would be a great leader to have on this trip. He saw Liam and Jackson head towards the bus as well as Kylie and Emma. Seth followed behind the girls. He also liked Jeff and Becca. They were excellent college leaders in their church. They hadn't been married very long when they felt God calling them to work with the college ministry. Pastor Bill Nash was glad to welcome them on board. He thought with a smile on his face that this was a great team of people who were headed to Mexico.

Holly put her backpack under her seat when Kylie started laughing at something Emma said. Holly looked at them both and said, "What's so funny, Emma?"

"I was telling Kylie about my younger brother's note to me. He asked me to read it on my way to the airport. He was being sweet when he said he would miss me and sent me a pack of candy in the envelope. He told me to eat one each day and that way I wouldn't forget him because the candy would remind me of him. He's so cute."

"That was a really nice thing for him to do, Emma. I bet he's gonna miss you since you told me this was your first time going so far away, especially for a month."

"Yeah, it's kind of funny. He doesn't really seem to miss me too much while I'm at college. Maybe it's because he knows he can call me whenever he wants to whereas in Mexico he can't. We've always had a great relationship." Emma thought about how much she loved her brother and smiled.

"I will miss him as well."

Kylie echoed, "Yeah, I know what you mean. I miss my parents already and I haven't even left." She laughed. "It does seem different from going to college." She shook her head to get rid of the melancholy feeling.

"Anyway, we're going to have a great time, aren't we guys?" She turned and looked at the guys in the back of the bus waiting for their agreement which they gave enthusiastically.

Pastor Bill got on the bus along with the driver who was also a member of their church. One Sunday after worship, he came up to Bill and offered to drive them to the airport. Bill was grateful for his offer and took him up on it. He loved when members of his church excitedly offered to serve.

"Everybody got everything tucked away?" Jeff, have you checked to be sure that everybody's luggage is secure in the storage compartment?"

"Yes Bill. We have plenty of room down there as well as here in the bus." He was sitting in the seat next to his wife Becca. Everybody seemed to be settled in so Bill took his seat and told the driver it was time to get going. They had approximately two hours so a couple of the guys put in their earplugs to listen to music. Others engaged in conversation. The bus driver turned the ceiling lights off and darkness surrounded them.

Holly whispered a silent prayer for God's protection as the bus pulled away from the church. She would take advantage of sitting by herself for now. She was hoping to sit with one of the girls to get to know better, but by the end of the trip she had no doubt they would all know each other very well.

CHAPTER 6

As they got closer to the airport Holly noticed that it had gotten quiet on the bus. The kids must have drifted off to sleep which was good because they would need all their energy for the long day ahead of them. She could just see the sun coming up over the horizon becoming a silvery horizon as night was turning into day. It looked like it would be a great day for air travel. She noticed Becca and Jeff were resting as well. Bill was in a quiet conversation with the driver so Holly decided she better rest during the little time they had left before arriving at the airport. She turned to her side and wedged her pillow between the side of her head and the window. Things would get busy as soon as they reached the airport.

~~~~~~~~~~

In Mexico City, Zach was getting the van ready to pick up the Americans at the airport. Pastor Abraham was going to drive the second van to carry the luggage. He looked forward to meeting this new group of people from the United States. The Mexican people looked forward every summer to the Americans' visits. They loved hanging out with the Americans as well as working with them.

Zach secretly looked forward to spending time with his own countrymen. Even though he loved being in

Mexico City, he missed the United States, especially his parents. He looked forward to spending the last few weeks of the summer with them before returning to seminary for his last year. He couldn't wait to share his stories and photographs with his parents. He knew his mom would enjoy hearing about his trip since she hadn't been able to visit Mexico for several years. His mom and dad were hoping to take a trip to Mexico next year.

"Is everything ready for the welcome celebration this evening, Abraham?" questioned Zach.

"Yes Zach. Julio will bring the pizzas to the church and Lilliana will bring the sodas. Fernando will bring ice cream later for dessert. I believe many of the church families will be attending even if they aren't hosting an American. They will start coming around 6 p.m."

"Great. That will give the Americans time to relax a little and do their group devotions before everyone gets here. We should probably leave for the airport around 12:30 since their flights gets in at 1:15. That will give them time to get their luggage and go through customs. We will wait for them outside the customs area."

"Sounds good, Zach." I need to do some errands before we leave. I will be back in about an hour and then we can leave."

"See you then. I am going to do some last minute things in the church and then I will meet you here at noon."

After Pastor Abraham left Zach entered the church building to be sure they had everything ready for the Americans. He looked forward to meeting them as well as getting a lot accomplished for the church over the next month.

CHAPTER 7

Jeff and Bill got off the bus first and started hauling out the luggage from under the bus. The college students picked up their luggage and went into the airport. Becca and Holly checked the interior of the bus to be sure no one left anything. They got off and grabbed their luggage and went into the airport terminal where the others were waiting for them.

Bill was seeing the bus driver off while Jeff started handing out the envelopes to each of the team members so they could get their passports and airline tickets ready to check in.

"Does everyone have what they need to check in, Jeff?" asked Bill.

"I gave them their envelopes to hold until we get through Mexican customs and then I will collect them to give to you."

"Thanks for taking care of that. I wanted to be sure the bus driver knew when to pick us up next month." Getting everyone's attention Bill said, "Okay, let's head over to the United Airlines' passenger check in."

Bill and Jeff led the way with the guys and girls close behind chatting. Holly and Becca followed last to be sure everyone stayed together.

"Becca, have you ever been on a mission trip before?" Holly asked as they were walking. She loved watching the people in the airport, as they came and went, talking on cell phones, hanging onto their children and rushing by on a cart.

"No I haven't." I'm really excited about this trip. Jeff and I have talked about doing a short term mission trip sometime but never had the opportunity until now. Working with the college ministry has been great and this trip is an added blessing. What about you?"

"I have taken several trips in the past as a college student. I love going to Mexico. The people are so warm and caring. It was amazing to me on my first trip as I thought I was mainly going to minister to the people but I was the one who ended up being ministered to. I think that's what is so special about short term mission trips. I believe we are blessed even more than those we serve. Anyway, I am excited to see the friends that I have made over the years as well as minister to the street people which I haven't done before."

Hurrying along behind the others they noticed the check in lines were long so they waited patiently. They had plenty of time before their plane was scheduled to leave.

The line moved along fairly quickly as the people got checked in. Bill, Chris and Seth checked in first and then waited for the rest of their team. Jeff, Liam and Jackson were next in line and when they finished they joined Bill, Chris and Seth. Kylie, Emma and Becca then checked in next and Holly was last. They hurried to join the guys and then headed toward their gate. They had to catch a tram that would take them to the other side of the terminal. Once they arrived there they had to locate their boarding gate.

They were all relieved to have gotten through the security checks without a lot of fuss. Fortunately they had plenty of time as their flight was not scheduled to take off for another hour. After they arrived at their boarding gate, some of them decided to get coffee and something to eat at Starbucks. Holly and Becca headed off with the college students while Jeff and Bill waited.

Bill called to Holly as she walked away. She turned back when she heard him call her name. "Will you bring me back a latte and a muffin, Holly?"

"I'd be happy to. Any special kind of muffin?"

"No anything's fine. Thanks. I'll pay you for it when you get back."

Holly nodded and ran to catch Becca and the others. Becca knew Jeff would want a café au lait and a cinnamon bun. The college students were already in line so Holly and Becca got in line behind them. As Holly waited in line she imagined the taste of a café au lait with Irish cream flowing down her throat. She also decided that a blueberry scone sounded good.

As soon as everyone got their order they headed back to the boarding gate where Bill and Jeff were engrossed in conversation. Holly gave Bill his latte and muffin and he paid her and then enjoyed his first drink of it.

As Bill took a break from eating his muffin he said to everyone, "Be sure to keep your backpacks close to you. Don't leave anything alone. Keep an eye on each other's stuff as well."

They all took seats and thoroughly enjoyed their food and drink while waiting for their flight to be called.

CHAPTER 8

"Flight 543 is now boarding at Gate 23. All passengers with first class tickets begin boarding now," said a voice over the loud speaker. "In a few minutes we will begin boarding the rest of you by the group number on your boarding pass."

"Everyone got your stuff together?" Holly asked her team. A couple of the guys were playing cards and the rest were playing speed scrabble. "You need to finish up whatever you're doing and get ready to board when it's our turn."

Jackson started gathering everyone's trash with Kylie helping him. They wanted to be ready when their group number was called.

Emma exclaimed with joy in her voice, "This is it guys. We are on our way. I can't believe it! We all worked so hard and for so long and now we begin. We are going to have so much fun with each other and serving others!"

Everyone laughed and agreed. Then a voice over the loud speakers announced their boarding time.

Bill said, "That's us. Let's get going." Everyone grabbed their stuff and got in line to board the plane. As they boarded the officials pulled Emma aside to search her luggage and the same happened to Jackson. Jeff waited for them while the others boarded the plane. Once their luggage was searched Emma and Jackson joined Jeff and headed onto the plane.

Everyone put their backpacks under the seat in front of them or in the overhead storage compartments. Becca and Emma were sitting together as were Holly and Kylie. The guys were in the two rows behind them. The flight attendants were getting people comfortable, especially the elderly and children. Holly looked forward to her time on the plane with Kylie. They were in their seats when announcements started coming over the loudspeaker. Everyone needed to buckle their seat belts, listen to the attendants show them safety information and turn off all electronic devices. Over the loudspeaker the pilot welcomed everyone and told them about the upcoming flight particulars. If the passengers had any problems they were to ask the flight attendants for help. He hoped they enjoyed their flight.

Holly enjoyed watching the college students interact with the other people sitting around them. Emma was sharing about their trip with an elderly lady behind her. She pointed out to her the other people who would be participating in this trip. The lady was very attentive to what Emma said. The conversation then turned towards Emma's faith. It was a blessing for Holly to hear Emma share her faith and to see the lady's receptiveness to Emma.

Seth and Jackson were playing a card game on their dinner trays and were having a great time. There were a few people sitting around them enjoying watching them play the game.

Kylie asked Holly when she came to know the Lord and it was a great opportunity for Holly to share her testimony. Holly loved sharing about her family and how God used circumstances in her life to strengthen her walk with Him. She told Kylie of her father's death and she loved talking about her brother Micah and his family. Holly's eyes lit up when she spoke about her niece and nephew. Kylie enjoyed listening to Holly.

When it was Kylie's turn to share her testimony she told Holly she was just getting to know God more intimately. She enjoyed college but it was a challenge dealing with the promiscuity of other college students in her dorm. She met God through Inter Varsity and she had made a few good friends there. She was in a good Bible study and was learning more about God through studying different attributes each week. Kylie shared her love of children with Holly and looked forward to working with the Mexican children at the church.

After their conversation Kylie was asked a question by Emma and she turned to talk to her for a minute. Holly knew they would be arriving in Houston shortly and decided to pull out her Bible to work on the devotional that they would be sharing with each other sometime this evening. She wanted to study the passage of Scripture they would be discussing and since Kylie was involved in another conversation Holly thought it would be a good time.

The pilot came over the loudspeaker later and instructed everyone to put their trays up, turn off their electronic devices and to buckle their seat belts as they were making their descent to the Houston Airport.

Everyone put away their stuff and hooked their seat belts in preparation for landing. Holly knew when they landed that they had to hurry to find their next boarding gate and then they could relax for about thirty minutes before their final flight to Mexico City.

CHAPTER 9

As soon as the plane landed everyone got their backpacks. Once the team got off the plane they followed Holly and Becca to the next gate with Jeff and Bill being the last ones. The guys were talking with the girls as they walked. They had to travel down a long hallway, take one of the moving walk ways, take a few turns and finally found their boarding gate.

Holly enjoyed watching the people as they made their way to the next destination. One mom was hurriedly pushing a stroller with a sleeping baby inside while dragging a smaller child along as he ate a peanut butter and jelly sandwich which was smeared over his mouth. She looked like she could use some help. Another man was busy talking on his cell phone as he hurried to his destination. Some people didn't enjoy the hustle and bustle of airports, but Holly loved it! She enjoyed people watching and this was a great place to do it.

Bill noticed his team putting their backpacks on the seats at their boarding gate to wait for their next flight. Thinking that the college students might decide to go somewhere he said, "Hey everyone, we have approximately thirty minutes before they ask us to start boarding the flight. It's really not enough time to go wandering. They will be serving lunch on the plane so let's stay put until they call us to board."

The college students picked up their backpacks and sat down while their backpacks rested at their feet. They started talking to each other but Bill still had a few more things to share with them.

"Please double check that you have your envelopes in a safe place in your backpack. When we get to Mexico City we have to move quickly. You need to have your documents ready when we get to customs. After customs we will go and get our luggage and then move to the "red light/green light" area. Remember, that's where we either walk through with the green light or get stopped by the red light. If you get stopped, your luggage will get searched. It will only take a few minutes and then they will let you go through. Becca and Jeff will take the lead through the "light" area. As soon as you make it through look for them on the other side and stay with them until we all get through. Holly and I will be last and will wait for anyone who may get stopped. Any questions?"

Kylie asked, "How do you know which light you will get?"

"You don't. It's strictly by chance. It's nothing to worry about though. It's their method of randomly checking luggage coming into their country," replied Bill. He looked around to the others to see if there were any other questions and there were none.

"Okay, let's relax for a few minutes."

Jackson pulled out his cards. "Does anyone want to play a quick game of Slap?"

Chris shook his head laughing. "Jackson, I think you really enjoy playing cards, don't you? Every time we have a few minutes you pull those cards out."

Jackson just smiled and shuffled the deck of cards. The rest of the team except for the leaders gathered around him and started playing cards as they waited for their flight to be announced.

Holly decided to take this opportunity to visit with Becca. She walked over to where Becca was sitting and asked, "Becca, can I sit by you while we wait?"

"Sure. I'd enjoy the company. Jeff is going to talk with Bill about the plans for when we arrive."

Holly sat down and they started sharing their lives with each other. Holly commented, "I really enjoy watching you and Jeff interact with these kids. Have you worked with college students before?"

"No we haven't. While we were in college we attended a great church with a wonderful college ministry. I came to know the Lord there and met Jeff during one of the Bible studies through that ministry. Later, when we got married, we prayed about where God would use us in ministry. We both decided that wherever we attended church, we wanted to work with high school or college students."

"I just recently graduated from college and I enjoyed coming to Mexico as a college student," Holly said. "Bill started taking college students to Mexico shortly after he came to our church as our Youth Pastor. I have been on the last three trips with him. Since he knew how much I loved Mexico, he asked me to come as a leader this year. I know I'm only a few years older than these students, but since they're freshmen Bill felt it would be okay."

"I think it's great that you love going to Mexico. I have never been and I'm looking forward to meeting and serving the people. We just moved to Cheyenne Wells last year because of Jeff's job. We've enjoyed the church and feel blessed to be a part of the ministry to college students. Jeff is happy with his job at the Community College because he gets to work with college students there too. Sometimes I have to travel with my job at the computer store so I miss some events. There's a wonderful group of people in our church and we're glad to be a part of the congregation."

Holly looked at her watch to check the time. They still had a couple of minutes before their flight would be announced. She noticed the kids were still involved in their card game. It looked pretty intense as they were slapping at different cards. She hadn't played that game yet but she knew there would be plenty of time in Mexico.

She continued her conversation with Becca. "How long have you and Jeff been married?"

"We just celebrated our fourth anniversary in March. We met in college and got married shortly after graduation. I found my job with the computer store about three months after we got here. I'm okay with it but I am looking forward to when we start having kids so that I can quit and stay home. I'm so excited for that time!" Becca smiled as she spoke of those plans and Holly could see the excitement in her eyes.

"Flight 656 is ready to board. Please get your tickets ready and we ask that parents with small children and those with special needs be the first to board. Then we will move on with first class followed by economy."

Several parents picked up their kids and headed to the boarding line. One little girl was crying because she didn't want to get on the plane. Her mom was trying to calm her down by giving her a piece of candy. Fortunately, the ticket agent was very patient with each of them. One gentleman was being transported in a wheel chair by an airport attendant. People made sufficient room for him to get through.

Jackson picked up the cards and stuck them in his backpack while everyone else got their tickets ready. When their group assignments were called they all got in line anxious to make this last part of their trip. Holly looked around at all the people traveling on this flight. She wondered about the stories that were their lives and started imagining what her story would be at the end of this trip. The line moved along fairly quickly and it didn't seem like many were being pulled out of line for baggage searches. As the team walked onto the plane, she hung back a little praying for safe traveling mercies and God's protection on this flight.

CHAPTER 10

This flight wasn't quite as pleasant as the first one. There were several unhappy children crying throughout the flight. There was a gentleman not too far from Holly who constantly sneezed, coughed and sniffled. Hopefully he didn't have anything too contagious.

Later as the plane got closer to Mexico City, Holly looked out the window and still couldn't help being amazed at the size of this city. It stretched out for what seemed like hundreds of miles. It also reminded Holly of a matchbox car city that went on forever as the plane started its descent into the airport. There are 25 million people living in Mexico City. People had to live on the sides of the mountains due to lack of space. It was quite an awesome sight from the airplane.

The first time Holly visited Mexico City she rarely saw green grass. The streets were lined with what looked like side-by-side townhouses and there was barely enough room for streets. In the better areas of Mexico City, true townhouses had little gated courtyards where they parked their little cars surrounded by little flower gardens. Mexico City was made up of many people, lots of cement, and very little greenery of any kind.

As they descended, Holly watched Kylie talk with a young Mexican boy in the seat in front of hers. It appeared to Holly that Kylie got attached easily to children. The little boy took to her right away as well. It was a blessing to the little boy's mom to have his attention distracted for a while so she could care for his little sister. Holly believed Kylie would make a great teacher someday.

The voice of one of the flight attendants came over the loud speaker telling everyone to be sure to stay buckled until the plane landed safely. Once the plane landed and taxied to the gate the seat belt light went off so everyone could unbuckle and leave the airplane.

The team members were talking a lot and she could feel their excitement as they realized they would be meeting their Mexican hosts soon. She checked one last time to be sure she had her passport ready. Jeff had earlier told everyone to be sure their passports were handy and to have their backpacks ready because as soon as they landed they would have to hurry.

They all felt the jolt when the landing gear hit the ground and a mighty force pushing them back in their seats as the pilots applied the brakes as the plane was slowed down and came to a stop. It was a pretty rough landing. The seat belt light went off after a few minutes and everyone started a frenzy of grabbing their luggage and getting off the plane. Holly and Kylie were the first team members off the plane so they stepped to the side to wait for the others. Soon Kylie saw Chris and Seth followed by Becca, Emma, Bill and Jeff. They all walked over to Holly and Kylie and then they waited for Liam and Jackson who happened to be near the end of a group of people filing out of the plane. They came over with big smiles on their faces. Everyone was pretty tired by now but their adrenaline was pumping so their energy level was still high.

"Does everyone have their passport ready?" asked Bill. They all affirmatively shook their heads.

"Okay, let's get moving. We need to follow the signs to customs. Jeff and I will be in the front and Holly and Becca will follow everyone else. Stay between us. We will go to customs first, pick up our luggage next and then make our way to security. Once we start it will be hard to stop since we want to get through customs as quickly as possible. Thankfully, the plane was on time so our friends shouldn't have to wait too long. If we can get through customs in a relatively short period of time we should be at the church by four o'clock. Let's move!"

Becca and Holly smiled at each other as they started walking behind the college students. Everyone walked fast to keep up with those in front. While they were hurrying Becca asked Holly, "Did you enjoy the flight?"

"Yeah, I did. It was a nice opportunity to get to know Kylie better. I loved watching her interact with the little Mexican boy in front of her. She wants to be a teacher and I can see why. How about you?"

"It was nice. I enjoyed getting to know Emma better. She loves sports and it's amazing how many statistics she knows about her favorite teams. Her favorite sport is basketball. She played in high school and apparently was really good at it. She's going to be a lot of fun on this trip. I believe she has a pretty competitive spirit though so that should prove to be interesting among the guys."

"That's great! The Mexican children love to play soccer with our college students and they are pretty competitive as well. It'll be interesting to see if she mixes it up with them. I know our guys will love it. Does Jeff like sports?"

"He does but he's a football fan more than anything. He played high school football and really did well from what his mom tells me. He's not extremely competitive though. He just enjoys playing the game as well as watching it."

Holly noticed they were rounding the last corner to customs. Looking at the lines that were already formed, Holly knew this would take at least a half an hour to get through. The last time she was here she felt like she was a cow being herded through stalls as you had to follow everyone through all the twists and turns in customs. She looked up at Bill and he nodded his head towards her in acknowledgement of the situation. Holly told Becca about how long she thought it would take for them to get through with the number of people already in line. They should still be close to keeping with their schedule. She knew that in Mexico schedules often did not mean a lot.

The college students were doing great as they waited patiently and passed the time by talking to each other. The girls were told not to speak to any Mexican men as they took that as a sign that American girls were interested in them and may try to pursue the girls. Holly was glad that the guys were keeping the girls in between them as they made their way through the lines.

Once the team got through customs without any problems, Holly and Becca led the way to the baggage claim area with Bill and Jeff following everyone else. They all found their luggage and were relieved that all made it through this part of the trip. Then Holly led them toward the red light/green light security area which would be their last stop before leaving the airport. It was just a coin toss as to the light color one got.

They all stood watching the people going through the lights. Some pushed carts that held their luggage while others pushed in front of people carrying their luggage. Holly turned to the team as they watched and said, "Okay everyone the only thing you can do is go to one of the lines and as the attendant waves you through you wait to see what color light you get. If you get the red light they will move you over to one of those tables and the attendant will open your luggage, go through it and then wave you through. We aren't carrying anything that would be a problem so it should be fine. If you get the green light just go through and wait for us on the other side. I believe our Mexican hosts will be waiting for us on the other side of that door and they'll be looking for us. Please don't worry if you get the red light. Jeff and Bill will come through last in case anyone has any problems. It's quite an experience but nothing to be afraid of or worried about. Everyone okay?"

They nodded but Holly could see a little apprehension on the girls' faces. She understood that feeling. The first time she came to this area she didn't want to go through the lines because she was scared she would get the red light. She was never so grateful the moment she received the green light. On her second trip she got the red light and had her luggage searched. It turned out to be no big deal so she wanted to reassure everyone the best she could but she also realized they wouldn't relax until they went through it the first time.

There were so many people crowding in line before their team, but when it was their turn everything went well. Liam and Chris were the only two team members to get the red light. Bill waited on them as their luggage was checked and then they were waved through. Holly got through immediately and found Pastor Abraham waiting for them with a good looking man that she didn't know.

Pastor Abraham came over to her embraced her and kissed her cheek. "Buenas noches, Holly. It is so good to see you again. I am glad you came back to spend time with us this summer."

Smiling, she said, "Buenas noches. It's great to see you again Pastor Abraham. I am so glad to be back. I've really missed everyone."

He turned to the good looking man next to him and said, "Holly, I would like to introduce Zachary Benson to you. He is our intern for the summer."

Holly smiled and turned to Zachary, holding out her hand to shake his. "It's nice to meet you Zach." Her first thought was that he was drop dead gorgeous. He was well over six feet tall and Holly noticed he was very muscular. He had a head full of curly, russet hair but his eyes were what fascinated her most. They were gray blue and beautiful with long lashes that only girls should have. They just looked at each other for a moment as if there were no other people around. Zach recovered first from that special moment.

"It's nice to meet you as well Holly." His first thought was what a lovely woman she was and how her smile reached up to her sparkling bright blue eyes. He noticed she came up to his shoulders in height, had an athletic build with a crown of wheat colored hair braided down her back with a creamy complexion and rosy cheeks. Those blue eyes captivated him the most because of their sparkle. He held her hand an extra moment and then she turned and introduced the other team members to Pastor Abraham and Zach. Bill, Chris and Liam just joined them as they were getting acquainted.

Pastor Abraham turned towards Bill and gave him a big hug. "Buenas noches Bill. It is good to see you again. We have missed you and Holly and so glad to have you back again." Bill introduced Chris and Liam and they met Zach, too.

"We have two vans outside to take you to the church. We will put your luggage in the van that I will be driving and your team will travel in the second van which Zach will be driving." Zach looked at Holly again. It was hard to keep his eyes off her.

Pastor Abraham smiled at everyone and said, "As Bill and Holly know we have quite a hike to get to the vans so we need to get going. We will change money at one of the money exchanges as we exit the airport. They have a better exchange rate than the banks in the city. If you need to exchange more money during your stay with us, we will make a trip to a bank during the middle of your stay here. Before we go to Taxco and the market you can decide if you want to exchange more money at that time. If everyone's ready we can get going."

Bill nodded in affirmation. They all picked up their luggage and followed Pastor Abraham and Zach. The guys kept the girls between them including Holly. Becca walked with her husband Jeff. Bill was talking with Pastor

Abraham and Zach as they walked towards one of the
money exchanges. Holly noticed that Zach would turn and
look at her every now and again. There was a silent
message passing between them and she was excited about
the possibilities. She said a silent prayer asking God to
guide her when it came to this man Zachary Benson.

CHAPTER 11

After getting their money exchanged and making their way to the vans everyone noticed that the streets of Mexico City were lined with cars, mostly small ones. There wasn't much space in between the cars either. It was an amazing adventure driving through these streets as buses plowed their way through and inched their way between the cars. No one paid much attention to traffic signals which made some of the ride a bit harrowing. Cars squeezed in front of each other where there was very little room and horns were constantly blaring at someone's poor driving skills or rudeness.

Holly laughed at the comments the college students were making as they watched the way people drove their cars. No one took seriously traffic lights as cars would sometimes lightly graze the side of a car as they tried to squeeze in front and then they would just keep going. Pedestrians had to be extremely careful as cars never paid attention to them. Cars seemed to have the right of way and people had to be careful not to get in front of a car because they would most likely get hit.

The comment that tickled Holly was how little all the cars were in Mexico City. Kylie jumped in and said that was because the bigger ones could never squeeze in between the other cars. Everyone laughed at her comment. Having 25 million people in this city didn't leave a lot of room for big cars. Holly smiled at that comment. The other interesting comment was that there weren't many policemen around to keep the traffic in order.

Holly enjoyed observing Zach from the back of the van without him noticing. He was busy talking with Bill, giving him details for this evening at the church. He seemed to be comfortable with people and seemed excited about what he was telling Bill. It would be fun working with him this summer although she had to remind herself that this was not the time for romance. She silently asked God to remind her when she forgot.

After an eventful ride the vans arrived at the church about an hour after they departed from the airport. Before they got out of the van Bill turned and looked at everyone and said, "Please get your luggage out of the other van and follow Holly into the church. She will show you where to put your stuff for now. As soon as we get everything unloaded we'll get together and talk about what's happening this evening. Zach's been filling me in on the details. He'll be sharing more specific details regarding what we'll be doing over the next month as well." Zach's eyes connected with Holly's from the rear view mirror and she smiled at him. He noticed her cheeks get red and knew she was blushing from his attention.

Holly picked up her backpack and got out of the van first as Zach's eyes followed her all the way. The college students started getting off with their backpacks and headed over to the other van to get their luggage. They followed Holly into the church where they all piled the backpacks and luggage into the kitchen area. This was a one room building with a courtyard area outside.

Emma asked Holly as she put her luggage in the corner. "Will we be meeting our host families right away?"

"I don't think so Emma. I believe we'll be meeting as a team with Zach first. Then we will have our group devotions. I believe the Mexican families will come later with food and welcome us Mexican style. That's when we'll meet our host families. At least that's the way it's been done in the past. Every year things change but I believe that's what will happen. We'll learn more in a few minutes."

"Thanks Holly. This is so exciting!" She moved out the door and joined Kylie and the others in the courtyard area. Holly overheard Kylie telling Emma she thought Zach Benson was such a great looking guy. Emma smiled and nodded in agreement. Holly couldn't help but smile and silently agree with the girls.

Once everyone was in the courtyard she decided to go back in to check bags and be sure everything was stacked up neatly and along the walls so there was space for everyone to get around easily. After taking a deep breath she went out to join the team and Zach Benson.

Everyone sat in a circle of chairs that had been set up for them. Holly joined them as they talked with each other. The courtyard had changed since last year. She noticed that a spot had been cleared out for the bathroom building and that more tarps had been put up in the courtyard to keep rain off the tables and chairs. Otherwise everything else was as Holly remembered.

Bill finished his conversation with Zach and asked everyone to quiet down so that the meeting could begin.

"Jeff, would you open us with prayer?"

"Sure. Let's pray. Father we thank You for bringing us safely to Mexico City today. We appreciate that everything went smoothly for us. We are excited to be here and to see the things that You will accomplish through us. Please help us to be flexible in what You call us to do. We pray that You will enable us to share the gospel with all the people we will be spending time with. Help us with the construction work that we'll be doing and help us to get everything done in a timely manner. We desire to give You all the praise and glory. Please be with us now in this meeting. We pray Your will be done. Thanks for choosing to use broken vessels like us to further Your kingdom here in Mexico City. In Christ's name we pray, Amen."

"Thanks Jeff. Okay everyone, Zach is going to share with us what the rest of the evening looks like. He will give us an overview of the month and then more specific details of the week ahead of us. Zach, I'll turn the meeting over to you now."

Zach stole a quick look at Holly and she shared a quick smile.

"Thanks Bill." Looking at everyone Zach continued, "We are so grateful to have you here this summer. I have only been here myself a few weeks. I'm a seminary student from Florida and I'm interning here this summer as part of my program. I've been here since the beginning of June. I am primarily involved with the children's ministry which includes a street ministry as well. There are a few people at the church who have organized this ministry and you will be working with them. We'll talk more about that later. The biggest part of what you'll be doing here is helping to construct a two stall bathroom building with a toilet in each one near the church building. We have people from the church who will be working with

59

us. They will be responsible for the main construction. You will be doing things like hammering nails, painting, running for supplies, etc. You will also help build some cabinets in the kitchen area for storage. The ladies will be putting on a bible school in the park next door with help from some of you. They usually hold bible school here but they don't want any Mexican children to get hurt while the construction is going on. So the first two weeks will involve construction and bible school. The second two weeks will consist of painting the bathrooms, the new cabinets and all the walls."

Addressing the guys he said, "During the physical activities of bible school you will take a break from the construction work and lead that part. The Mexican children will love playing games with you."

Looking at the ladies he said, "A couple of you will be responsible for making curtains for the kitchen windows. I have the measurements so you will just have to buy the material and sew them. We will have two sewing machines available for you and they will be set up in the church. Any questions so far?" He looked around and everyone was listening and taking in what he said but no one had any questions.

"Okay then. The other thing that you will be participating in as I said earlier is a street ministry. That will happen every Friday and Saturday afternoon. Every Friday morning when we finish the construction work and bible school we will have lunch and then head downtown for the afternoon to minister to the street people. Then on Saturday morning we will meet here to have morning devotions and bible time with the Mexican children. We will provide a meal for them around noon and then we will have our own lunch once the children leave. Then in the afternoon we will go back to the street people. With the street people we begin with soccer, then we have a time of singing songs and sharing God's word and finally we will feed them a light lunch. One weekend in the middle of your trip we will travel to Taxco for some souvenir shopping and sightseeing. It's a small silver mining town in the mountains approximately three hours from here. That will be a time of relaxation and rest. For those of you who like silver jewelry this is the place to buy it." The girls clapped. "We will also take one afternoon off and travel to what is called the Market in the City for some more souvenir shopping. It has all kinds of things that you can purchase from leather goods to jewelry to clothes and lots of other stuff. So, that's an overview of your month here. I'll give you more specifics as time goes on."

Kylie raised her hand to ask a question. "Zach, do you have the supplies for our crafts for bible school or do we need to go to the store and buy them ourselves? I for one would love to go to a Mexican store and purchase the items we need."

Zach smiled as he replied, "You will have the opportunity to shop Kylie. We haven't had time to get the materials yet as well as some food for the lunches and snacks. You'll be meeting your teachers Sunday afternoon to talk about the theme for the week and discuss the crafts and snacks. Then you'll go out and purchase what is needed."

"Great!" Kylie was excited to get into a Mexican store and use her limited Spanish to make purchases.

Zach smiled. "Any other questions?"

"How does it work with the street people?" asked Liam.

"Basically, we walk down the streets and the street people begin to follow us. We will lead them to an open parking lot where we play soccer with them. Afterward I will share devotions with them, sing some songs and then usually we feed them tortillas, beans, bread and drink. We'll talk more about that before we go."

"I'm really looking forward to participating in that ministry." Liam smiled as he looked around at his team. "I hope to be a youth pastor in the future but I don't know whether it's to be on the mission field in something like this or in a church in the states."

"That's great Liam." Zach was encouraged by Liam's statement.

Zach wanted to finish up so they could get to their group devotions before the Mexicans started arriving at the church to welcome the American team.

"Lastly this evening the Mexican host families will be bringing food and giving you a welcome party. In Spanish the word for welcome is bienvenido. The food will consist of Mexican pizza and ice cream. The families are excited to meet you and have you in their homes. They'll be here around seven so you need to have your group devotions now before they start coming. You'll hang out with your host families tonight and possibly around ten you'll go to their homes with them. Just as an aside, Holly and Bill may have already told you this, but Mexican people don't live by the clock. You will need to be flexible while you're here as they move at a slower pace compared to our culture. So don't worry if at ten your family isn't ready to leave. It's okay. Don't worry if you happen to be late in the morning. We'll wait for you."

Bill looked at everyone as they talked. "Okay, let's get our bibles and devotion books and meet back here in five minutes."

Zach stopped them before they started for their things. "One thing I almost forgot to mention. The only toilet you can use here is in the little room next door. A family lives there but there are very kind in letting us use it when needed. It has an outside door so you don't have to go through their residence. Please don't put toilet paper down the toilet. There will be a trash can next to the toilet to deposit your paper. This is true for your host families' homes as well." He chuckled at the expressions on their faces. He remembered the first time he heard that as a young boy visiting Mexico City with his parents. He thought it was disgusting. They nodded their heads as they remembered being told that during their monthly prep meetings.

Bill looked at Zach and said, "Thanks for all the preparation you've been doing on our behalf." Everyone said thanks and nodded their heads in agreement with Bill.

"I think I can speak for all of us when I say it's great to be here and we are all excited about what we will be doing." Chuckling he added, "Even with the bathroom situations". Once again everybody nodded their heads in agreement.

"It's been my pleasure. I'm enjoying being here and I have looked forward to getting to know each of you." Zach looked at Holly as he said that and she smiled shyly.

Holly sat there thinking about how much she wanted to get to know him. She just had to be careful since this was not why she came to Mexico City. Everyone went to get their bibles and devotion books in order to meet in a few minutes. Zach had some things to do before the Mexican people arrived so he told them he would join them later. Holly watched him leave and then joined the team. He looked back at the same moment she was watching him and nodded his head slightly to acknowledge her and then walked through the door. Holly gave him a tentative smile in return as she walked over to join the team for devotions.

Zach knew he would have to be careful about Holly. He felt an immediate attraction to her but knew this was not the time or place to act on that attraction. He would have to get to know her only as a friend for now and trust God with the rest.

CHAPTER 12

Miguel talked with his thugs while Gabriel cleaned off the table. Miguel had a woman come in and cook for them every night. On this evening they had just finished eating tacos. Gabriel listened as Miguel outlined his plan to get rid of the "Americanos". He learned of their arrival in Mexico City today and knew they would be coming to his area of the streets soon. He was confident that he would be able to get rid of them and this time for good. He just had to wait and be patient for the right opportunity. Gabriel knew Miguel was good at waiting.

Gabriel washed the dishes while listening to what they said. The house they lived in was not much but it was better than most people had in the area. He hoped to finish cleaning the dishes so he could go to the church and get a look at the "Americanos". He had to be very careful that Miguel didn't see him or find out.

When Gabriel finished cleaning he looked over to Miguel who was talking with one of his body guards. Gabriel left quietly through the back door and knew he wouldn't be missed for a while. Taking some shortcuts he walked about two miles to the small church building. While he walked he thought back to the last group of people that came from the United States. He enjoyed listening to their stories about God and His Son Jesus. He had a difficult time understanding what they said but he remembered feeling good being around them, much better than he felt being with Miguel. He just didn't know why. Hopefully this new group of people would talk more about

Jesus so that he could understand better why they loved Him so much and were willing to come to a different country to share about Him. For the first time in a long time Gabriel had a little smile on his face as he continued walking to the church.

~~~~~~~~~~

Bill looked at his watch as they closed their group devotions in prayer and realized that the Mexican families would be arriving soon. He thought he even heard some people milling around outside the fence. The church and courtyard were surrounded by an eleven foot wrought iron fence with a large blue metal door that was locked when people weren't permitted inside. There had been a lot of vandalism in the church so the members paid to have the fence and door put up for security.

Bill knew Pastor Abraham would be returning any minute to open the door to allow people to come in. Bill was pleased at how well group devotions went because there was a lot of good discussion. He looked forward to more of their time together as a team. It was a real bonding time for them as well as helping everyone to keep their focus on the Lord.

Before the Mexican families arrived Bill wanted to get the attention of his team since they were talking to each other. "The families will be arriving soon. I think I already heard some people here outside. You each have your host family names so be looking for them as you introduce yourselves. They have your names and will be looking for you as well but Pastor Abraham said earlier that he will be introducing everyone later just in case you can't find your host family. Just remember to use your Spanish when you can. They are looking forward to getting to know each of you while you're here. Please put bibles and devotion books back with your luggage now."

Pastor Abraham noticed the Americans putting their stuff away as he arrived with his wife. He wanted to introduce her to them but knew he needed to unlock the blue metal door first. After unlocking the door Pastor Abraham and his wife greeted their friends as they entered the courtyard.

As soon as some of the men arrived they started putting up tables and chairs. The ladies got busy putting paper products and silverware on the tables. Holly was excited to see the Sandoval family who were her host family. She stayed with them last year and grew to love them. They wanted her to stay with them again this year and Becca would be staying with them as well.

Holly looked to see if they had arrived so she could introduce them to Becca but she didn't see them yet. She noticed Emma and Kylie talking to some younger girls. The guys were kicking around a soccer ball with some younger boys in the courtyard. She decided to take this opportunity to run over and use the bathroom before it got crowded.

Before she went inside she noticed some changes that had been made to the small dwelling that was home to a family she came to know last year. It had a yellow tarp as a roof last year and every time it rained they had to tighten the tarp so it wouldn't blow off. This year she noticed they had replaced the tarp with several long pieces of hard plastic. She couldn't tell how it was secured to the side but she hoped it did a better job of keeping out the rain. She noticed someone had planted some bright colored flowers along the side of the dwelling giving it a cheerier appearance. The family who lived here had very little income so it was nice to see that they could make some improvements for better living conditions.

As the sounds picked up in the church she quickly slipped inside the little room and shut the door behind her being thankful for the few moments of quiet. She heard a noise from the other side of the wall that sounded like a baby but she wasn't sure. She prayed no one would come through the door even as she remembered being surprised last year that this family always seemed to know when someone was using their toilet. She never did figure it out.

One of the most challenging things for her on a mission trip was having time alone. She liked being by herself sometimes and that was rarely possible on these trips. She washed her hands and headed out to renew old friendships and to make new ones.

As she stepped out the door she saw the Sandoval family walking into the courtyard and ran over to them. They turned and saw her when she called their name. They were so happy to see her and hugged and kissed her. It was so great to see them she thought. She caught Becca's eye and signaled for her to come over to meet this terrific family.

Becca noticed their reunion as Holly waved to her. "Becca, I want to introduce you to the Sandoval family."

Looking at each one individually Holly pointed out each of the children first. "This is Angelica, Marta, Juanita and Jose." They each shook Becca's hand and kissed her cheek. Turning to their parents Holly continued, "This is Iliana and Julio." Becca shook their hands as they also kissed her cheek.

Julio, as the head of his family, addressed Becca in his broken English, "We are pleased to meet you Becca. My English is not so good but I am trying. We are glad to have you in our home."

"Mucho gusto y gracias. I am very happy to meet you all. Thank you for having me in your home." She said this in Spanish and English and they were pleased at her use of their language. Holly was impressed as well. She knew Becca had been practicing her Spanish and it seemed to have paid off.

As Becca and the Sandovals got to know each other Holly noticed Zach walk into the courtyard with his hands full of groceries and drinks. No one else seemed to see him so she excused herself to go help him. As she walked over to Zach she noticed a young boy standing at the edge of the outside door looking in. She stopped for a moment wondering if she should go over to ask him if he would like to come in and join them. She kept looking at him as she smiled and started towards him. She hurried when she saw him back away from the door. When she got there he was nowhere to be seen. She looked up and down the street but didn't see him. Oh well, she thought, maybe he will come back another day. She started back to help Zach.

"Hi Zach, can I help you with some of that?" she asked him, a little bit distracted.

He smiled. "Thanks. I thought I might drop it all before I made it through the door." He handed her a bag of drinks to carry over to the tables.

"Hey Zach, did you see that little boy standing at the doorway when you came in just now?"

"No, what did he look like?"

"He was a small boy, dark curly hair, maybe seven or eight."

"That sounds like a lot of little boys around here. I'm sorry I didn't notice any little boy by the door."

Shrugging her shoulders Holly said, "Maybe he'll come back later."

~~~~~~~~~~

Gabriel ran across the street and hid behind the building when the girl came to the door. He didn't want to talk to her but he wanted to see what was happening at the church. He watched her looking for him up and down the street before she went back inside. When everyone was inside the building and it didn't look like any more people were coming, Gabriel carefully climbed up onto the top of the roof across the street from the church so he could look over the fence at what was happening. From the roof top he could see lots of people in the courtyard. He saw tables decorated with flowers and covered with lots of food and drink. He could easily tell the Americanos from the Mexicans because their skin was lighter than his. He spotted the girl who was looking for him talking to the man that comes to his area and tells stories about Jesus. He tried to remember the man's name but couldn't at the moment.

As Gabriel watched them he thought the girl was very pretty. She was much smaller than the man. He was fascinated by the color of her hair. He knew Mexican men liked Americano girls with light colored hair. The thought crossed his mind that Miguel would like this Americano girl a lot. Gabriel didn't like that idea at all because he knew about Miguel's plan to get rid of these Americanos. He hoped Miguel never had the chance to see this girl. He physically shook his head to get rid of that uncomfortable thought. He liked how she smiled while talking to the man. Maybe he would get a chance to meet her later if she was one of the people who came to his neighborhood and if Miguel wasn't around because he definitely didn't want Miguel watching this girl. There it was again that same disconcerting thought and it made Gabriel feel a little anxious.

Gabriel knew it was getting late and thought he better get back home. Miguel would be wondering where he was and he didn't want to tell him anything about his visit to the church.

~~~~~~~~~~

"So how many people are you expecting tonight Zach," questioned Holly?

While the Mexican women emptied the bags and set the food on the table Zach replied to Holly. "All of the host families will be here although some will arrive a little later. So I would say approximately thirty to forty people. We will probably eat in about a half an hour or so and hopefully by then everyone will be here. Pastor Abraham wants to introduce the host families to your team just in case everyone hasn't met each other."

He put the empty bags under the tables to collect trash later. He was glad for these few moments to be with Holly and wanted to take the opportunity to get to know her better.

Taking Holly's elbow he guided her over to the side of the courtyard. "I understand you were here last year Holly. Was that your first time in Mexico City?"

"No, I have come here the last three years. The first year Bill came to our church he planned a mission trip here. It was the first mission trip I had ever been on. I absolutely loved it."

"I took some mission trips as well when I was an undergrad student. When I found out I had to do an internship as part of my seminary studies I decided I wanted to do it here. My mother is from Mexico and I thought it would be cool to have the opportunity to serve her people and get to know them and their culture better. She hasn't been here in years though and hopes to visit in the near future."

"Really," Holly exclaimed. "It's great that you were able to get this opportunity then. Did your mom know any of the families at this church?"

"Not really. She is from Veracruz which is several hours from Mexico City. But it's nice getting to know the Mexican people here. I have really enjoyed it so far."

"I bet your mom was excited when she knew you would be interning here."

"Yeah, she was. My dad wants to bring her here next year so I hope it works out for them." Zach became silent for a moment as he thought about his parents.

"I hope so too." Holly enjoyed talking to him. She noticed he was quiet for a few moments. He probably missed his parents a lot. She was really comfortable being with him. He kept looking at her and smiling. Once again she noticed he had beautiful eyes.

Holly broke the silence between the two of them as they looked at each other. "I probably ought to get back to the Sandovals. Becca and I were talking with them when you came in. I stayed with them last year and I'm looking forward to being with them again this year."

"You're right. We should be mingling with everyone." As she walked away Zach put his hand on her arm to stop her.

"Holly, do you think we could talk some more later," he asked softly and with some hesitation?

She smiled with desire shining from her eyes and replied softly, "Yeah Zach. I'd like that."

"Good. I'll look forward to it. Tomorrow might be a good time when we're on the boats in Xochimilco. Jaime will be serving his shrimp and rice dinner."

"That sounds good. I'll see you later." She walked over to greet some other people. She whispered a prayer thanking God for the little bit of time she just had with Zach and looked forward to tomorrow.

As Holly walked away Zach prayed as well thanking God for the opportunity to talk to her. He also prayed that God would guide him in his time with her. Just being with Holly for a few moments blessed Zach because he recognized that she was a very special young woman but he knew they were both here for service and not romance. Even though he couldn't wait to know more about her he would have to be very, very careful.

Zach whistled as he walked over and greeted some families. Anyone watching Holly and Zach probably wondered what was going on between the two of them. She was smiling and he was whistling.

Pastor Abraham got everyone's attention so they could pray for the dinner that had been prepared for them. He hoped the Americans would enjoy Mexican pizza and ice cream. He asked them to bow as he prayed. "Father, we thank you for giving us this time together as sisters and brothers in Christ and thank you for bringing our American friends safely here. I pray that you would bless their time with us. We pray for sweet fellowship as we make new friends and we thank You for this food. Please strengthen and nourish our bodies to serve You better. In Christ's name we pray, Amen." Then he announced that the women and children would go first through the line and then the men would follow.

The women and children started through the line filling their plates with pizza. There was plenty of food so no one was in a big hurry. The men continued their conversations while waiting. Holly was so tickled to be eating Mexican pizza because their sauce had a different flavor than back home. They also had several pizzas with ham and pineapple and some others had different mixtures for toppings. It was sure different from American pizza but just as tasty. She didn't like the ice cream they had because of the flavors. One was pink in color and the flavor was rose which tasted like perfume to her. Another one tasted like cucumbers. She could do without the ice cream. She went over to join Kylie and Emma and a group of Mexican ladies that they were visiting with while eating. Holly looked forward to going home with the Sandovals and catching up with them. She was sure a lot had happened in their family since last year. She was glad Becca had the time earlier to spend with them.

As the evening progressed people were having fun with each other and sharing about their families. As Holly looked around her she loved seeing the interaction between the Americans and the Mexicans. Her team members seemed to be fitting right in, using their Spanish when necessary and enjoying these new people in their lives.

Soon after people finished eating Pastor Abraham got everyone's attention so that he could formally introduce the Americans to the Mexicans. It looked like the host families found the Americans that would be staying with them but Pastor Abraham wanted to be sure. After the introductions people got ready to leave. Bill wanted to see the Americans as a group before they left with their host families so he got them together as the Mexicans cleaned up the leftover food.

Bill asked the team to gather together in the church sanctuary. He could tell that everyone was tired and knew it was good that they were able to leave with their host families earlier than planned.

"You each have the phone number of the host family where Jeff and I will be staying. You also have

Holly and Becca's host family number as well. If you have any questions or problems, please don't hesitate to call any one of us." If anybody gets sick, please let us know immediately. I also want to say how much I enjoyed watching you interact with the Mexican people tonight. It was such a joy seeing your willingness to use your Spanish." Becca, Holly and Jeff nodded in agreement. "Jeff, will you pray for us before we leave?"

Jeff nodded. "Everyone, let's bow before our Lord. Father, we thank you for this wonderful evening and for giving us this opportunity to meet these dear people. Thank you for the safe travels of today and we ask that you protect us as we depart and keep us safe while we are apart from each other. Please bring us safely back together tomorrow. It's in Jesus' name that we pray, Amen."

"Thanks Jeff. One last thing, tomorrow morning we will be meeting here around ten and your host families will bring you to the church. Don't worry if you're running behind schedule because, as I said before, most of the time Mexicans are on a different time schedule than we are and that's fine. We will be helping with the Saturday morning children's bible study and then serving a meal. After that we will go to Xochimilco and enjoy the afternoon boating on the floating gardens with Jaime serving his shrimp and rice dinner. You will probably need to come here several times with your host families to get familiar with the route and then you will be able to come by yourselves. So keep track of how you get here. Have a great time with your families and we'll see you tomorrow morning around ten."

Everyone grabbed their luggage and went out to meet their host families to head home with them. Some would be taking a taxi, some would be riding in cars and the rest would be taking the bus.

Holly, Becca, Jeff and Bill waited for their kids to leave with their host families to be sure everyone was accounted for before they left. The Sandovals were ready to go home so Becca went over to say goodbye to her husband before she left. As Holly waited with the Sandovals for Becca she looked over and saw Zach looking at her. She quickly waved her hand to say goodbye and he waved back. She smiled because she looked forward to getting to know him better tomorrow at Xochimilco. Becca came over and they left for the Sandovals' home by riding the bus. Holly knew riding the bus was a very unique experience because people would jump on buses even when they were full. The bus drivers ignore traffic signals and tried to load as many passengers as possible in order to make as much money as possible. It could be dangerous so you had to be very observant. Riding the bus in the evening was even more challenging then during the day. But it was a blessing to be with the Sandovals as they headed home. While they were in Mexico City she knew Bill and Jeff would also ride the bus back to the Sandovals with them in the evenings to be sure they got there safely.

Zach was excited as he watched Holly leave and he thanked God for bringing this young woman into his life. Zach didn't have much experience with women. He didn't date in high school because he did a lot of group activities that included guys and girls. In college his mom encouraged him to get to know young women through campus ministries but none of them caught his eye the way Holly had. Zach hoped tomorrow would be the beginning of a special relationship with Holly.   Silently he lifted up a prayer to that end as well as for Holly's time with her host family and for their time together tomorrow.   He started whistling as Pastor Abraham came up behind him and said, "Zach, I noticed twice tonight you were whistling a happy tune. Does a lovely, young, blonde American woman have anything to do with your whistling?" Pastor Abraham had a twinkle in his eye as he walked off to put away the last few chairs. Zach felt the blood rushing to his face as he walked over to help put the rest of the chairs away and lock up before they left the church. Zach knew he was smitten and asked God to protect both of them as he and Pastor Abraham turned off the lights and walked out of the church.

CHAPTER 13

Holly was the first to get up on Saturday morning. She remembered from last year that the Sandoval's water was cut off from midnight to 5 a.m. and she wanted to take advantage of it coming on as soon as possible. She liked to get up early, finish her toiletries and spend some time alone with God. Becca said she wanted to get up around 7 a.m. so Holly had plenty of time. They were to use the downstairs bathroom and their host family would use the upstairs bathroom.

Becca and Holly shared a small room with two twin beds and a small nightstand between the beds. There was just enough room at the end of the beds to lay their suitcases on the floor. With their luggage on the floor there was very little walking space. She laid her clothes out last night so she wouldn't have to make a lot of noise getting into her suitcase. She didn't want to wake Becca up too early.

Holly walked quietly down the stairs to the bathroom which was at the end of the stairs on the left side just before the entrance door. This room was just large enough for a toilet, sink and small shower stall. She noticed the small trash can next to the toilet where toilet tissue was supposed to go instead of down the toilet. There wasn't enough water pressure in Mexico to flush paper down the toilet so they used small trash cans for that reason. She shrugged thinking this was all part of serving the Lord in a foreign country and Mrs. Sandoval was very good at emptying the trash cans regularly. Every time she returned home to the United States after these trips she had a special appreciation for being able to flush toilet paper down the toilet.

As she got into the shower she reminded herself to keep her mouth closed so she didn't swallow any water. She didn't want to experience "Montezuma's Revenge" as the Americans called the awful stomach ache and diarrhea that one got after drinking the water in Mexico City. When Holly finished with her shower she got dressed and went back to her room and woke Becca up. While Becca was in the shower Holly got her Bible and did her quiet time with God. Becca came quietly into their room respecting Holly's time with God and got into her quiet time as well.

Iliana Sandoval got up early and was downstairs preparing breakfast for her guests so they could get to the church by 10 a.m. She was glad to have Holly in their home again and she liked Becca as well. Iliana admired how Becca spoke Spanish with her family and was impressed with Holly's improvement in her Spanish too. Her girls were going to join Becca and Holly to help with the children at the church this morning.

Holly and Becca came down later to breakfast and enjoyed conversation with Iliana. Holly loved Iliana and enjoyed their time together. She didn't get a lot of time with Iliana, mostly at meals. Iliana didn't speak English very well but with Holly's Spanish/English dictionary they seemed to make out alright. With her improved Spanish this year and Becca's knowledge of Spanish they were able to have a delightful breakfast with Iliana. She shared a lot about what had been happening with her family over the past year.

Iliana made them scrambled eggs and refried beans. She served them a small bowl of cereal with liquid yogurt poured over the top. She also had mango cut up in small pieces along with some sweet breads and fresh squeezed orange juice. Holly knew she could trust Iliana when it came to being careful with their food and water.

Breakfast was soon over and Becca and Holly needed to leave for the church. Marta and Angelica would be going with them to the church. Juanita would be joining them later at the church. The girls would show Holly and Becca what bus to get on so that during the week they could do it themselves. The girls came down the stairs, grabbed a quick bite to eat and they all headed out the door.

As they left Becca whispered to Holly, "Did the girls get enough to eat? They seemed to be in a hurry and their hair wasn't even dry yet."

"Becca, here in Mexico they don't worry about things like their hair not being dry before leaving the house. The temperature is so nice that their hair will dry in no time. You'll probably see quite a few ladies and young girls with wet hair. The Mexican culture is extremely laid back. I think the girls are making an effort to get us to the church on time but they didn't get up early enough. They will probably eat some of the stuff we have at the church for the kids if they get hungry."

Becca nodded okay as they walked out the door. Holly looked back at Iliana and thanked her for breakfast. Becca did too. They shut the door and walked down the five flights of stairs to the ground level. Angelica and Marta were chatting up a storm and hurrying so Becca and

Holly hurried as well. The girls wanted to catch the next bus so they had to get to the bus stop quickly.

Traffic was not as heavy as it normally would be during the weekdays so that was a blessing. The streets were like the spokes of a bicycle wheel rolling out from the center. The streets came from five different directions with the center being the best place to catch a bus. It was easier crossing the big streets this time of day, especially on the weekend rather than during the week. Pedestrians did not have the right of way here so the girls had to be really careful watching all directions before crossing to the bus stop.

Holly and Becca jumped on the bus that the girls picked out and found some seats together. Holly sat with Angelica and Becca sat with Marta. They were talking about the Mexican children they would be working with that morning and what the Americans would be serving for a snack. Becca thought it was more of a meal than a snack but Holly knew that this meal was the only meal that a lot of these Mexican children would get today. There were a lot of poor families in this church. Even the host families didn't have a lot but what they had they were more than happy to share with the American team. Holly was glad the team would be giving each host family an envelope with $150 to help defray the costs of hosting the Americans for a month.

The girls told Holly and Becca they would be getting off at the next bus stop and then walk the rest of the way to the church. It was good for Holly and Becca to learn this route and what bus to take so that during the week when the girls were in school they could get to the church by themselves.

As they walked to the church from the bus stop Angelica and Marta shared about their school. Angelica would be graduating this year, Marta had one more year and Juanita had two more years. Jose, their brother, was enjoying his first year of college and doing really well. He wouldn't be too involved with the team this year because of his studies. He hoped to spend some time with them during the street ministry.

They arrived at the church after a few of the others had gotten there. There was already a flurry of activity in the kitchen and in the courtyard. Holly saw some of the Mexican children playing ball in the street with Kylie, Emma, Chris and Liam. Jackson and Seth were inside helping set up chairs and tables. They had already set up little chairs in separate areas of the courtyard for individual classes and a few tables in the center for crafts.

The ages of the Mexican children today ranged from 4-11 year olds. Chris and Seth would help with the 10-11 year old boys while Jackson and Liam would help with the 7-9 year old boys. Bill and Jeff would work with the 4-6 year old boys. Kylie was going to help with the 10-11 year old girls and Emma the 7-9 year old girls. A couple of the Mexican women had the 4-6 year old girls and Holly and Becca would be helping them. Everyone would help with the games but crafts were done in the individual groups.

It was a great morning and everything seemed to move along nicely without any hitches. When it was close to serving lunch Emma and Kylie went to help. Some of the children were finishing their crafts and some of them were outside playing games. There were several Mexican women preparing the meal in the kitchen.

As Emma and Kylie set the tables with napkins and cups with drinks the kids came running into the courtyard and quickly sat at the tables. Emma and Kylie started serving plates with a hotdog, chips, apple and cookies for dessert. Chris, Seth, Jackson and Liam came in after rounding up a few stragglers and put the balls away to help serve the children as well. They served extra drinks when the children finished what they had and there were extra hotdogs to share as well. Children were waving their hands and calling out for more food. The children loved the hotdogs and the Americans loved watching them enjoy the food so much!

It was an amazing thing to behold 60 children chow down their food so quickly. It seemed liked they hardly took a breath while eating. It was also sad to think that this could be the only meal for the day that some of them would eat. It was difficult for Holly to think about while she watched them eat. She constantly lifted them up in prayer.

After everyone finished eating the Americans cleaned up and dumped paper plates and cups in the trash. Some of the children wanted to wrap up extra hotdogs in napkins and take them home. So a couple of the Mexican women found the plastic bags that the hotdog rolls came in and put the napkin wrapped hotdogs in them for the children. Some took apples as well. There were no leftover cookies.

Holly happened to look up from serving one of the children when she noticed the young boy she saw last night leaning against the metal door. She wasn't sure what to do because she didn't want him to run away like last night. She smiled at him and waved. He smiled back and then left. Holly wanted to find out who he was but there wasn't anyone close to ask. Everyone was busy helping the Mexican children finish cleaning up. One of the children shouted to her for more drink so she picked up her pitcher and walked over to serve the child. She sent up a prayer asking God to give her the opportunity to find out who that little boy was and to have a chance to talk to him. Something about him pulled at her heart.

Liam walked over to Holly when they had finished serving the children and when the tables were cleaned and stacked. "Holly, is it really true that this is the only meal that some of these children will eat today?"

"Unfortunately it is Liam. Some of these families live on 12 cents a day if you can believe it. It's hard to comprehend. They can't afford to eat but one meal a day. Some don't even get one meal a day. That's one of the reasons the church sponsors this Saturday morning bible club so that the Mexican children have the opportunity to hear about God and also get a good meal. That's also why the church hosts bible school each summer. This year because we're here for an extended amount of time they are sponsoring bible school for two weeks instead of one. Some of the money we raised at home in preparation for this trip will go toward paying for the meals like today. We also get to plan the meals and buy the food during those two weeks."

Holly gave Liam a few moments to digest this and then continued their conversation, "I really love this part of the trip. Being able to give these Mexican children a good meal is a real blessing while at the same time it is fun to go to the market and shop for the food. It's an experience that I'm sure everyone will enjoy. The first time I visited one of their stores I was shocked to see a lot of armed guards wearing bullet proof vests and carrying machine guns walking everywhere to guard the entrances and everything in sight. The last couple of years there didn't seem to be quite so many guards as that first year. I know it's hard but we have to remember that God is in control here and we do what we can while we're here."

The look in Liam's eyes spoke volumes to Holly about this young man's heart. He will make a great pastor one day she thought. She wouldn't be surprised if God had other plans for him as well. "Thanks Holly. It is hard to know people live like this when we have so much."

Speaking with conviction he continued, "But certainly you're right. We can only do so much for them while we're here and we can, most importantly, keep them in our prayers. We can't change everything at once to make it better, can we?"

"No, we sure can't. We get the privilege to come along side God in His work and do what He gives us to do. It sort of reminds me of Jesus. He did a lot of healing but he didn't heal everyone. There were so many people that needed Him, but God gave Him a purpose, a ministry and a time frame, and that's what He accomplished while He was on this earth. He left the rest in God's hands and at the end was able to say it is finished. Just like we have to do during the time He has given us here. Does that make sense Liam?"

"It does and thanks. It helps to remember that when I see so much suffering, God will use me when and where He chooses and the rest I will leave up to Him." He walked away with a determined look in his eyes. Holly knew that God would do wonderful things with that young man.

After the last of the Mexican children left and the door was locked, Bill and Jeff got everyone together for their group devotions. They decided to do it now before they left for Xochilmilco. It would be a long afternoon and they wouldn't arrive back to the church until later that evening when Berta, their cook, would have dinner ready for them. She was a member of this church and was hired by the Americans to cook for them while in Mexico. She knew what to cook and how to cook it so that it wouldn't be difficult for their digestive systems. She always used bottled water and certain spices that would protect them from stomach ailments. Everybody would be pretty tired by the evening so Bill wanted to work on their devotions now while they were still fresh.

Pastor Abraham and Zach were in the church talking while the team gathered up their bibles and devotion books and made a circle out in the courtyard. The door had been locked so they wouldn't be interrupted by anyone. Jeff was leading today's devotion.

Last evening Bill began their devotions by looking at James 1:1-8. He talked about profiting from trials, counting it all joy when we have trials knowing that the testing of our faith produces patience. He had several questions during the course of that devotion that produced great discussion.

Today Jeff would be sharing James 1:9-11 about the perspective of being rich or poor. As they began reading this Scripture, Holly remembered her conversation with Liam. She was constantly amazed at God's perfect timing. This part of James talked about God not being a respecter of persons and that both rich and poor have the privilege of being identified with Christ. Both groups of people are on the same level with each other and God wants to keep them from being preoccupied with earthly things. As the team discussed this, Liam shared that he believed genuine happiness and contentment depended on the true riches of God's grace, not earthly wealth. Everyone nodded in agreement. Jackson shared that even the poor can rejoice in their high spiritual standing before God because of His grace and the hope that comes with that grace. During this discussion Liam's eyes met Holly's in understanding. The opportunity to be with God's people, sharing in the understanding of His word as well as working and serving in His kingdom is what these times were all about. What a blessing!

Jeff closed their time together in prayer and briefly went over what the rest of the day looked like. They would travel to Xochimilco by bus and Jaime and his family would meet them at the boats with his shrimp, rice and drinks. Everyone was to grab their backpacks and be ready when Pastor Abraham and Zach were ready to leave.

They each grabbed their backpacks and waited in the courtyard. The ladies were gone and the kitchen had been completely cleaned without any evidence of anything having taken place this morning. Everyone was hungry so they were anxious to be on their way. Just then Pastor

Abraham and Zach came out of the building ready to leave. Walking to the bus stop Holly watched Kylie and Chris talking while the others walked behind them chatting with each other. She was sure their conversations were about the morning's activities. She liked to be behind everyone so she could keep an eye on the team as it allowed her to encourage anyone who fell behind. Bill talked with Pastor Abraham while Jeff and Becca were busy talking to each other. It was hard for them not staying together at night but they were accepting it well. Holly saw Zach lagging behind the rest of the group. She hoped they could talk while they walked.

Zach initiated the conversation when she caught up with him. Looking at her he said, "Hey. How did things go last night with your host family?"

"Great!" she said with a smile. "I stayed with them last year and I love their family. I'm glad I'm able to stay with them again this year." She looked at him and then she looked away as she continued to talk. "Iliana doesn't speak much English as you know, but I have been studying my Spanish a lot more this past year. Becca does really well with her Spanish so we were able to have a nice conversation with her this morning at breakfast. I think she appreciated that we spoke, as best we could, in her language. She even used some of the English that she's been learning. In the past one of her kids would translate for us but it was nice not to have to do that today."

"Good, I'm glad." You know you have a great team. They seemed to enjoy themselves last night. I didn't hear anyone complain of being tired after such a long day of travel. Today they really pitched in and were a big help."

"Thanks. I think so too. I'm just getting to know each of them. As I told you earlier this is my first time here as a leader and I've never worked with any of these college students before. Jeff and Becca work with the youth in our church so they know them better than I do. I've had some great conversations with some of them already though."

He smiled as they continued following everyone to the bus. Holly asked him, "Where in the states are you from Zach?"

"San Antonio, Texas. I was born and raised there. When my dad was in college he took a mission trip to Mexico with Campus Crusade. He met my mom on that trip. He came back to Mexico for the next couple of years, they fell in love and when he graduated he came back and proposed. They had to jump through a lot of hoops to get her a visa and passport to be able to live in America but it finally worked out. They had a wedding in Mexico City and then later in the states for all my relatives. Several years later, she got a permanent visa because of her marriage to an American. Now she can leave the states anytime for Mexico and return to the states without any problem. It took them a long time to get it all worked out though."

She turned and looked at Zach as they walked. "That's a great story Zach. When was the last time your mom was back here?"

"It's probably been about ten years. She came back when her father died. Her mother died when she was a young girl. She doesn't have any brothers or sisters which is unusual for Mexican families. They're usually pretty large."

"Do you have any brothers or sisters?" Holly asked.

"I have a younger brother in high school. His name is Elias, Eli for short. He's great. He loves basketball and soccer. We're really close and I miss him when I'm at seminary."

Holly enjoyed listening to Zach talk. He had such a soft yet strong voice. She loved watching his eyes when he shared about his family. She liked this man which caused her to smile a lot. Zach looked at her when he finished talking and they enjoyed a few minutes of silence thinking about each other.

They were getting close to the bus stop so Holly kept her eyes on the college students as they approached the stop. Zach, too, was being sure everyone was together. Getting on a city bus, a pasero as they were called in Mexico City was a challenge because they were so overcrowded. Pastor Abraham signaled to Zach to take the rear as he took the lead being sure the Americans all boarded the same bus. Bill hurried the team onto the bus when it arrived and Holly and Zach got on last.

This bus wasn't as crowded as some of the buses that Holly had taken in the past, probably because it was a Saturday. She was glad because it meant that she could relax a little bit more. She and Zach continued their conversation as they stood. There weren't any more seats left and Holly didn't want one of the college students giving up their seat for her. She secretly wanted to talk some more with Zach anyway.

Continuing their conversation Zach asked Holly, "Do you have any siblings?"

"I do. I have one brother Micah. He's married with two children. His wife Ellie is great and I lovvvve my niece and nephew Katie and Caleb. They are so cool." Zach loved seeing the sparkle in her eyes when she talked about her family. "My mom and I live on a ranch and my brother and his family live down the road from us. I get to see them often and I enjoy babysitting for Katie and Caleb."

"What kind of work do you do?"

"I just graduated college and I haven't decided what I want to do yet. My degree is in Psychology and I thought I might like to do counseling with women but I would have to get my Master's first. Our church is starting a lay counseling program and I thought I might participate in that and get my feet wet first. At one time I thought I might like to be a guidance counselor in the school system and I might still decide to do that. I wanted to wait before I settled into a job so I could participate in this longer mission trip."

Zach looked at Holly for what seemed an eternity but was really only a few seconds. "Well I'm sure glad you decided to wait and come on this trip." Holly noticed his face blushing and she thought that was sweet.

"Thanks Zach. Me too." She smiled and then looked away.

They were coming up to the bus stop for Xochimilco. Everyone had to get off quickly and then walk over to the boats. They were excited as Holly watched the girls talking with the guys. It was nice to see the guys being protective of the girls. Right before they left the church Bill made it a point to remind the guys to keep the girls in their sight at all times. Whenever they were on buses he told them to keep the girls between them. Everyone was to watch each other's back and backpacks. Mexican guys liked American girls and pick pocketing was a pretty common occurrence in Mexico City.

Once they got to the boats Pastor Abraham told them that Jaime had not arrived yet so that if the Americans wanted to do some shopping at the local booths they had some time. The team noticed there were several little outdoor booths filled with everything from jewelry, clothing, hats and water colors to hammocks. Bill reminded them to go in pairs and that they had to be back in half an hour. He noticed that the guys stuck with the girls when they walked off toward the booths and he was glad about that. It was good that the guys were taking seriously his words about protecting the girls. The little booths were in the vicinity of the boats so they couldn't go very far. Zach, Bill, Jeff and Pastor Abraham talked as everyone took off for the little booths. Becca and Holly headed off together as well. Holly wanted to find a nice water color print for Micah and Ellie. She also wanted to get Katie a Mexican beaded bracelet because she loved girlie jewelry. Caleb was still a baby but she thought she could find him a wooden carved truck for when he was a little older. Becca wanted to find something for Jeff as a remembrance of their trip together. It was fun shopping but they had to keep track of the time because they wanted to be ready when Jaime arrived.

CHAPTER 14

Everyone had a wonderful time that afternoon. When they finished their shopping they returned to the boats to find Jaime and his family waiting with the food. They took turns climbing onboard a flat bottom boat with a colorful painted sign arched over the entrance of the boat with the name Angelica painted across it. All the boats had small wooden canopies so that they had shelter if it rained which it generally did every afternoon. There were two long tables the length of the boat with ten chairs along both sides of the table. The canal had at least 35 different boats that came or went and were docked. Like their boat the others each had a woman's name painted on the floral archway leading onto the boat.

After everyone found a seat the Mexican man standing at the end of the boat started moving the boat with a long pole that he would put into the water to move the boat. Jaime and his wife, with the help of others, started serving the food. He had cooked his shrimp in tomatoes with a few jalapeno peppers. It was served over rice with sliced avocados on top. There were saltine crackers for those who wanted them. Later, a Mexican dessert called flan was served. It was a congealed custard pudding and people either liked it or not. The Americans ate and found it delicious.

While they floated on the canal and ate the delicious food a boat carrying a mariachi band floated nearby and Jaime paid the band to play music as they floated alongside their boat. Some of the college students got up and started to dance at one end of the boat. It was really enjoyable! Holly noticed another boat floating by selling baskets of flowers to people on other boats. Zach sat next to her as they ate their food and then they got up to dance to the music. There wasn't much room to dance but it was fun just the same. Holly had enjoyed coming here last year but this year with Zach present it was even better. The more they shared about each other the more she liked him. She was pretty sure he felt the same way about her.

On the way back to the church everyone shared about the gifts they bought as souvenirs. They looked forward to giving them to their families when they got back home. When they arrived at the church someone from each of their host families was there to take them home for the evening. Holly looked forward to spending some time with the Sandovals but was sorry to leave Zach.

Bill gathered everyone together before they left. "Listen everyone, tomorrow is church. You will be coming with your families and probably arriving at different times. The service usually lasts about two hours. We won't be returning to our host homes until later in the evening so be sure to bring a change of clothes so you can change after church for our trip to the pyramids. We will also meet with the bible school teachers after lunch for a few minutes to see what supplies we will need. If we need to get supplies, we will buy them when we get back from the pyramids. We will explore the pyramids in the afternoon and then spend the remainder of the evening going over last minute details for the week. Also be sure to bring your devotional notebooks. Any questions?" No one had any questions.

Jeff asked, "Did everyone enjoy themselves today?"
A general murmur of agreement went through the group.
"Good. Have fun with your families, get some good rest
and we'll see you tomorrow."

Everybody said goodbye to each other and left for
the evening. Holly looked for Becca as she saw Julio walk
through the door to take them home. She didn't want to
keep him waiting. She nodded to Julio in recognition that
he was there for them. She found Becca talking with Jeff,
probably saying good night, so Holly picked up her stuff
and walked over to Julio.

"Hi Julio, did you have a nice day today?" she
asked him.

"Yes I did Holly. Did you enjoy the floating
gardens?"

"I sure did. They were as wonderful as the last time
I visited. What a great spot!" Looking over towards Becca
Holly turned to Julio and said, "Becca is saying good night
to her husband and she should be here in a minute."

"It is not a problem to wait." Julio sat down in the
chair and Holly said she would be right back when she
spotted Zach alone by the water cooler.

She walked over to Zach as he watched her walk
toward him. He was glad she didn't leave without saying
good night. "Hey Zach, I wanted to tell you before I left
how much I enjoyed the day." She held out her hand to
shake his. He gently grasped her hand within his and held
it for a moment longer than was probably necessary as he
looked into her eyes. "I enjoyed it too. I hope you have a
restful night Holly. I'll look forward to seeing you
tomorrow."

"Me too," Her hand was still in his, not wanting to let go. She looked over and saw Becca with Julio and knew it was time to leave. Recognizing it was time for her to leave Zach reluctantly let go of her hand. Walking away she turned back and said to Zach "see ya." He smiled and waved to her. She did the same with a wonderful feeling bubbling in her heart. She hoped she had some time to talk with Becca about Zach this evening before bed. Zach watched her leave all the way through the door. Boy did he have it bad! He turned and smiled as he shook his head in wonder.

Becca, Julio and Holly walked to the bus stop to catch their bus. Each one was quietly meditating on their own thoughts. Julio knew the girls must be tired so he respected their need for silence. It was nice for his family to have the girls staying with them. He enjoyed Holly because she was like one of his daughters. It was nice having her back in their home. He thought Becca was a fine young woman as well. He hoped to get to know her husband a little better while they were here.

Once they arrived home the girls spent some time with the family and decided they needed to get to bed. Julio said they would leave for church at 8:30 so they said good night and went to their room. Becca and Holly decided to get their showers quickly before the water was turned off and then they wouldn't have to worry about it in the morning.

Becca took her shower first. When Holly returned to their room after her shower she found Becca reading.

"Becca, do you have a minute to talk about something?" asked Holly.

97

Putting her book down, Becca said, "Sure, what's up?"

"Well, I don't know if you've noticed but I spent some time today with Zach walking to the bus stop and then on the boats."

Becca had watched them today wondering if something was developing between the two because she noticed them together a few times. She didn't want to initiate a conversation since she didn't know Holly well enough yet and didn't want to offend her. She was honored that Holly wanted to talk to her about it.

"I did notice you two a couple of times today but didn't want to intrude by asking any questions."

"Thanks Becca. We talked about our families, basically getting to know each other better."

Holly looked away while playing with a piece of her wet hair. She turned back to Becca and said earnestly, "I really like him Becca. I know this isn't the place or the time for something like this to happen and I'm not sure what to do about it. It's ironic that we spent time during our monthly meetings addressing so many issues, one being boy/girl relationships on a mission trip and here I am contemplating what we've cautioned the kids against. I think he's feeling the same way but I think he knows this isn't the time either."

"I can see what you mean, Holly, but I also believe there is nothing wrong with you two getting to know each other. If there is something developing you have to turn it over to God. You want to handle it with discretion and not let it become the focus of this trip, but I can tell you already know that. If God has planned this for you two then you can trust Him to work out the details. I think, maybe, you should tell Bill so that it wouldn't take him by surprise if someone else said something."

"You're right Becca. Thanks. That's helpful. Everyone seems to like Zach and I sure don't want to monopolize his time so I want to be careful how much time we spend with each other."

"Can I pray for you, Holly?" Becca asked tentatively.

"Thanks, I would love that."

Becca moved over to Holly's bed and put her hand on Holly's hand. "Father, thank You for the wonderful day we've all had. Thanks for taking us safely to and from Xochimilco. Thank You for the sweet fellowship we enjoyed with each other and the Mexicans. Thank You for Holly and her sensitivity to the group and to You for what You might have planned for her and Zach. Please speak peace into her heart and comfort her with the knowledge that You will work out all things for her good and Your glory. If Zach is the man You have for her please help them to both walk cautiously and prayerfully. Please protect them and this group. Guide and direct them both and fill them with Your wisdom and peace. Please bless us with a good night's sleep and help us to focus on You tomorrow as we worship together with our new Mexican brothers and sisters. Help us to honor You in all that we say and do. In Christ's name we pray, Amen."

"Thanks Becca. I appreciate your willingness to listen and to pray for me and Zach. Jeff's a blessed man to have you." Holly hugged Becca.

"You're welcome Holly. I'm blessed as well to have him. Sleep well."

Holly turned the overhead light off and snuggled under the covers. With a smile on her face sleep quickly came.

~~~~~~~~~

As Holly drifted off to sleep Zach was at his place praying for their relationship. He felt like this was the woman God had for him and he knew he had to be careful how he proceeded. He didn't want his focus to be on Holly and not on the ministry God gave him to do here. He would talk with Pastor Abraham tomorrow after church to let him know what he was feeling and to get his advice as well. He felt like it would be appropriate to speak about this with Bill as well. The Americans were here for a purpose and he didn't want that to get messed up.

CHAPTER 15

On Sunday morning everyone arrived at church at different times with their host families. Since the service usually lasted a couple of hours many Mexican people strolled in throughout the service. The church service was wonderful with one of the members translating so the Americans could understand. After the service many Mexican families introduced themselves to the Americans and told them how much they appreciated them coming to help their church.

Holly enjoyed meeting different families, having known some from her previous trips. As people left the church the Americans got ready to meet with the teachers before going to the pyramids. Their host families had packed them bag lunches to take and when they returned later this afternoon Berta would fix a meal for them.

Later when the team met with the bible school teachers the ladies split up with the teachers they would be assisting while the men got together and discussed their projects. It was a productive hour and a half as they made notes of supplies they needed to pick up later on their way back from the pyramids. After their meeting ended the team got in the van. Holly remembered that Zach was going to be their tour guide today so she prayed for wisdom and caution for their budding relationship. She didn't want to occupy all of his time because the guys on her team enjoyed spending time with him, too.

Emma and Kylie sat with the guys getting ready to play some cards while they traveled to the pyramids. Holly noticed that they did that whenever they had free time or traveled. Bill and Zach were sharing a seat talking and Becca and Jeff were together as well. Zach turned to locate Holly and his eyes captured hers. He winked at her and then continued his conversation with Bill. Holly hid that wink in her heart and thought now would be a good time to catch up writing in her journal. She loved to capture her thoughts on paper so she could reflect on them at a later time and remember the details, details she would probably forget if she hadn't written them down.

The trip was so pleasant with not too much traffic and nice weather. After an hour or so of driving they arrived at the pyramids. Holly put away her journal and wondered how many team members would try to run up to the top of the pyramid. She knew she would be walking up to the top. She loved the view from the top of the pyramid. They usually tried to get a team picture from the top if everyone climbed the pyramid.

As they walked Holly felt someone come up behind her and she turned to see Zach smiling at her. Bill was talking with Jeff while Becca walked with Emma and Kylie.

"Hey Zach," Holly said as they continued to walk.

"Hi Holly, I was hoping we would get some time to talk. How's everyone doing at their host families?"

"They're having so much fun," she replied. They walked a little faster to keep up with the rest of the team. "They're enjoying the food and they love using their Spanish to communicate. You did a great job of matching people up."

"I appreciated Bill's insights about everyone. It made it easier to match families with your team members. The guys seem to be pretty protective over the two girls and that's good."

Looking at the college students she agreed. "Bill was very specific when addressing that issue of protecting each other whenever we travel." Thinking about the guys and girls she smiled. "They're a great group of young people and I'm really enjoying them."

As they got closer to the pyramid Zach turned as he continued walking and said to Holly, "I'm sure glad you decided to be a leader this year. It's given me an opportunity to get to know you."

Her heart soared with his words. She looked at him shyly and smiled. "I'm glad too Zach. I want to get to know you as well. I want us to be careful not to be too focused on getting to know each other and forget the real reason we are here. Do you understand what I'm saying?" She prayed he understood because she needed him to be strong about how to pursue their relationship.

"I do and I agree with you. We have a lot of work to do while you're here and I don't want to get sidetracked either." He gently grabbed her arm to stop her. She looked at him and she could tell he was serious. "But I also know that I want to spend time with you Holly."

They gazed into each other's eyes detecting the desire one for the other building. Feeling a little bit uncomfortable Holly broke the moment by turning and walking over to the group getting ready to climb the pyramid. Zach knew he had to be very careful so he didn't frighten her off. He knew his feelings were strong and he hoped hers were too. He watched her talk with her teammates and quietly joined the group a minute later.

Seth told everyone he was going to try to run to the top and if anyone wanted to join him they could. Running up to the top of the pyramid meant running up 200 narrow stone steps. "Is anyone else game to try?" Chris jumped in and said "Sure, I'm with you Seth." No one else took the bait so up Chris and Seth went while everyone else started walking up the steps.

Once they all got to the top they congratulated Chris and Seth for being able to run the distance. It was hard enough to walk up let alone run. There was silence from the team as they looked out over the countryside from the top of the pyramid. It was an awesome sight! Holly was amazed at God's creation and knew the others were experiencing the same sense of wonder since no one was talking at the moment. What a beautiful scene they saw from the top of the pyramid. There was another pyramid in the distance that looked like it was surrounded by a cotton ball of clouds. She learned from one of their Mexican hosts that the pyramid they were on was called The Sun and the one in the distance was called The Moon. The distant pyramid was enshrouded with sun rays falling from the clouds as the sun shone brightly. The back drop of that pyramid was a beautiful ridge of mountains.

Bill finally interrupted everyone's thoughts and said "Let's get someone to take a group photo of us over here with the mountains and the other pyramid in the background." Zach offered to take the photo. "Thanks Zach, but I want to have you in the photo with us as well." Bill asked a gentleman who happened to be walking by if he would take a couple of pictures of their team and he agreed. Each of the kids gave him their cameras so the kind and patient gentleman ended up taking pictures on everyone's camera.

Afterward they gathered together on a corner of the pyramid and ate their packed lunches. Later, after taking more pictures, they started their descent down the pyramid. It was late in the afternoon and they needed to get back to the church to talk over the final details for the upcoming week. They also needed to have their group devotions and pick up supplies at the store so Bill got everyone moving back toward the van. It was a great afternoon for everyone.

On the van Bill, Jeff and Zach sat with the guys sharing stories while getting to know each other better. Becca, Holly and the young ladies sat together talking and sharing girl things. Holly enjoyed her time with Kylie and Emma. They were neat young women. She also remembered that Kylie and Chris were spending more time together. She couldn't help but wonder if any of the other team members noticed that about her and Zach.

As they drove closer to the city she enjoyed listening to Kylie talk about becoming a teacher. She loved working with children and had worked in summer camps the last couple of years as a counselor. Emma loved sports and played basketball in school. She hurt her ankle during a game once and was fascinated at how the physical therapy she received restored her ankle perfectly. She decided then that she wanted to be able to do the same for other athletes. She hoped to work mostly with athletes as a physical therapist. Smiling, Holly watched Becca interact with the girls and knew why she worked with the youth.

She had a great way about her and the girls warmed up to her quickly. She was sure that her time with Becca, as a roommate, would produce a special friendship for years to come.

When the team arrived back at the church everyone got off the van and went into the church to prepare for devotions. Their cook, Berta, said she would have dinner ready for them around 8 p.m. so they had plenty of time. Everyone looked forward to Berta's meals because they were authentic Mexican food and always tasty. Getting use to the time difference in eating their meals was somewhat challenging but they tried to be flexible. No one complained.

It was Holly's turn to lead devotions this evening and it was a little intimidating for her because she had never led plus Zach would join them. Bill asked Zach who said he would love to attend devotions with them. Each leader was supposed to prepare three devotions to share with the team. Bill was leading devotions the majority of the time but asked the other leaders to help out as well. They could choose their topics and Holly's first devotion was on the importance of getting to know God intimately. She opened with prayer and then started talking about the difference of intimately knowing God as in a personal relationship versus intellectually knowing about God which was considered head knowledge. Heart knowledge versus head knowledge was an easy way of describing the difference between personally knowing God and intellectually knowing about Him. When the knowledge of God becomes intimate it becomes heart knowledge which then changes attitudes and behaviors. With head knowledge you have intellect but rarely is there change in attitude or behavior. With the intellect of knowing about God a person can appear to have an intimate relationship because of the knowledge, but the outward changes in a person's behavior or attitude aren't present. Holly suggested that a person's view of God dictates their view of everything else. What they believe about God is reflected in their responses to people and circumstances. She told them that growing in the knowledge of God is a lifetime pursuit.

Holly had asked Jackson before devotions if he would be willing to read Psalm 27:8 and he agreed. Jackson began reading the verse, *"When You said, 'seek My face' my heart said to You, 'Your face, Lord, will I seek.'"*

"Thanks Jackson."

She had also asked Kylie beforehand if she would read Jeremiah 29:13 and she agreed. Kylie found the verse in her bible and began reading. *"And you will seek Me and find Me when you search for Me with all your heart."*

"Thank you Kylie for reading that verse."

Holly's analogy for an intimate relationship with God was that of a human relationship that you cultivate. The people that you spend more time with while cultivating a personal relationship are those you go to when trouble comes versus the people that are just acquaintances. You don't spend much time with acquaintances and they aren't the first ones you run to when facing trials. In intimate relationships which are developed over time you share personal details, struggles and challenges of your life and the joys of life. They are your support system. You grow to trust them as you grow to know them by spending time with them. Holly continued to say that it is the same way in a relationship with God. You grow to trust Him the more you spend time with Him and get to know His character by spending time studying and reading His Word and praying.. She concluded by saying that God delights in spending time with His children and promises that if you seek Him, you will find Him and He will let Himself be known. She closed with prayer encouraging everyone to spend time every day with God with the desire to know Him more intimately.

After devotions they decided to take a five minute break and then begin work on the details for the upcoming week. They saw Berta cooking in the kitchen and waited expectantly for dinner later that evening.

They got back together after the break and talked about the work the guys would do tomorrow. Zach asked Berta if the team had enough time to run over to the store for supplies before dinner and she told him dinner would ready in about 45 minutes so they had plenty of time. The team left with a list of supplies as they walked to the Carrefore, the name of the local supermarket which was a couple of blocks away.

As they walked into the Carrefore everyone was amazed at how big it was. In the United States Super Wal Marts were starting to be built and the Carrefore was similar here in Mexico. In the front part of the Carrefore they had a small jewelry shop, an ice cream shop, a toy shop, a beauty shop, a bakery and a dairy queen. There were several armed security guards standing all along the front of the store with machine guns and wearing bullet proof vests.   The Carrefore was one of the largest stores any of the Americans had been in and they had fun trying to find their way around.

Kylie had a wonderful time shopping for materials for the crafts they would be making with the Mexican children during bible school. She really enjoyed using her Spanish and enjoyed all the unique things they had in the store. Liam and Seth found a coffee shop at the back of the store that sold unique coffees and sweet rolls. They shared their discovery with the others and they all decided to come to this store and sample the different coffees whenever they had an opportunity. After filling up two shopping carts with supplies and food for the next several days they headed back to the church. They each carried two or three bags of groceries and supplies.

When they got back to the church the ladies decided to get together to be sure they had all their craft supplies ready so they would know exactly what they would be doing tomorrow. They knew several Mexican women would be leading bible school and they would be helping with the crafts and anything else that was needed.

Holly was asked to prepare some bible studies for the moms that would be waiting while their children participated in bible school. It was decided that she and Becca would share the responsibility of leading these studies. Pastor Abraham wanted to take full advantage of this time with the moms since it wasn't something that happened very often. There would be a translator for the women during the bible studies and that would be a new experience for both women. The translator wasn't able to make the meeting today so Holly and Becca would meet with her tomorrow before the bible study. Becca hoped that when she led the study she would be able to use some of her Spanish and not have to use the translator too much.

Everyone took a break when Berta announced dinner was ready. Zach offered up a prayer of thanksgiving for a wonderful day of worship, fellowship and fun. The men let the women serve themselves first and then they followed. Zach came over and sat by Holly after he got his food.

Berta had made a salad and Mexican tacos. She took corn tortillas, rolled them up with chicken inside and then fried them. She provided salsa, sour cream and grated cheese that was to be served over the tacos. She served delicious sweet breads as well.

After Holly ate her tacos and licked her fingers she questioned Zach. "Do you know who will be translating for Becca and me this week when we lead the women's bible studies?"

Swallowing the bite of food in his mouth he replied, "Her name is Laura Herrera. She's a really nice lady and is bilingual. You will like her a lot."

"To tell you the truth, Zach, it's a little intimidating to think about teaching with a translator."

"You'll do fine Holly. She's real easy to work with and she's looking forward to helping you and Becca. She was sorry she couldn't be here tonight. It's a nice thing you're doing for the women here. Rarely do they have the opportunity to participate in bible studies because they are always taking care of their children. The women I have talked with are really excited about this opportunity."

"Well please be praying for me as it is a little scary to think about. I know God will equip me but, boy, doing this was not one of the things I thought I would be doing. It's totally out of my comfort zone."

"I know what you mean. God seems to enjoy taking us out of our comfort zone so that we can depend on Him more than on ourselves. Over the years my parents loved to share with me and my brother the different times God put them out of their comfort zone. But they always said He was faithful and they were blessed beyond what they had imagined."

"You're right. I know that God is faithful to accomplish His purposes in our lives and that it's a privilege to be used by Him. I have experienced His faithfulness too, but I still get scared sometimes. I have to remember to ask the Holy Spirit to remind me quickly of God's faithfulness to me in the past." She smiled as she looked at him taking the last bite of her salad.

They finished eating their meal in silence. Holly wiped her fingers with the napkin and glanced quickly at Zach. "I guess we need to clean up and finish with our plans for tomorrow. We were hoping to get everyone back to their host families early so they could spend some time with them and then get a good night's rest."

They picked up their plates and walked over to the trash can to throw them away. Everyone else was doing the same thing. Holly noticed that Chris and Seth were licking their fingers with smiles on their faces as they finished up the last of their food. She enjoyed watching her team members soak up the culture. Chris looked up as she watched them with a gleam in his eye. She winked at him and continued to throw her trash away.

Bill had Berta by his side. "Everyone, let's show Berta how much we enjoyed our meal." Everyone clapped and whistled enthusiastically. Berta's face turned red but she was so pleased that the Americans liked her food. She returned to the kitchen to finish cleaning up while Bill got everyone together and wanted to know if anyone had questions about what their responsibilities were for the next week. It appeared everyone felt comfortable with what they would be doing and so they got ready to leave for their host families a little early. Bill and Jeff would walk Kylie and Emma home because it was on their way to their host family. Chris, Seth, Jackson and Liam would walk to their homes because they were in the same direction. Zach was taking Becca and Holly to their family's home by bus. Everyone said goodbye and left the church. There was a lot of excitement for tomorrow since that's why they came to Mexico City. A lot of silent prayers were floating up to God on their way home.

As Holly stepped outside the church with Becca and Zach she looked around the street. She had a funny feeling they were being watched. She couldn't put her finger on it but there was a tingling sensation going up her neck. She kept looking around but didn't see anyone. Zach and Becca asked her what was wrong when she stopped walking. She shrugged her shoulders and said nothing. Holly started walking but looked back a few times, seeing nothing.

Gabriel watched the blonde lady look around as if she was looking for something or someone. Gabriel enjoyed watching the "Americanos" at the church. He waited for them all afternoon to return to the church. When he saw them arrive he watched from the roof top of the same building across the street. He was undetectable there so he felt comfortable watching from that spot. He liked watching the blonde lady. He would like to get to know her. Maybe he would try to visit the bible school they were putting on in the park tomorrow. He saw one of the posters advertising the bible school and he desired to participate if he was able. He had to be very careful though so that Miguel did not find out. After the blonde lady, her friend and the man that was called Zach rounded the corner Gabriel climbed down from the roof to walk home. With his hands in his pockets he hoped that if there was a Jesus like Zach said that He would make a way for him to attend the Bible School and meet the blonde lady. Gabriel didn't know then that God had a plan for his life and it included meeting Holly Brady which would completely change his life.

CHAPTER 16

Holly woke up Monday morning with sunshine streaming through the bedroom window. Becca was still sleeping so Holly decided to run downstairs and get her shower. The house was quiet as she headed toward the bathroom so she knew everyone was still asleep. Holly liked to get an early start, especially knowing they were going to be extremely busy today. She couldn't wait to meet the Mexican children at bible school.

Showering was always an experience as she worked hard not to get any water in her mouth. She sure didn't want to deal with "Montezuma's Revenge". During her trip last year several team members came down with vomiting and diarrhea from drinking the water even though they were told not to drink any water in Mexico unless it was bottled. It was a pretty awful for those who experienced it and they stayed far away from the water after that experience.

When she finished her shower and walked back to her room she heard Iliana in the kitchen preparing breakfast. She smelled bacon cooking mixed with the fragrance of strawberries and mangos floating through the whole apartment. Becca was already getting her stuff together for her shower when Holly returned to their room.

Holly looked over at Becca as she put her clothes in her laundry bag. "Did you sleep well Becca?"

"I did. Thanks. I am so excited about getting started today." Her eyes were bright with anticipation and excitement.

"I know what you mean. I always get excited about meeting and working with the Mexican children. Hopefully we'll have a good attendance." She thought for a moment as she continued speaking to Becca. "Usually the first day we don't have quite as many children as we do by the end of the week. Each day as the Mexican children feel more comfortable with us they bring more children with them, especially when they tell others they get food at bible school. We could have as many as 120 children by the end of the first week. Fixing the snacks for them will be challenging but we can always get more food if we need it. It's so much fun!"

Becca nodded in affirmation, grabbed her stuff and went down to the bathroom for her shower. Holly decided to spend some time in the Bible while Becca showered. She decided to read a Psalm and then pray for a while. She prayed for God's pleasure as they served the Mexican people. She also prayed that God would allow her to impact one child's life in a significant way. Unbeknownst to Holly, God had already been working out the details of that prayer request to use her in Gabriel's life.

After finishing their showers and getting their backpacks ready Holly and Becca went down for breakfast. They would be taking the bus by themselves for the first time so they wanted to be sure to leave a little early in case they missed the first bus. Iliana served them cereal and yogurt first and then added bacon, strawberries and mangos. The girls ate a hearty breakfast while conversing with Iliana in Spanish. Holly was improving in her Spanish with Becca's help. When they finished Iliana gave them each a bag lunch, they said goodbye and then headed out to catch their bus.

When they arrived at the church Holly noticed everyone was already there. They were milling around getting their supplies organized to begin the day. There were several Mexican men and women helping her team members. Holly and Becca put their stuff in the corner by the kitchen and went over to Emma and Kylie.

"Hi everyone!" Becca said enthusiastically. Kylie and Emma hugged both Becca and Holly. She and Holly asked at the same time, "What can we do to help?"

"We're getting our supplies together to take next door to the park. Some of the guys have already set up tables and chairs for us so we need to take our stuff over when the ladies are ready," answered Kylie.

Holly asked the next question. "Which of the ladies is overseeing bible school? Is she here yet?"

Emma responded, "The nice looking woman with the curly dark hair over in the corner." She pointed to the woman speaking to a group of Mexican women. "She is giving them their final instructions. She told Kylie and me to get the materials together for the craft we will be doing today. So that's what we've been doing. Her name is Maria."

"How will we prepare snacks when the time comes?" asked Becca.

Kylie looked up and answered, "From what Maria said a few minutes ago, a couple of the Mexican women will be here to prepare the snacks which is really a lunch and then when they're ready, we'll come over and help them bring the food back to the park to serve."

"Sounds like a plan. I'm going over to speak to Jeff for a moment and then I'll be right back to help." Becca said.

Kylie, Emma and Holly watched her go over and give her husband a hug. They each longed for what Jeff and Becca had for themselves at some time in the future. Holly decided that it would be really nice if one day she had the right to do the same thing with Zach. That was her last thought before going back to work.

After a few minutes Holly, Kylie and Emma had their stuff organized and ready to take to the park. Holly watched the guys as they got their supplies together for the construction work they would do today. She nodded and smiled at Zach as he looked over at her. He returned a smile.

Bill came over a moment later and told the girls they would be having their group devotions after lunch today. Everyone would take a break for lunch and a siesta which was a rest time and then they would get back to work around 3:00. The ladies would begin to work on the curtains for the church. Holly remembered her conversation with Becca about talking to Bill about Zach. As he walked back to join the guys Holly stopped him. "Bill, during the siesta can I talk to you about something?"

"Sure, right after we have lunch we can take a walk and talk then. Okay?"

"Yes that's fine. Thanks."

Bill returned to join the guys and Holly continued her work with the ladies. In about a half an hour the children would start arriving so they needed to get their stuff over to the park and set up so they would be ready.

Maria came over and introduced herself to Becca and Holly. She also introduced the Mexican women to the American women. The ladies gathered up their materials and headed next door to the park. Kylie and Emma were so animated in their excitement.

When the ladies got to the park they noticed some children already waiting there with their mothers. Maria pointed the women to particular tables and chairs for their age group so they could get ready for their kids. Some of the Mexican ladies brought balloons to decorate their tables so the children would be even more excited. Kylie, Emma and Becca split up to help the different women while Holly went over to Laura Herrera and introduced herself.

Laura looked up as Holly walked over to her. "Hi, are you Laura?" Holly tentatively asked. Laura smiled and hugged her. "I am and you must be Holly." Laura stated.

"Yes I am. Maria pointed you out to me so I thought I should come introduce myself and talk about what we will be studying during the women's bible study. Would you like to look over the scripture passage I'll be using with the women today before get started?"

"Thank you, I would."

"How does this translating work exactly Laura? I've never done this before and I don't mind saying I'm a little nervous."

"After every few words stop and let me translate and then continue. When you want the passage read in its entirety just let me read it in Spanish. Then as you continue with your lesson I will translate whatever you say or read in the Bible. It takes a little getting used to but you will be fine."

"Thanks for the vote of confidence. Okay, so I'll be using Micah 6:8 for my text today. I will start with prayer and then read the scripture and go from there. Does that sound okay?"

Laura nodded, "It does. We will get started after the children are settled down. I don't know how many women you will have but even a couple will be blessed by their time with you. Thanks for being willing to do this Holly."

Holly got a few chairs together for the women and watched as the children started coming in. After several minutes there were at least 50 Mexican children ready to get started. Maria and the other women leaders got the children together, opened in prayer and then sang a couple of Spanish songs before the children were dismissed to the different areas for their age group. Emma and Kylie went to their assigned groups to help the teachers while Becca went to join Holly with the women.

After the children got settled, Holly, Becca and Laura met with a group of four women for their bible study. Holly opened up their time with prayer as Laura translated. Holly was tentative as she began to speak. She would stop periodically and wait for Laura to translate every few phrases. A couple of times she interrupted Laura, thinking she was finished, but eventually they started clicking and worked well together. The Mexican ladies were very patient and just soaked up everything Holly shared. A couple of times she lost her train of thought while Laura translated but God was gracious and allowed her to gain her momentum back. She found the most difficult thing during translation was keeping her mind focused on what she was going to say next.

While the ladies and children were busy in the park the men were busy working at the church building. Bill and Jeff helped some of the Mexican men set the studs for the two stall bathroom building while Seth and Jackson helped some men get the lumber together for the kitchen cabinets. Chris and Liam dug some holes for some more poles which would help hang more tarps in the courtyard for protection against the rain. There was great camaraderie between the Mexicans and Americans. They worked hard trying to get accomplished what needed to be done to keep on schedule. Bill looked around and loved watching everyone working well together. He knew God was smiling with pleasure as He looked down on all of them. He prayed for the women, hoping things were going as well with them. He knew Holly was tentative about leading a women's bible study using a translator but he knew God had equipped her for just this moment. He had watched her develop into a godly young woman over the last few years. He was glad she was able to come on this trip as a leader and whispered a special prayer for her at that moment.

CHAPTER 17

Glancing at the time on her watch Holly knew she had to bring her discussion to a conclusion. In closing, she wanted to encourage the women by using the scriptural text and said, "Since our time is about over, I want to conclude by reiterating what Micah 6:8 says. 'God has shown us what is good and what does He require of us but to do justice, to love mercy and to walk humbly with our God.'" She stopped and waited for Laura to translate and then continued. "I hope this has given you something to take home and meditate on and be in prayer about. I wanted to tell you that when I came here this morning to share God's word with you I was really nervous. But, if I believe what Micah 6:8 says that I am to strive to do what is right, to show kindness to others, then I must walk humbly with God, trusting Him to equip me to do what He sets before me." She waited for the translation and noticed a couple of women nodding their heads in agreement.

"So I want to take this opportunity to challenge you that whatever God has set before you, whatever the circumstances of your life, you can trust that He will show you what is right and good so that you can walk humbly with Him, trusting Him to care for you in the midst of your life." Laura finished translating and then Holly prayed.

"Thank you, Father, for this opportunity to be together with these new friends and to study Your word." Holly paused long enough for Laura to translate. "I am grateful to have the privilege to be with these dear sisters in Christ and to learn more about You." Laura continued to translate. "Please help each one of us to live in a manner worthy of You and that we will bring praise, honor and glory to Your name alone." Holly paused while Laura translated. "Please continue to unite us as women who love You and teach us more about You this week so that we can experience a more intimate walk with You. In Jesus' name I pray, Amen." Laura concluded the prayer in Spanish.

As a couple of the ladies came over to Holly to hug and thank her she noticed a little boy standing in the distance behind a tree. He looked familiar to her but she couldn't see him clearly enough to remember. Another lady hugged her and Holly smiled at her. She took another quick glance over to the boy again and he was still there. The other ladies had gotten their belongings together and left to help their children get ready for lunch. Laura came over to thank Holly and to find out the Scripture text for tomorrow's lesson. Holly tried to focus on Laura's request but she was still distracted by the little boy. As he moved from behind the tree she saw him clearly and remembered seeing him at the church a couple of times.

"I'm sorry, Laura, for being distracted but do you see a little boy over there by the tree?" Holly pointed in the direction she wanted Laura to look. "Do you know who he is?" Laura glanced over her shoulder. "I am sorry but I do not." Holly shrugged off her reply. "Oh well that's okay. When we're finished maybe I'll walk over to him and find out who he is. I noticed him at the church a couple of times this weekend but he always disappeared before I had a chance to find out who he was. He seems intent on watching the children in the group closest to him but doesn't seem to want to join them. Anyway, back to tomorrow's lesson. I will be using Hebrews 13:21 as my text." She looked back at the little boy surprised to see he was still there.

"I want to thank you, Laura, for helping me and being patient with me throughout your translating. It was a little hard at first to keep my focus while you translated, but after I got used to it I think it went pretty well." Laura gave her a hug of agreement and walked over to the other women. Holly looked over to Becca, Emma and Kylie as they prepared to serve lunch. She caught Becca's eye and nodded towards the little boy at the tree and started walking over towards him praying he wouldn't take off again.

Gabriel saw the blonde lady walking to him but he couldn't seem to move his feet to run away from her as he did at the church. She came up to him with a smile on her face and he thought she was the most beautiful girl he had ever seen.

"Hola, habla Ingles? Do you speak English?" Holly hoped he spoke English. He nodded his head yes. She said, "Me llama es Holly, my name is Holly. What is your name, como te llama?"

He was so mesmerized by Holly that he couldn't answer her for a moment. "Do you speak English? Habla Ingles?" She asked him again to be sure she understood him correctly the first time.

He nodded his head affirming again. "My name is Gabriel," he said slowly in English. Holly held her hand out to shake his. "It is nice to meet you Gabriel. I think I saw you at the church the other night. Was that you?" She spoke slowly in English so that he would understand her.

He seemed to speak English but to what extent she couldn't tell.

He nodded yes again. "Did you come to attend bible school today?" She hoped to get him to talk a little bit more.

"I would like to but," he replied as he shrugged his shoulders and looked down at the ground. Holly could tell he was hesitant and she sensed he was getting ready to leave.

"Would you like to at least have some lunch with me, with us?"

He shook his head no. She wanted to get him to come back. Something about this little boy pulled at her heart. "I hope you will come back tomorrow. I would like to get to know you better."

As he began to back away he quietly said, "Maybe I will try, but I do not know if I can get away." As he got further away Holly called out to him. "Thanks for coming today, Gabriel. I hope I get to see you tomorrow." He slightly nodded in acknowledgement of her words and then took off running.

Holly stood watching him leave thinking about their encounter. She prayed God would bring him back tomorrow. She went back to help the others serve lunch and looked forward to tomorrow with anticipation as she thought about Gabriel.

After lunch was served to the children the Mexican ladies finished cleaning up while Holly and her team members brought their supplies back to the church. They wanted to see how the rest of their team made out at the church and knew that their lunch would be ready for them in an hour or so.

Holly remembered that she would be meeting with Bill after lunch and was a little nervous about that talk. As she walked into the church she prayed for courage to share with Bill about Zach. She prayed for their team and the work they were involved with at the church. She also said a special prayer for Gabriel hoping he would be back tomorrow.

CHAPTER 18

Gabriel began to run home but as he got closer to home he started walking so he would be able to think more clearly about Holly. She sure was nice but for some reason he already knew she would be. He was glad he could speak enough English to communicate with her. At least that was one positive thing Miguel did in making Gabriel learn English. He decided as he walked that he would go back tomorrow just to see her. He liked hearing about Jesus too. He listened to the lady talking to the group of children that he was standing close to and she said that Jesus wanted to be their friend. He was surprised about that because he could not imagine anyone wanting to be his friend given his relationship with Miguel. No one liked Miguel except those who associated with him and that was just because of money. She also said that Jesus died on a cross so that people could become his friends. Gabriel was amazed and perplexed by that because how could someone who died be his friend? And since no one ever did anything nice for him, why would someone die for him? For some reason those questions gave him such a nice feeling inside, which was something he did not experience much. As he got to his house he still thought about all that he heard today. Before he could open the door Miguel threw it open and Gabriel knew he was in trouble. Miguel grabbed him by the shirt and pulled him inside the house slamming the door behind him.

"Where have you been Gabriel?" Gabriel backed away from him as he answered. Thinking quickly he said,

"I was out walking, looking for new people who might need your services. You always said I should keep a look out for new business so I did. I did not find anyone yet but I thought I could look every once in a while." He waited for the explosion. Miguel liked the idea and the fact that Gabriel was taking a little more initiative to get new business. Miguel walked closer to Gabriel who wasn't sure that he bought his story, and waited for a blow to his body. Miguel then suddenly backhanded Gabriel across the cheek. "Next time,' he began roughly, "do not be gone all morning. I had some errands I needed you to do and I had to send one of the other guys. You know I do not like to waste their time with your jobs." Gabriel rubbed his cheek, grateful that Miguel only slapped him. Gabriel didn't cower and that always amazed Miguel as he secretly respected Gabriel because of that. Gabriel took his punishment like a man should rather than as an eight year old boy and he never begged for mercy. As Miguel left, it crossed Gabriel's mind that maybe Jesus might have just helped him not get a beating. He had this thought but wasn't sure why it came to him. Rarely did Gabriel only get a slap across the face from Miguel. This was a new and very comforting thought to him. He thought about that more as he went about his chores.

~~~~~~~~~~

After lunch Holly and Bill took a walk to follow up on their earlier conversation. They talked about how the morning went and what got accomplished. They both enjoyed watching their team work together with the Mexicans.

Looking at Holly, Bill asked, "Holly, what was it you wanted to talk about?" She appeared a little nervous.

Holly started walking slower as she looked at Bill. "I need to get your counsel, Bill. It's kind of hard to know how to say this but I want to be honest with you. I believe there is a special connection developing between Zach and me. One of my concerns is that during our monthly meetings we cautioned the college students about getting attached to one another or to any Mexicans in a romantic sense and here I am in the exact situation and it bothers me." She quickly added as she looked at Bill. "Not the relationship as I am very excited about what God might have for us, but about the timing. My other concern is that I would like to see how it develops, but I don't want it to take precedence over what we are here to do and neither does Zach. So there it is. I'm not sure what to do next. I need your help Bill." She looked at him hoping he would understand after slightly shuddering while blurting it all out to him.

Bill was praying the moment Holly started talking. "I appreciate your being honest with me Holly. Most of the time, we have no control over our emotional responses when it comes to romance. After all, what you do have control over is how you handle yourself while you're here. I see nothing wrong with you and Zach developing a friendship and getting to know each other. Actually, I'm happy for you. Zach seems like a great guy, one who loves the Lord and desires to be in a lifetime of ministry for Him.

I know I don't have to say this since you've already stated it yourself, but be careful how much time you spend with each other and do not exclude the others. We don't want any of the college students seeing you consumed with this relationship and especially since you pointed out earlier that we cautioned them against this very thing happening."

She breathed a sigh of relief. "Thanks Bill for listening and understanding. I came here to serve God and that's what I plan to do. I am also looking forward to what God does with my relationship with Zach, but I know that's not why I'm here. I wanted you to know so that I would be held accountable. I shared this with Becca who encouraged me to discuss this with you."

"Thanks for your confidence in me Holly."

When they returned to the church the team was getting ready to have their group devotions. Becca was leading today and Holly looked forward to what she would be sharing. As she and Bill walked through the church door Zach came over to them. Bill smiled at him and walked over to see some of the boys.

"Hey Holly."

"Hey Zach."

"I wanted to say goodbye to you before I left. I know your group is getting ready for devotions and I have several errands to do before we can continue our work here later this afternoon."

"Thanks. I'll look forward to seeing you later today." She walked toward the group as Zach walked to the door. They both turned to look at each other for a moment and then Zach left and Holly joined her team.

After devotions the guys went back to work while Becca gathered the girls to discuss what they would be doing tomorrow at bible school. Holly decided to spend her time on the women's bible study for tomorrow so she let Becca know she was going back to the park for some time alone to prepare her lesson. Since the park was next door it was fine for her to go by herself. Holly picked out a nice park bench that was fairly isolated. She wanted to pray and then do an outline.

After some prayer time she opened her bible to Hebrews to plan her lesson. As Holly read Hebrews 13:21, *"He who equips you in every good thing to do His will working in us that which is pleasing in His sight through Jesus,"* she thought about what she wanted the women to learn from this lesson. She questioned herself about what this meant to her in light of her walk with God. As she meditated on the scripture over the years she gained confidence to step out and serve God in whatever way He chose to use her. It also gave her hope that God would accomplish His purposes through her. She realized she wasn't doing anything on her own as she remembered what John 15:5 says, *"I am the Vine, you are the branches; he who abides in Me and I am in him, bears much fruit for apart from Me you can do nothing."* In our own strength we can't accomplish anything, but we must have the Holy Spirit working in our lives to accomplish that which is pleasing to God.

Knowing that the daily lives of these dear women were challenging and difficult Holly wanted to encourage them to find their strength in God and not seek it within themselves or in anyone else. She looked up a few more scriptures to share and was just finishing when she was surprised to see Gabriel watching her from a distance. She closed her bible and prayed that God would give Gabriel the courage to come over and speak to her.

Gabriel had been watching Holly read her book and didn't want to interrupt her. He liked looking at her. He knew he shouldn't have come back after the episode with Miguel, but when he finished his chores he knew Miguel would be gone for the rest of the day so he found himself walking toward the church. He noticed Holly put her book down and wondered whether she would care if he walked over to her. He decided to take a chance and started toward her.

Holly noticed him coming closer so she gave him a tentative smile, hoping to encourage him. As he got nearer Holly said, "Gabriel, what a nice surprise to see you again today! I was hoping you would come back tomorrow so this is even nicer."

"You remembered my name," Gabriel said in awe.

"Of course I remembered your name. I was happy to meet you this afternoon. How have you been?"

"I am okay." Without looking at her he asked, "What were you reading?"

"That's my Bible. I was preparing for tomorrow's lesson with the women. Every day while we are here another lady named Becca and I will be sharing God's word with some of the ladies while their children are in their own groups." Holly saw a puzzled look on Gabriel's face and wondered what was going through his mind.

"How do you know it is God's word?" he questioned as he kicked at some stones.

Holly silently prayed that God would give her the right words that would ignite a desire in Gabriel to know more about God. Opening her bible to Hebrews she said to Gabriel, "He tells us in Hebrews 4:12 *that the word of God is living and active and sharper than any two-edged sword.* The Bible is the word of God and as we read it we get to know God better and it changes our heart."

She stopped so he could think about that for a few minutes and then she continued. "Gabriel, the Bible is God's love letter to His people." She waited and watched his expressions, wishing she knew what he was thinking.

"Why would we want to know God better?" Gabriel asked.

"Because Luke 16:15 tells us that God wants to know our hearts." She gently took her finger and put it under his chin to raise his eyes to her own. She really wanted him to understand this part. Softly she said, "And Gabriel because He wants to know our hearts He wants us to know His heart as well." She turned to another verse in the Bible and pointed it out to Gabriel.

"Psalm 25:4 says *make me know Your ways God and teach me Your path; lead me in Your truth and teach me for You are the God of my salvation and for You I wait all day.* " As she continued to share scripture with Gabriel she encouraged him to look at the bible as she read the passages to him even if he couldn't read.

"What is salvation?" he questioned looking directly into her eyes.

Holly was thrilled that he asked that question. "It is when you ask Jesus, who is God's Son, into your heart. God says in the Bible that the only way to know Him is to know His Son, Jesus." She talked slowly so that Gabriel would understand every word she said. "First you ask Jesus to forgive your sins which include all the bad things you have ever done or will ever do. Then you tell Him that you want Him to be in control of your life. That's salvation." She prayed that she was sharing this at a level he would understand. She could see him pondering this and she rested in the silence, praying that God would work mightily in this little boy's heart.

"How do you know that Jesus is God's Son?" he boldly questioned Holly.

"Because there are many places in the bible that God says Jesus is His Son. I wish I had more time to read some of them to you."

As Gabriel thought about this his next question was, "How does Jesus get into your heart?"

She responded by saying, "You just ask Him. You pray and ask Him to live in your heart and help you live a better life that pleases Him." Holly knew she had to get back to the church but wanted to give Gabriel a few more moments to think about what she said.

Gabriel finally spoke to her saying, "Thank you for telling me that. I never heard much about Jesus. I am going to think about what you said today. It seems hard to believe that Jesus would forgive all the bad things I have done and then love me forever. But I sure like how it sounds." Holly's heart melted as he said this to her. She could see he was mature beyond his age and wondered what life experiences he had encountered to make him grow up so quickly. She knew life on the streets was extremely difficult and it made her sad believing Gabriel's life was probably very bad.

Gabriel knew it was time for him to get back. He didn't want to upset Miguel again. He thought he was pretty lucky to get off so easily the last time but felt certain he wouldn't get off that easily if he was caught again. As he began to back away from her Holly knew he was ready to leave.

"I hope you will think about what we have talked about today Gabriel and come back tomorrow to join us. You will learn more about Jesus plus I would like to see you again."

He gave her a small smile in response to her comment about wanting to see him again. "I do not know if I can make it or not, but I will try." For the first time he looked like a little boy as he shuffled his feet while wandering away.

Holly got up and went back to the church. She didn't realize she'd been gone for over two hours. The guys had gotten quite a lot accomplished and now everyone was in the process of cleaning up. She quickly got her camera from her backpack so she could take some pictures of her team members hard at work. Chris and Jackson noticed her taking pictures and started clowning around. She got some great shots of the two of them. Becca was talking to Jeff so Holly snapped a couple pictures of them. Kylie was having some fun with Seth so Holly caught them on film as well. She looked forward to an evening with the Sandovals because they were going to play games and Iliana was going to make some special Mexican dishes for dinner.

Holly put her camera away and started helping with the cleanup so they could finish quickly. She felt confident in God about her lesson for tomorrow and thought again about her encounter with Gabriel. She silently prayed that God would take care of that little boy and that while she was here he would ask Jesus into his heart. She looked over at Zach at the same time he caught her eye and winked at her. He also gave her that terrific smile. All in all her day was very successful! She couldn't wait to write everything down in her journal. With that last thought she walked over to join in the fun her team was having with each other as they continued to finish cleaning up the church.

CHAPTER 19

Holly and Becca were the first to arrive at the church the following morning. They had a great evening with the Sandoval family and Jeff had surprised Becca by joining them. Becca was surprised because the Sandovals had invited Jeff the previous night without telling her. They thought she was probably missing some time with her husband so they extended the invitation and he gladly accepted.

Holly noticed Liam and Emma arriving and talking with each other. Since she hadn't gotten any pictures of them yesterday she grabbed her camera and snapped some while they were talking. She wanted to remember to take her camera to the park today so she could get some pictures of the ladies in her bible study as well as the children. She hoped Gabriel showed up so she could get some pictures of him too. After the rest of the team arrived Bill prayed for everyone and for the day ahead of them. Then they all went about preparing for the day and their jobs. The ladies took their supplies over to the park with the Mexican women and couldn't wait to greet the children as they arrived.

Laura came over to Holly and gave her a hug to greet her. Holly shared more scripture references with Laura so that she could be more prepared when she translated. Holly thought about Zach but didn't get a chance to see him before they left the church for the park. Hopefully she would see him later in the afternoon.

Bible school went smoothly that morning in the park. More Mexican children showed up and more women attended the bible study too. Holly kept scanning the park for Gabriel but didn't see him anywhere. She couldn't help but be disappointed when he didn't show up. She continually asked the Holly Spirit to remind her that this was all in God's hands. Right now she needed to concentrate on her lesson and not get distracted by thoughts of Gabriel. It wasn't fair to the ladies for her not to be focused on what she was sharing with them about God. Halfway through her lesson with the ladies Holly noticed Gabriel standing by a tree not too far from some of the children. She stopped in the middle of her sentence and looked at Laura to excuse herself for a moment. Laura nodded and translated to the women as they watched her walk over to a little boy.

Holding out her hand to him she said, "Hi Gabriel. I'm so glad you came today." He shook her hand and smiled. "Can I take you to that group of children over there so that you can listen to the lesson?"

He nodded affirmatively and they walked over to the group. "They also do a craft," Holly commented.

"I cannot stay very long," he said abruptly. She was puzzled as she responded, "Okay. Well, stay as long as you can. Hopefully you can stay through the lesson."

When they got to the group of children she introduced him to the leader and to the children. He sat down quietly and watched her as she headed back to her group of women. She could tell he didn't want her to leave but she had other responsibilities and hoped he would stay long enough to hear God's word. She left it in God's hands.

She continued with her lesson once she rejoined the group and explained why she went over to Gabriel. She didn't realize the ladies had watched her talk to Gabriel and take him over to the children. None of the ladies knew him but because Holly took the time to help him their respect for her grew. They listened even more intently as she spoke and began to trust her more.

Gabriel kept watching Holly while he listened to the woman leading his group and sharing about God. He liked it better when Holly was with him but he knew she was busy with the women so he tried to listen more closely to what his leader was saying.

Gabriel liked hearing his leader sharing the story of Noah from the Bible, especially that God had instructed him to build a big boat called the Ark. She said Noah listened to God because he had a relationship with Him and he trusted God. Even when people gave Noah a hard time and told him he was stupid to build such a large boat he still trusted God. Even when God told him how big the Ark was supposed to be and that it would take him about 100 years to build it he still trusted God. Gabriel sat on the edge of his seat taking in every word the leader said and actually forgot about Holly at that moment. He could hardly believe that building a boat could take 100 years and that Noah would do it just because God told him to do so. Noah didn't care that people treated him and his family bad, but he just continued to do what God commanded.

Noah's story made a big impression on Gabriel as he thought about his own life and how often Miguel gave him a hard time because he was nice to someone. He thought about the times Miguel punished him for doing some act of kindness. Noah didn't care what other people thought or how he was treated because he wanted to do what was right in God's eyes. Gabriel thought Noah was really impressive and he wanted to think about Noah some more.

After his leader finished her lesson and the group was ready to make a craft Gabriel decided he better leave. Holly saw him get up and she assumed he was leaving. She had just finished praying with her ladies so she excused herself once again. The ladies were talking about the lesson so it was a good opportunity for her to see Gabriel before he left. She grabbed her camera because she wanted to get his picture.

"Hey Gabriel," Holly called to him. He turned and looked at her. "Are you leaving now?" she asked as he stopped.

"Si, I mean yes, I need to get home." He wanted to talk with her more but knew he had to get going. He was moving dirt with his shoes and looking at the ground.

She lifted his chin so he would look at her. "It was good to see you today Gabriel. I am glad you came." He nodded. "Me too." He gave her a sweet smile.

"I hope you enjoyed the lesson," Holly replied.

"I did. It was a great story about a man called Noah. I would like to ask you some questions about him sometime." She noticed his eyes light up as he talked about Noah.

"I would like that too. Maybe tomorrow if you come back we could spend some time after the lesson when the others are making a craft."

Shyly he said, "Gracias Holly. I hope I can come back tomorrow. It is hard to get away sometimes." He turned to leave and then he turned back to her. "That lady said Noah was a man of prayer. You talked about prayer yesterday." He stopped as though he was thinking about what he wanted to say next. Holly waited because she knew he had more to say.

"Do you think you could pray for me Holly?" he asked her with hesitation laced through his voice. Holly was so excited that he would even ask her to pray for him because that meant he was beginning to trust her and nothing could have blessed her more at that moment.

With tears glistening in her eyes she replied, "You bet I will Gabriel. Nothing would give me greater pleasure than to talk to God for you. Actually, to tell you the truth, I've already been praying for you."

"Really," he said in awe. Holly could tell that she had surprised him with that revelation. He shared another sweet smile with her that warmed her to the tips of her toes. Then she remembered she still had her camera in her hand. "Gabriel, would you mind if I took your picture?" He looked at her a little funny but nodded yes, so she quickly took a couple pictures of him and then asked one of the ladies near to them to take a picture of the two of them. Gabriel couldn't believe she wanted a picture of them together. Maybe she would give him a copy. He could only hope and he decided to pray for one to see if God would answer him. Holly thanked him for coming and said she looked forward to seeing him tomorrow as he walked away. Holly was so excited about what happened with Gabriel that she couldn't wait to write about it in her journal that evening. She also couldn't wait to share it with Zach. She silently thanked God and looked forward to her next opportunity with Gabriel.

Holly decided to get this particular roll of film developed so that she could see if anyone knew more about Gabriel when she showed them his picture. A thought crossed her mind that maybe he would like a copy of the one with the two of them so she decided to have two copies made of that particular photo.

CHAPTER 20

Holly enjoyed the routine of the following days. The women's study continued to go well and she felt more comfortable with Laura translating. Gabriel showed up Wednesday and Thursday long enough for the bible lesson and then left.

Holly thought back to their conversation about Noah. Gabriel wanted to know why Noah would trust God enough to make the Ark even when everyone else made fun of him, called him stupid and wouldn't have anything to do with his family. Holly enjoyed sharing with Gabriel about Noah's relationship with God and His desire to be obedient. She wanted to impress upon Gabriel the importance of getting to know God and being obedient to His word. They talked about prayer and before Gabriel left he let Holly pray for him.

~~~~~~~~~~

Gabriel left bible school Thursday excited about what Holly shared with him. He enjoyed learning about Noah because Noah didn't care about what other people thought. He didn't care how other people treated him either. He only cared about what God thought of him and about being obedient to what God called him to do. Gabriel thought that would be a great way to live life. No

142

more being scared of Miguel but just doing what God wanted him to do.

As Gabriel walked in the front door Miguel came out of the kitchen. "Where have you been this time?" Gabriel could hear the anger in his voice.

Gabriel thought quickly saying, "I was over at the grocery store."

"What did you buy there? I do not see any bags in your hands and you have been gone an awful long time to be at the grocery store." Miguel walked closer to Gabriel with a menacing look on his face.

Gabriel started backing away from Miguel. Miguel reached for him, caught him by the shirt and backhanded him across the face. "I know you were not at the grocery store because I had Antonio follow you when you left today." Gabriel rubbed his cheek. Miguel saw the fear in Gabriel's eyes. He liked the power he possessed to cause people to be afraid of him.

"I was not doing anything wrong Miguel. I just wanted to hear a story about Noah." He knew he shouldn't have said that but something compelled him to be honest with Miguel. Miguel backhanded him again and Gabriel fell over the small table next to the chair.

As Miguel walked toward Gabriel he said, "I told you before that I am working to get rid of those people who come to our streets and you go to the park to listen to them. Why is that?"

Gabriel's lip was bleeding but he continued to be honest with Miguel. "I wanted to know more about why Noah would build an Ark when so many people were mean to him. I wanted to know why he would obey God like that."

Miguel questioned him softly but with anger in his words. "And did you find an answer to your question?" He could not believe that Gabriel was telling him all this.

"Yes. He wanted to obey God because he trusted Him." Not sure where his courage was coming from Gabriel stood straight up and looked Miguel in the eyes. He knew he was in for a beating anyway so he was going to be like Noah and not worry about what Miguel thought or did. The more Gabriel thought about Noah as he shared with Miguel the more he wanted to be like Noah. In that moment Gabriel was determined to know more about this God that could compel an old man to be obedient in building an Ark and not caring about what anyone else thought.

Miguel grabbed Gabriel by the shirt and took him into the room. As Miguel beat Gabriel he never muttered a word. He kept thinking of God and hoped to meet Him someday soon.

~~~~~~~~~

Thursday evening after everything was put away at the church and they were getting ready to do their group devotions, Holly thought about what tomorrow was going to be like. She couldn't wait to see what they were going to do with the street people. Taking a few minutes before devotions she got out her journal to record a few thoughts.

She was amazed at how much the guys had accomplished in the last four days. The cabinets were coming together nicely and so was the structure that would house two toilets. Everyone was pretty tired but really excited about what they had accomplished. They were interacting well with the Mexican people and for that they praised God.

The girls loved participating in bible school and were getting to know the Mexican children better. Each day brought more children. Holly was thoroughly enjoying the women's bible study even more than she had anticipated. By Thursday she had 15 women in her study. After each study they would discuss with each other what she had shared with them. She was finally comfortable with the translating as she and Laura were more in tune with each other every day.

As she recorded these thoughts she stopped and thought about her conversations with Gabriel. She picked up the pictures today and especially loved the shots of her and Gabriel. The next time she saw him she would give him one. She was so glad he came back today and appeared to be really interested in Noah. He kept asking her how Noah knew God well enough to want to please Him and no one else. She had been searching for a small Spanish bible for Gabriel and she asked Zach earlier to try and find one for her. Hopefully he would get it before the next bible school and at that moment she lifted up a silent prayer that Gabriel would soon come to know Jesus as his Lord and Savior.

As she thought about Zach she realized that in the last two days they hadn't spent much time together. During the day they were both busy with their individual projects and when the evening came her team members spent a lot of time together sharing about the day's activities. He would be leading the street ministry tomorrow so she hoped they would be able to find some time together to talk even if it was walking to or coming from the streets. Bill was calling everyone together so she finished her last thought, closed her journal and went to join the others.

CHAPTER 21

Gabriel woke up Friday morning with a fat lip, a black eye and a bruised arm. He was really sore as he quietly crawled out of his bed. Miguel was snoring in the corner and Gabriel didn't want to wake him. He wanted some time to himself before the day started. It was at times like this that he really hated Miguel, but he didn't have anywhere else to go so he put up with him. Miguel left last night after he beat Gabriel and didn't return until early this morning. He was in a foul mood last night when he left and Gabriel was glad he didn't come back right away.

Today Gabriel had to collect some money that was owed to Miguel. He wanted to finish his chores and get out of the house before Miguel woke up. Later he would return with the money that he knew would make Miguel happy. He didn't want to stop going to bible school but he wasn't sure how he would be able to continue now that Miguel knew about it. He wanted to find out more about Jesus and God. Maybe knowing Jesus and God would help him find a better life than he had with Miguel.

CHAPTER 22

Everyone was ready and waiting at the church when Zach arrived. He spotted Holly talking to Jackson and Seth. He'd been praying about their relationship last night and hoped God would open up some time for them to talk today. They hadn't seen each other much the last couple of days and he missed talking with her. He hoped she felt the same way.

Zach gathered everyone together to tell them what they would be doing on the streets since this would be new to them. "We will walk to the corner by the shopping mall and catch the bus that will take us to Quintera Street. There are little markets along that street so once we get off the bus we will walk to an abandoned lot. You'll notice that the street people will start following us as soon as we get off the bus. The abandoned lot is where we will sit in a large circle and sing some Spanish songs. I brought some song sheets for each of you. Then I will share a message in Spanish. I'm sorry there's no translation today. When I'm finished we will walk to a large parking lot next to a grocery store where we will start up a soccer game. The people will follow us to the parking lot. This group of people will consist of children and young adults. The young adults, especially the guys, love to play soccer and some of the women will watch the children while we play. Any of you that would like to play is welcome. I will say, though, that it can get a little rough. These girls and guys live a tough life on the streets and they play soccer the same way." He directed his last comments toward the girls.

"Another thing for you guys that is really important is that I want you to keep a close eye on our girls. I don't believe anything will happen but some of the Mexican guys can be pretty aggressive when it comes to American women."

Kylie raised her hand to ask a question. "One of the Mexican ladies told me yesterday while we were talking about the street ministry that we will be feeding them as well. Is that right?"

"Yes, Kylie, we will be feeding the group. Pastor Abraham will be bringing a van down to the parking lot sometime while we're playing soccer. In the back of the van there will be two large pots of beans and jugs of juice. Laura will be coming with Pastor Abraham to help serve the food. She will get tortillas and cookies from the grocery store when they get here. When we're finished playing you will help serve the Mexicans. Laura will help you while Pastor Abraham and I talk individually to some of the people and hopefully we'll get to share the Gospel. Basically Laura will spoon beans into the tortillas on a paper plate, add a few cookies to the plate and prepare a drink. Then each of you will take the plates and serve until everyone has a plate and a drink. It's pretty easy and the people know what to expect when they come to be served as other teams from other churches have ministered in this area before. Good question Kylie. Any other questions?"

No one had any questions because they didn't know what questions to ask. Everyone was mentally thinking about what they would see in a little while. Holly, too, wondered how anyone lived on the streets. This was something she hadn't done on her former mission trips so she was a little anxious about what was to come.

Everyone got their backpacks and started for the bus stop. Zach looked for Holly who was in front of him talking to Becca. He wanted to walk with her so they could talk. Holly smiled as he caught up with her. Becca smiled and said she wanted to take advantage of this time to talk with Jeff and hurried to catch up with him. Holly knew Becca also wanted to give her and Zach some time together. The rest of the team was walking ahead and the guys looked like they were keeping an eye on the girls which pleased Holly.

Zach offered to carry Holly's backpack. It was something Holly noticed that their Mexican hosts did for them whenever they were around. She noticed a couple of the guys in their group carrying Kylie and Emma's backpack so she was grateful Zach offered and she gave it to him because they got heavy after a while.

Zach looked at her as they were walking and said, "Holly, I've missed talking with you these last few days."

"Thanks Zach. I've missed talking with you as well. It's funny after talking with Bill about our situation and his only caution was about how much time we spend with each other to the exclusion of anyone else, we really haven't had any time with each other. We've both been so busy."

"How have things been going for you in your women's study?" He knew she was nervous about meeting with the women and having someone translate for her.

Looking at him with excitement sparkling from her eyes, she turned and touched his arm. "It has been great! Laura and I are working well with each other. The first day or two was challenging but it's been fine since then. I had fifteen women yesterday. Each day a few more women come and it's the same with the Mexican children. We have about sixty children now."

Her enthusiasm was contagious and Zach said, "That's great! I'm glad it's going well for you. We are making a lot of progress on the structure for the toilets and the cabinets. Your guys work really hard and they're a nice group of guys to work with. The Mexicans are enjoying them a lot. It's fun to watch and I'm amazed at how much we're getting accomplished."

"You're right Zach. They are a great group of guys and I noticed how nice the toilet structure and cabinets are coming. I was pleasantly surprised at how much has been accomplished thus far." Zach nodded in agreement with a smile.

"Zach, I wanted to tell you about this little boy that I am growing fond of. He was the little boy I told you about who was at the church that first night we arrived. His name is Gabriel. I don't know anything else about him but he has taken captured my heart. He attends bible school, listens to the lesson and then leaves quickly. We have talked a couple of times about Noah because that was the lesson he heard the first day. He seemed intrigued by Noah and has asked some good questions. I hope to get to know him better next week. There's something about him that draws me to him." She pulled out the picture of the two of them and showed Zach.

"He looks like a cute little boy. I will be praying for your time with him Holly." They continued walking and talking. Zach smiled and said, "It's wonderful to see your college students relating to the Mexican children here. Today will be a special opportunity for that as well. It's different because life in Mexico is hard but life on the streets is almost impossible. Your heart will break when you see the way they live, especially the little ones. The first time I participated in the street ministry several years ago, talk about taking hold of your heart. Just seeing the conditions these young people live in is hard and I really wanted to help in some way. When I had the opportunity to intern here, during my interview, I told Pastor Abraham I wanted to be involved with the street ministry. I don't know yet what God will be doing with me in the future but I know I have a heart for the people here on the streets."

Walking through the streets of Mexico City was an interesting and sometimes challenging endeavor. Some might call it a real adventure to get through the streets of Mexico City simply because twenty five million people live there. The streets were lined with hundreds of little Volkswagon cars whizzing past them while people were running right and left across the street as they hoped to beat the traffic. Cars didn't wait for pedestrians, pedestrians waited for the cars. Couples were lined up and down the street embracing and kissing mixed in with many other public displays of affection. People had no inhibitions in Mexico City.

The team was getting close to the bus stop so Zach needed to take the lead in getting them quickly onto the right bus. He and Holly moved quickly to the front of the group so he could direct them. After getting everyone on the bus with the girls sitting and the guys standing next to them, they continued their conversations. Zach and Holly got separated getting on the bus so she had some time to think over some of the things he shared with her. It was good to have those few minutes to talk with him. She noticed Bill talking with him now. Zach sure was a terrific guy! His looks brought a smile to her face.

Emma sat next to Holly and commented on seeing her walking with Zach. Holly agreed with Emma's precious description of Zach being "drop dead gorgeous", but Holly was more impressed with his heart. He reminded her of her brother Micah. Micah was a great looking man as well but it was his heart that was most impressive. Micah was the most gentle, sensitive man Holly had ever known. He loved his family well because he loved the Lord more.

When the team arrived at Quintera Street they got off the bus quickly because buses in Mexico City were always in a hurry. The buses had long routes and lots of people to deal with so drivers didn't like to wait too long for them to get off the buses. When the team got off the bus they noticed the little stands lined up and down the street with vendors selling meats, fruits, candies, jewelry, and anything one could want. Smells of grilled meats, barbecued meats, frying vegetables, and sweet fruits permeated the air. There were some stands that displayed cool T-shirts with all kinds of Mexican designs. People were everywhere shopping and eating.

Once the bus left Zach took the lead and everyone followed. Sure enough, just as Zach said, Holly noticed people begin to follow them. Most of them wore ragged clothing, some had sandals, some sneakers, and some barefoot. They didn't look like they'd bathed in a long time either. The heart wrenching sight for Holly was seeing little children following them as well looking the same. Some of the smaller children had no pants on, just shirts. Holly noticed Kylie, Emma and Becca watching the people as well. She noticed tears in Kylie's eyes. Holly was glad to see the guys near the girls because some of the Mexican men looked pretty rough.

Holly noticed cardboard boxes cut in half lying over rope that was extended from tree to tree or pole to pole. They had ragged blankets with holes in them draped over some of the boxes. The boxes extended almost to the ground on either side of the rope. She noticed that there were people sitting or sleeping under the boxes with blankets around them or under them. She realized that she was looking at their homes.

At that moment Holly caught Zach's eye and the depth of compassion she saw there nearly took her breath away. He shared with her the sweetest smile she'd ever received from anyone. She continued to keep her eyes on Zach because somehow that was enough to give her the courage she needed here on the streets. She silently prayed God would look out for each of them today. She turned and noticed Bill was right behind her. He smiled a sad sort of smile at her in that moment. She knew he was feeling the same thing she was feeling as they observed the people they would be ministering to today.

When they arrived at the abandoned lot they noticed a lot of broken glass bottles and trash. They had to be very careful where they walked and also where they could sit. They needed to form a circle which was a challenge. Some of the street people sat in the circle while others stood in the background. Some of the women watched the smaller children as had been predicted.

Holly noticed many of the people putting their fists to their noses. She was told earlier that people on the streets sniffed paint thinner because it was cheap, easy to obtain and it worked like any other drug to give a high. She noticed several people with loose fitting shirts or pants that concealed a small can of paint thinner. Every once in a while they would take the can out, pour some on a small shredded piece of tissue that they carried in their hands, make a fist and sniff. Closer observation revealed that some of their hands seemed to almost be deformed from holding balled up, paint thinner soaked tissues in their fists. When she ventured to look at some of the faces of the people she could tell they were high. Their eyes were half open and they appeared to be in a different world just by the way they walked or held their heads. She noticed one woman in particular who would pull out a paint thinner can while several other people would come up to her with their outstretched hands desiring a dose of the thinner. It was hard to believe people lived every day like this.

Zach began to pass out song sheets and got his guitar out to begin the singing. He started to lead the singing with a song called "Shout to the Lord". Holly watched as everyone sang, the Americans also even though the song sheets were in Spanish. Since everyone had some language training in Spanish it wasn't too difficult to follow and pronounce the words. She loved watching the

Mexicans sing and when they sang the chorus they really did shout to the Lord. They continued to worship God by singing three more songs that Zach chose. As everyone sang Holly noticed a little boy whose diaper fell off. He was playing in the dirt and having a great time. Tears clouded her eyes as the scene played out before her.

When they finished singing Zach put his guitar away and got his bible out to share some scripture verses and a message. Just after praying Holly noticed a disturbance by the far fence when a man yelled something in Spanish, but she couldn't make out what he was saying. Before she knew what happened they were about ten men dressed in bullet proof vests and armed with machine guns rushing through the fence at them. They were the Mexican police who quickly surrounded the group.

The guy who was yelling in Spanish initially talked and pointed at some of the street people. The police started to pull some of the Mexican guys from the group and frisk them. It appeared that the guy who was yelling and pointing brought the police for a particular reason. Holly looked at Zach who was quietly telling everyone to be cool. Her team members were frightened by the look on their faces. Bill was also telling everyone to just be calm and relax. Pastor Abraham started talking to one of the policemen. Zach looked at Holly and gave her a reassuring smile. Holly knew that sometimes Mexican police arrested foreigners just to get bribe money and Holly prayed this would not happen to their group. She believed others in her team were praying as well.

Chris and Seth sat close to Kylie while Jackson and Liam saddled up closer to Emma. Jeff was already sitting by Becca. One of the street kids sitting next to Holly reached for her hand and Holly looked down into some very frightened eyes. She squeezed the little girl's hand and the child gave her a tender smile. They all waited while the police frisked each Mexican street person sitting in their circle. Holly was amazed that the police weren't finding the paint thinner that some of these people kept hidden in their pants. Somehow when they saw the police coming they disposed of the cans. The frisking lasted a few minutes more and then the police filed back out through the fence.

Everyone let out a sigh of relief as Zach got up and opened their time in prayer. As he spoke in Spanish each of the Americans said their own prayer of thanksgiving for God's protection over them at that moment. A lot of the street people watched Zach as he spoke. Holly wished she knew better Spanish because Zach seemed to be keeping their attention with whatever he was sharing with them. It was amazing that Zach could keep their attention with all the commotion going on around them. There were children yelling and laughing, trains were coming and going, and traffic speeding about.

After Zach finished his message they ended in prayer and then sang another song. Then Zach proceeded to tell the street people they were welcome to join in a game of soccer at the Careforre parking lot. It was a large grocery store about a mile away. Holly could sense the excitement in the street people and in her team members as well. She was glad to see that her team members were putting the incident with the police behind them and joining in the excitement of playing soccer with the Mexicans. She couldn't help but wonder if dealing with the police like this was a common occurrence for these people. Holly saw Bill talking with Pastor Abraham for a moment before he and Zach walked toward the grocery store. Everyone got up and followed while Bill lagged behind to talk with Holly and be sure his team was following Zach.

As Holly walked up to Bill she was glad to be leaving the abandoned parking lot and the experience with the police behind. Bill ran his hand through his hair and stretched his back as he waited for Holly. Holly could see he had something to say to her. "Holly, I wanted to tell you what Pastor Abraham said about the police incident and I plan to share it with everyone else later. Apparently that first guy was a snitch and when he saw several of the street people together in one location he decided to alert the police. It's not a common occurrence for the street people to come out of hiding into a public location except when teams come to minister in the streets which is rare. So this was the perfect opportunity for the police to look for drugs of any kind. Amazingly enough they didn't find whatever they were looking for since they didn't arrest anyone. I don't know about you but I wondered how and where they hid the stuff they carried so quickly."

"I know. I wondered the same thing and I was amazed that not one can of paint thinner was found."

Bill shrugged his shoulders saying, "Me too. Jeff and I were relieved that they didn't arrest anybody, especially our people. I didn't want to have to deal with bribes and all that would involve. I prayed the whole time the police were surrounding us."

"I was too." As they walked she looked around and couldn't believe how desolate everything was. "It's hard to believe people live like this and it's really sad Bill. It's been difficult for me knowing how hard life is for the people at Beth El but this is so much worse. No shelter, barely any clothing and not much food. I don't know how they can survive."

"Not many survive for very long from what Zach told me. There was a young woman that he has ministered to a few times since being involved in this ministry. A week before we came she killed herself by stepping in front of a subway train. She was only 18 years old and the mother of a two year old. The despair has to be great down here and I think that's why you see so much paint sniffing. It numbs them from the reality of life and they can't afford drugs." While Bill shared this story he shook his head because it was so hard for him to grasp the reality of how these people had to live and the despair they lived with day in and day out.

They continued to walk in silence until they reached the parking lot of the Careforre. Everybody walked to the far left of the parking lot where they would play their soccer game. Holly noticed the van and saw Laura standing beside it waving to her. Holly had no desire to play soccer so she walked over to Laura. Kylie, Becca and Emma followed. They all decided to help serve the meal once the game was over.

Laura gave them each a hug that was customary in Mexico upon greeting friends. "How has everything gone so far?" Laura asked. The women started talking at the same time as they shared what occurred with the police.

Finally Laura put her hand up because she couldn't understand anything they said. Becca finally shared the event as the others listened, agreed and nodded at appropriate times. Laura's eyes were big with amazement and Holly also saw sadness radiating from them as well.

After they talked awhile Emma and Kylie wanted to take a couple pictures of the soccer game. Becca and Laura went in to the grocery store to buy tortillas to serve with the beans and rice. Holly stood by the van and watched the soccer game. The guys were really getting into it. Some of the Mexicans took off their shirts because they were hot and sweaty. It was funny to watch the small Mexican guys when they would run up against Chris and Seth who were big guys. She kept hearing the word "grande", which meant large, from the Mexicans when they ran into either of these guys. They would literally bounce off of them and Holly couldn't help but smile to herself. She was glad for their size, especially when they were around a lot of these Mexican street guys. In the end the Mexicans won and walked around like proud peacocks. The Americans laughed and patted them on the back while congratulating them.

Becca and Laura brought out the tortillas and were in conversation when the game ended while the guys walked over to the van. Emma and Kylie came over to help serve the people. They served black beans and rice in the tortillas with a drink. The dessert came a few minutes later which was an assortment of cookies. Beside the guys who played the game they served several girls and a few children. There were a couple Mexican guys that were rude and mean to those around them and Holly kept her eyes on Emma and Kylie as they served them. She noticed that when Chris and Jackson came beside them to help these men backed away from the girls. They then turned their attention on a couple of the Mexican girls and forcibly took their plates in order to eat their food. The girls then came over for another plate of food. Many came back for seconds and thirds and finally Laura had to turn them away when the food was gone.

While Holly served them she thought she noticed a little boy who looked like Gabriel standing a good distance away at the end of the parking lot. She hadn't noticed him before and didn't know if he had been there the whole time or had just arrived. She put her hand above her eyes to shield them from the sun in order to get a better look at the boy. Holly wasn't sure it was Gabriel but she started walking toward him. Zach was watching her as she made her way over to the little boy. He didn't want her wandering off too far so he kept his eyes on her even during his conversation with one of the Mexicans.

Gabriel saw Holly coming toward him. He couldn't believe he happened to see her while he was walking home. He wasn't sure whether he should turn and run before she got to him, all the while keeping his eyes peeled for Miguel. He could be anywhere and the last thing Gabriel wanted was for him to see Holly. Gabriel found himself wanting to protect Holly from Miguel but he also didn't want to leave without saying hi to Holly. He liked being around Holly because she always made him feel good about himself.

When Holly got near to Gabriel she said, "Hi, what a nice surprise to see you! Do you live around here?" She thought he lived somewhere closer to the church. As she got closer to Gabriel she couldn't believe her eyes. Gabriel had a black eye and a fat lip. He didn't look so good either.

Holly kneeled before Gabriel and gently took his hand. "What happen to your face Gabriel?" she asked. She shuttered to think about what happened to him as she looked into his eyes but felt the need to ask anyway.

"I got into some trouble last night. That is all." Gabriel was uncomfortable with Holly seeing his bruises and he was pretty sore as well. Holly could tell he was hurting but she didn't know how to help him.

"Is there anything I can do for you? If you would walk over to the van I could put some ice on your lip." She gently ran her hand over his curly hair as he shook his head no. He knew he couldn't let her take care of him as nice as that sounded because they were too close to where Miguel hung out. He appreciated her caring about him because nobody had ever expressed any concern over his well-being.

"Thanks but I cannot. I need to get back." He started moving away. He hated to leave her but he did not want to take any chances that Miguel, or Miguel's thugs could see him with Holly. He kept looking around to check the area out as he talked to her. Holly could see he was uptight and nervous about something but, didn't know how to help him.

"Well, if there is anything I can do to help please let me know. You know where to find me and anyone at the church can get in touch with me. I hope you'll feel better soon Gabriel." She was reluctant to let him go but she knew she couldn't help him. There was something about this little boy that pulled at her heart.

As Gabriel started to walk away Holly remembered the photograph and called out to him. "Gabriel, wait, I have something for you." She pulled out the photograph from her pocket and gave it to him. He looked up at her in awe thinking of his prayer to God for a copy of the picture of the two of them. It was his first prayer and God answered it. He didn't know what to say except "gracias". Holly nodded, "You are welcome. I will be praying for you Gabriel. Remember God has His eyes on you every moment of every day. Sometimes it may not seem like it but you can be sure He is aware of every detail of your life, big and small. He will never turn His back on you and if you ever need help, Gabriel, just call on God. Remember that for me, will you?"

He just nodded, smiled and kept walking in awe of his answered prayer as well as having a picture of him and Holly. This God was really something and so was Holly. He turned to look at her a few times and then he was gone.

CHAPTER 23

As Holly made her way back to the group Zach was walking toward her. He was interested in finding out more about the little boy Holly talked to. He saw the boy leave and met Holly half way as she returned.

"Holly, who was that little boy you were talking to?"

"He was the little boy I saw at the church the first night, the one in the photograph I showed you. That was Gabriel."

Zach could see that she was concerned for Gabriel by the expression on her face. Holly twisted the end of her long braid with her fingers, a habit of hers when she was upset. "He looked like he had gotten into a fight Zach. He had a fat lip and a black eye. I noticed a few bruises on his legs and arms as well. He wouldn't go into detail but I could tell he was hurting."

Zach heard the distress in her words but didn't know how to comfort her because he knew this was very normal for life on the streets. He gently rubbed her arm and looked at her with something in his eyes that Holly couldn't quite put her finger on. She was so concerned about Gabriel that she didn't think too much about it at that moment. They turned to walk toward the van as everyone finished the meal. Some of the Mexican people had already left. She noticed Liam talking with a couple of the guys while Kylie and Emma talked to a couple of young girls. It looked like the mean Mexican guys left which was fine with Holly.

Everyone cleaned up the trash and got their belongings together to make their way back to the bus stop. They needed to get back to the church for the meal that Berta had been preparing for them. Bill was leading group devotions tonight and he wanted to talk about their day as well. Zach was staying for group devotions so Holly looked forward to having more time with him. It was hard for her to keep her mind off Gabriel so she whispered a prayer of protection for him.

~~~~~~~~~~

Gabriel sure enjoyed seeing Holly so unexpectedly today. He hated that she saw the marks from Miguel's beating though and he was embarrassed wondering what Holly thought. She did say she would pray for him and that was strangely comforting to him. He looked forward to seeing her in the future and he cherished the picture but he needed to hide it in a safe place so Miguel never found it.

He dug some paper out of the trash around the corner from his house. He wrapped the picture very gently in the paper and decided to hide it in the loose floorboard in his room where he hid his special treasures. There weren't many but this photo was his greatest treasure yet and he needed to be very careful that Miguel never saw it. He knew what that would mean if he did.

~~~~~~~~~~

Miguel and his guys had been watching the soccer game from a distance. They had been following the Americanos and the Mexicans from the time they arrived at the abandoned lot. Miguel was so angry that they were in his territory again. He was even angrier when he spotted Gabriel talking to an American woman. He had to put a stop to these people coming and talking to these street people once and for all. Maybe Gabriel and this woman would be his way to stop them from ever coming back. He would watch Gabriel and not let him know he was aware of what was happening. When the time came he would play his ace in the hole whatever that turned out to be but, imagined it would have something to do with this woman. From a distance she looked beautiful and he decided to get a closer look at her somehow. With that thought in mind he and his men left the area, but his thoughts about these Americanos lingered in his mind.

CHAPTER 24

Back at the church after a long day of ministering to the street people Berta had prepared a wonderful meal of chicken tortillas with guacamole sauce, sour cream, salad and rolls. For the dessert they were going to have Mexican ice cream. Everyone was exhausted and felt sadness so they ate in silence. No one had much to say and Bill looked forward to their devotions, praying that God would encourage his group and speak peace to their hearts like only He could do. Tomorrow was another day to serve the street people and Bill prayed that God would renew his team members spiritually and emotionally tonight. They all seemed to be withdrawn and he knew that was because of what they experienced today.

After they finished cleaning up from their meal Bill got everyone together for their devotions before host families showed up to escort everyone home. Zach was sharing God's word tonight and Bill knew that he could use God's peace and encouragement as well and looked forward to what Zach would be sharing.

Zach gathered his bible and notes together and headed to a chair as the team got their devotional materials together. He decided to change his devotion tonight because of the weariness he saw on their faces. He began by sharing the verses God laid on his heart a few moments ago. "We are all pretty tired after today's events so God put on my heart to share a different devotion than what I had originally intended. Jesus is speaking in Matthew 11:28-29 where He tells us to *come to Him, all that labor and are heavy laden, and I will give you rest. Take My yoke upon you and learn from me; for I am meek and lowly in heart; and you share find rest for your souls.* Let's pray." Zach prayed for the team, for the street people, for the ministry of the church before he closed by praying for their weary hearts and tired bodies.

During his devotion Zach spoke about the weariness of the disciples as they ministered and shared the Gospel. He noted that they were able to do what God gave them to do because they constantly went back to God who was their source of energy. Zach proclaimed that even when life is at its most difficult God is the source of energy, peace and joy for all. His children will be depleted if they try to minister in their own strength. They will be weary and heavy laden when they see the hardships in life and the horrible situations many experience. But with God all things are possible even in such times and situations. His children can rise above their circumstances or situations. He will lead His children as He equips them to accomplish His purposes in each situation and in each person's life.

After he finished his devotion Zach asked the team if anyone wanted to share anything about the day whether it was disappointment, fear, joy, heartache or something that God revealed about Himself. There were a few that shared and then Jeff prayed for each of them. The host families started arriving so everyone got their belongings together and got ready to leave. Zach sought Holly out to say good night and Holly was grateful that he did. Their hearts were becoming more and more entwined with each other and both of them felt that this was a very good thing.

Tomorrow would be a new day and God alone knew what opportunities would be ahead for their team.

CHAPTER 25

Gabriel snuck into the house later in the afternoon hoping that Miguel was not home yet. He quietly shut the door behind him as he looked cautiously around the small living area. He breathed a sigh of relief when he realized that Miguel was not there and he quickly took the treasured picture to his room and hid it in the floorboard. He then relaxed as much as he could and set about getting dinner for Miguel and himself. Later he needed to get out and collect some more money for Miguel. He felt his pocket to be sure the money he collected earlier was still there. He took the money out of his pocket and put it on the table for Miguel. Gabriel knew that as soon as Miguel walked through the door he liked seeing money on the table. It always seemed to put him in a better mood.

Just as Gabriel stirred the beans and set out tortillas Miguel walked through the door. Gabriel's nerves were on high alert and he said a silent prayer that God would protect him from Miguel. Gabriel realized at that moment that he said his second prayer to God. He hoped God listened again because he knew he needed God's help.

Miguel immediately walked over to the table and began to count his money. "This is a good day's collection Gabriel."

Gabriel put down the dishes on the table and nodded. "I will finish up after dinner. I only have a few more stops."

"Have you had any trouble getting people to pay the money this week?" Miguel asked Gabriel.

Gabriel shook his head and replied somberly, "No. Everyone has been paying ever since you had Hector Ramirez beaten up and his store torched." Gabriel didn't want anyone else to have problems with Miguel so he neglected to mention any of the bad comments people had made about Miguel or his men.

Gabriel served Miguel his tortillas and beans. He noticed Miguel watching him. He wondered what was going on behind Miguel's eyes because it made Gabriel nervous not to know. Miguel continued to eat and Gabriel left quickly to collect the rest of the money. Miguel secretly watched Gabriel leave the room and knew his men would keep an eye on him whenever he left the house. When Gabriel left the house he thanked God for keeping him safe a little while longer.

Miguel thought about Gabriel's betrayal by speaking and hanging out with the American woman. He would teach them both a lesson they would never forget and then Gabriel will have wished he had never met that American woman. Miguel smiled and dug into his beans and tortillas because soon he would finally be rid of the Americano do-gooders and Gabriel would always know who was in control.

CHAPTER 26

Saturday morning went along pretty much the same as Friday. The Americans and some Mexican people from the church ministered together to the street people. Nothing as eventful as the police situation yesterday happened so everyone was very glad. There were more street people today than yesterday and Holly hoped they planned sufficient amount of food for everyone. Some of the mean Mexican guys were there again and it looked like they had a few extra guys with them so she checked to be sure that Chris, Liam, Jackson and Seth were fairly close to Emma and Kylie. Jeff and Becca were together as well and were talking to some young people. Holly kept looking for Gabriel but he wasn't there today. She was concerned about him, especially after seeing the bruises on his face. She silently prayed for his protection and that she would see him again soon.

From a distance Gabriel watched the Americanos and Mexicans playing soccer. He did not dare risk joining in today for fear Miguel would be notified. He saw Holly from a distance and thought again how beautiful and kind she was. Gabriel never had anyone speak to him the way she did and he felt she really cared about him. That was a new feeling as well. He looked at their picture a lot last night after Miguel went to sleep. He had to be very careful not to get her into trouble with Miguel. Gabriel sat back where he knew no one could see him and just watched Holly and the others. He hoped he would get to spend some more time with them in the future.

When the soccer game was over and the street people finished eating they started to leave. Holly and the girls cleaned up the back of the van while the guys cleaned up the trash. Every once in a while Holly caught Zach watching her and a pleasant feeling washed over her.

Zach came over to Holly as she was deep in thought. He watched her quietly for a moment and then gently touched her shoulder so he wouldn't startle her. She turned and found him smiling at her.

"Hey," she said quickly. "I was just thinking."

"You looked like you were thinking about something so I didn't want to startle you."

"Thanks." Holly finished putting the leftover food carefully into the back of the van as well as the paper products. Zach pulled the back of the van down and they both walked over to the rest of the team. Everyone had finished their jobs and they were ready to head back to the church.

As Holly and Zach walked toward the bus stop with the team she asked, "How do you think everything went today?"

Zach responded as he mentally made note that everyone was accounted for and walked ahead of him. "I think yesterday and today went well and actually went better than I expected given our sudden experience with the police. I was glad it was quieter today." He saw Bill and Jeff take the lead over the group as they got closer to the bus stop so he moved quickly with Holly in order to be sure everyone got on the same bus.

Everyone got on the bus without any problems and he made sure Holly had a seat next to him as he stood next to her. The bus was really crowded and the guys made sure the girls had seats and then stood around them in a protective manner. At times Mexican men took more freedom and liberty with their hands when they found themselves around American women.

Yesterday Bill had shared a story about Holly with Zach regarding an incident involving her last year when they were here. She and three other American women were shopping for some material to make towels for a family at the church. While they traveled back to the church on one of the buses Holly felt a hand rub the back side of her upper thigh. She was sitting on the outside seat next to the aisle. She whispered to her team mate to move further over in the seat so Holly could move further away from the aisle. She felt it again, turned around and as a Mexican man was getting off the bus he smiled slyly at her and then saluted her. She handled it okay but felt violated and was really angry.

Zach was angry for what had happened to Holly last year so he decided to be sure nothing like that happened to any of the American women while he was in charge and especially not to Holly. Zach felt her nervousness yesterday when she got on the bus and now understood why so he was especially careful with her.

After they arrived back at the church Bill encouraged the Americans to take some time and do their devotions if they hadn't already done them so they could gather as a group later to talk about it. They had about an hour before Berta was ready for them to eat. Zach said goodbye to everyone, winked at Holly and left. Holly loved that special wink of Zach's which she knew was meant only for her. She sighed, grabbed her bible and found a quiet spot to spent time with God.

As Holly read the scripture for today's devotion her mind wandered to Gabriel. She looked at their picture which she decided to carry in her bible so that she would be reminded to pray for him often even though she knew she would pray for him even without the reminder. She hoped to see him soon so she could be sure he was okay. Before she knew it Berta was calling everyone for dinner.

The evening was delightful for the Americans as Berta fixed a wonderful meal of tamales, salad and rolls. Everyone thoroughly enjoyed her cooking and applauded her when finished. Berta loved cooking for the Americans because they were always so appreciative. After their devotions the host families promptly arrived to take the Americans home. The Mexicans loved to hang around with the Americanos and were always on time or early when picking them up. As the Americans left Holly thought of Gabriel and said a silent pray for him, petitioning God to cause him to show up at bible school on Monday.

CHAPTER 27

While lying in bed that evening Holly thought back to her conversation with Zach. She enjoyed sharing about her family and learning more about his.

"Have you talked to your family since you've been here?" he had asked her.

"I have. I talked with my mom two nights ago and she said my niece keeps asking when I'm coming home. Katie is so precious and the cutest thing ever. She loves to talk and looks like Micah with dark hair and dimples. I can't wait to have kids of my own. Caleb is the sweetest thing and seems to have my brother's personality although he's a lot like his mom too. I think he will look more like my sister-in-law, Ellie, who has auburn hair and green eyes. I do miss them a lot."

"They sound like a great family Holly. I hope I get to meet them one day."

"I hope you will as well. How about your family? Do you get to talk with them much?"

"I did last weekend. I was glad to hear that my mom is feeling better. My brother, Eli, is busy getting ready for college and he's really excited about it. My parents will miss him a lot and especially with both of us gone. He's a great guy!"

They continued to talk about their families and their interests. Holly remembered his excitement for doing long term mission work in Mexico. The thought crossed her mind at how much fun it would be to do that with him. She started praying for wisdom from God because she was falling in love with Zach and she wanted to be sure that he was included in God's plan for her. A peaceful feeling came over her after her prayers and she turned over, sighed contently and fell fast asleep.

CHAPTER 28

Before Holly knew it Sunday morning came and the church worship service lasted over two hours which was normal for the churches in Mexico and a blessing to her team. Today Bill was asked to preach and he used a translator which took a little longer than usual. She loved using her dual translation bible. It had Spanish on one side and English on the other. She was able to follow along in Spanish and then quickly translate it by reading the English. When the service was over the Americans were surprised to see a meal set up out in the courtyard of the church for everyone. It was a wonderful array of tamales, tacos, chips, and sweet breads. They also had what was considered a specialty in Mexico. It was corn on the cob that had a stick stuck through the cob from one end to the other. Mayonnaise was spread over the corn and then rolled into grated white cheese. The corn cobs were much larger than what they got in United States. It was an acquired taste for the Americans but they had a wonderful time of fellowship with the Mexicans.

After church and the meal the team traveled to the open market and did a lot of souvenir shopping. At the market everyone found a maze of small vendors and shops selling sterling silver jewelry, leather bags and wallets, embroidered lace tablecloths, Mexican multi-colored blankets, pottery and many other things. They had to go in twos so that no one got lost and the guys went with the girls to look out for them. They agreed to meet back two hours later.

Walking into the jewelry shop was like walking into a sparkling silver room. There was so much silver that it was almost blinding though also breathtaking. Holly bought a pair of sterling silver hoops for Ellie and a sterling silver ink pen for Micah. Later in another stall she found a beautiful, multi colored blanket for her mom. In one of the clothing stalls she found a lovely white dress with embroidering on it for her niece Katie. It was more challenging to find something for her nephew Caleb but she finally decided on an extremely soft, stuffed dog that one of the stall owners made. He would enjoy sleeping with it at night. She bought a leather bag and wallet for herself and also a beautiful water color of the boats on the floating gardens. She would have it framed when she got back to the states. Holly was really happy with her souvenir choices.

Becca had gone with her because she wanted to get something special for Jeff while he went with Bill. Becca found a beautiful sterling silver money clip for Jeff as well as a sparkling sterling silver ink pen. Becca bought herself a lovely lace tablecloth and a multi-colored blanket in shades of grays and blues. As Becca and Holly walked back to the court square to join the others before heading back to the church they past a small stall that sold key chains. Glancing at their stuff Holly noticed a really nice sterling silver key chain that made her think of Zach. On impulse she told Becca to keep going and she would catch up with her in a minute. Becca slowed her pace as Holly slipped into the stall to purchase the key chain for Zach as a reminder of their time together.

Everyone gathered at the court square and then decided to stop on their way for some ice cream before catching their bus. All the college students talked at the same time about all the fun souvenirs they found for their families. Becca walked with Jeff while Bill and Zach talked. Emma and Kylie walked with Holly and shared about all the things they found at the market. They each bought sterling silver earrings for themselves and their girlfriends. Emma bought a blanket for her family and a special pocket knife for her brother. Everyone seemed content with their purchases but getting on and off the bus might prove to be challenging with all the packages the team carried.

They stopped at the ice cream store and everyone experimented with a different flavored ice cream. Some of the flavors that they didn't try were mainly because of their names. Several of the ice cream flavors were named for flowers and they didn't sound particularly tasty to anyone. Some of the fruity flavors were delicious such as Holly's blueberry and Becca's mango. Everyone had a great time and thoroughly enjoyed their ice cream as they continued walking to the bus. Zach came alongside Holly and offered to carry her packages. He hadn't bought anything so his hands were free. Some of the other guys did the same thing for the girls. It was a nice opportunity for Zach and Holly to visit.

As they walked Holly decided to give Zach the key chain. She reached into her pocket and pulled out the tissue wrapped package. "Zach, I saw this key chain and immediately thought of you. I wanted to give it to you as a reminder of our time together." She turned and handed it to him.

He was so touched by her thoughtfulness. "Thanks Holly. It's really nice. I will treasure it." He reached his hand into one of his pockets and pulled out a small tissue wrapped package of his own. "The minute I saw this I thought of you and I wanted to get it for you as a reminder of our time together as well." They both started laughing.

They slowed their pace so Holly could open his gift. As she unfolded the tissue her hands trembled and she hoped Zach didn't notice. She'd never received a gift from any guy other than her brother. Inside the tissue was a lovely, delicately woven sterling silver bracelet. She looked up at Zach with the most beautiful smile he'd ever seen on a woman. "It's absolutely beautiful Zach. I will treasure it always. Thank you for giving me such a lovely gift. As soon as I get back to the church I'm going to put it on." He was pleased with her reaction as she carefully wrapped it up and put it in her shirt pocket for safe keeping.

There was a comfortable silence between the two of them as they picked up their pace to catch up with the others. Tomorrow would be the beginning of another busy week with bible school and the construction projects which meant they probably wouldn't get to spend much time with each other so they especially enjoyed being with each other now.

All in all Holly thought this Sunday had been a great day! After they arrived at the church everyone got together for their devotional and team meeting. Holly hurried and put her packages down so she could put her new bracelet on. She couldn't believe how beautiful it was and how perfectly it fit. She kept twisting her arm around looking at it. As she joined the group she noticed Zach sitting next to Emma. They were talking and Emma was smiling. He looked up just as Holly looked at him and she smiled that shy smile of hers that was just for him

Zach noticed the bracelet on her arm. It gave him so much pleasure and joy to see her wearing it. She was lovely!

Holly looked over to Kylie who had just said something to her and she had to ask Kylie to repeat what she said since she didn't hear her the first time. She kept thinking of Zach and how he had taken time to pick the bracelet out for her. Thank you, God, she mumbled. She couldn't wait to get back to the Sandovals and capture the wonder of this day in her journal.

CHAPTER 29

Monday came with a flurry of activity at the church. The Mexican children started arriving earlier than they had the previous week and there were more of them. They were bursting with excitement and chattering among themselves as they waited for the activities to start. They loved being with the Americanos and looked forward to the events of the day. Holly believed that by the end of this second week they would double the number of Mexican children that there were now present.

The enthusiasm of the children was contagious as Holly noticed that Jackson and Chris were surrounded by the younger Mexican boys. She saw them coaxing the older guys to play some soccer with them before bible school started. She looked over and saw Liam and Seth working on the construction preparations for that day and they seemed to be waving Chris and Jackson off so they could play with the boys for a few minutes before the day's activities got going. Some of the little Mexican girls were helping Kylie and Emma with the craft supplies. Holly noticed the teachers smiling as they prepared their things as well. Holly could swear they each walked with a bounce in their steps. It was always wonderful to engage the children and know they were enjoying everything about bible school. She kept looking around for Gabriel but, thus far, he hadn't returned.

Laura and Becca had prepared lessons for the women this week and during Becca's lesson Holly noticed Gabriel leaning against a tree close to his class. He looked at her and slightly nodded. She winked back at him and wanted to go over to him but knew she needed to wait until Becca finish her study with the women first.

The women finished their study in time for the snack break with the children. The moms helped the leaders prepare the snacks and serve them to the children. Holly took this opportunity to go over to Gabriel who now sat with his class, albeit on the edge of the class, but just the same he was there. He smiled as he saw her walk over to him.

"Hey Gabriel, how are you today?" she asked as she carefully looked him over for any more bruises. She didn't want him to notice that she paid too much attention to his physical condition. Something told her he would be embarrassed by too much attention.

"Bien or fine," he said as he tried to remember to use his English

"I had hoped to see you when we were with the street people over the weekend."

"I could not make it. I had lots to do."

She could tell that he was uncomfortable talking about this but she decided to press him a little further.

"We had a great time. How was your weekend?"

He looked down as someone served him a Rice Krispie treat and drink. He fumbled with the napkin and then looked up at her. "My weekend was okay."

"Good. I hope you will be able to be here every day this week. It is the last week for bible school. Then we will be helping with the construction projects by making curtains and painting."

He looked up at her after taking a drink and another bite of his snack. "I will try. It is hard for me to get away." He took another bite of his snack, gulped his drink and then said, "I really do like coming here but I just have to be careful."

"Why is that Gabriel?"

"I can no say, Holly, but I just have to be." He quickly took another bite of his snack and Holly knew she wouldn't get anything else out of him. "Well I hope you will enjoy the bible study today. It is about David and Goliath. Goliath was this giant that a boy named David killed with a slingshot and a stone. He probably was not much older or bigger than you."

Gabriel looked up at her with wide eyes full of awe. "How could a boy kill a giant with a slingshot?" he asked Holly. Holly found he was absolutely amazed at the thought.

"I do not want to spoil the story for you because you will hear all about it today. If you have any questions about it afterwards, I would be happy to answer them if I can."

"Okay you got a deal," he said with more excitement than Holly had seen before in him. He quickly finished his snack and drink. "I no want to miss any part of the story."

"You can slow down Gabriel. You will not miss anything because they will not start until everyone is ready."

Gabriel was so excited! To think that a boy could kill a giant was beyond his understanding. To him Miguel was a giant and if only he could kill Miguel his life would be so much better. He would listen carefully today and pray that this new God he has been hearing about might help him kill Miguel as he got up to throw away his trash away returned and looked at Holly. "Gracias. I hope I can hear the whole story before I have to leave."

Gabriel was so conscious about time and Holly noticed how often he looked around as if he was checking to see who was present. He seemed fearful at times as well. "Gabriel, if you cannot hear the whole story let me know and I will finish what you miss."

Everyone was being called to their classes and as Gabriel moved away to his class he looked back at Holly and waved. She could tell he was really anxious to hear more about David and Goliath. She picked up her trash and deposited it in the bag. Emma, Kylie and some of the other ladies were cleaning up and preparing for the craft time. Holly decided to pitch in and help them since the women's bible study was finished and Laura left to do some errands for her family. Holly also wanted to tell Becca what a great job she did in leading the study and working with Laura.

~~~~~~~~~~~

Unbeknownst to Gabriel and Holly, one of Miguel's men was positioned far enough away so that no one even noticed him. He watched Gabriel talking to the blonde woman that Miguel mentioned. She was a beautiful Americano woman and the man thought in a nasty way that he would like to get to know this woman himself. Maybe

186

with what Miguel had in mind he might just get that opportunity. That thought put a smile on his face as he continued to watch her and Gabriel. Gabriel would not like what Miguel had in mind, but Gabriel also needed to be taught a lesson and Miguel was the one to be sure that he learned that lesson well.

CHAPTER 30

Later that evening, Miguel's man reported all that he observed that day between Gabriel and the blonde woman. Miguel was so angry it was hard for him to control himself. Several times he banged his fist on the table as his man reported the details of what happened. Miguel wanted to beat Gabriel to an inch of his life for his betrayal but if he let on that he knew what was going on it could blow his plans for the Americanos and the blonde lady. He would just have to play it cool and put his plan into action soon. Everything was falling into place nicely and he was placated by the fact that soon the Americanos would be out of his territory and Gabriel would be towing the line once again.

Miguel and his men got back to laying out the plans for getting rid of the Americanos. Miguel smiled more and more as the ideas became more of a reality as the plans took shape. Miguel was going to make sure that Gabriel wished he had never laid eyes on the blonde woman.

CHAPTER 31

Each day that week went pretty much as the previous day. The construction work was really looking good and the guys were feeling terrific about how much work had been accomplished this week. The cabinets would be ready to paint next week and so would the walls of both the little church building and the bathrooms. The girls could start the curtains too.

The Americans looked forward to the weekend because after their time with the street people on Saturday they would be heading to Taxco as a group for some rest, relaxation and souvenir shopping. Then they would return Sunday evening to their host families and prepare for the next week.

During the middle of the week Holly had an opportunity to talk more with Gabriel. He seemed to be at bible school during the bible story time and then he was gone. On Wednesday Holly had a few extra minutes because the women's study finished early so the women could prepare a special craft for the kids. Holly took this opportunity to spend some time with Gabriel. She wanted to find out what he thought about the bible story of David and Goliath.

Gabriel saw Holly walking toward him as he prepared to leave. He should leave immediately but he really enjoyed talking with her. Every time Gabriel left after being with Holly he felt better about himself and his life. He slowed up his pace so she could catch up with him.

"Hey Gabriel, wait up," Holly called after him. He turned to wait for her.

When she caught up with him she asked, "Are you leaving already?"

"Yes. I need to get back home. I have some things I need to get done before the evening." She noticed once again that he seemed to be looking around as if he was nervous about something or someone.

"Okay, I will not keep you. I just wondered what you thought about David and Goliath."

She saw him relax for just a moment before he started sharing what he learned. He positively lit up as he talked about how David defeated Goliath.

"I am amazed that David was able to kill Goliath because Goliath was so big and David was just a boy. He only used a sling shot and a stone!" he exclaimed. "How can that be?"

Holly responded and said, "He did it with God's help Gabriel. Remember when some people made fun of the fact that a boy like David wanted to kill Goliath. I love David's reply when he said that the Lord would deliver him from the hand of the Philistine which was Goliath. He also told Goliath later that he came to David with a sword, a spear and a javelin but that David came to him in the name of the Lord. He continued to tell Goliath that God would deliver him into his hand that day. All he used, Gabriel, was a slingshot and the five stones he had gathered earlier in the day, but he totally trusted God to help him kill Goliath."

Still amazed Gabriel replied, "I know it is hard for me to believe that someone so small could kill someone so large and powerful but I would love to be able to be like David and kill a giant." Holly didn't know that Gabriel was thinking of Miguel at that moment but she did wonder what was going through his mind and who the giant in his life could be.

"You know, Gabriel, God would not want us going around killing people. When someone treats us poorly we are supposed to ask God to help us and then we are supposed to let Him take care of that person. It is easy to want to take revenge on someone and it is hard to let God be the One to take revenge. But Gabriel, it is the very best thing and it is what we are supposed to do. We are to show love and kindness to people even when they are mean to us."

"No, I do not want to do that," Gabriel objected.

Holly could see that Gabriel was adamant about that statement when he continued to say, "I would rather get rid of someone myself," as he looked at the ground.

Holly bent over and gently lifted Gabriel's chin up so that their eyes met. "Gabriel, I do not know who has hurt you so deeply but pray and ask God to help that person not be so mean. It may not happen right away but I believe God will deliver you out of your situation if you ask Him."

Gabriel bent his head back down and quietly spoke in a whisper, "You do not know how hard it is Holly." She barely heard his words.

"No, I do not know, but you can be sure that God does know and I will continue to pray for you that God would help you and that He would protect you while you are in this situation. He loves you Gabriel and He just wants you to love Him back. It is a wonderful experience to be one of God's children and to know the joy of His love, care and protection."

Gabriel started feeling uneasy about being here so long and he was also uncomfortable listening to what Holly said because he would love to be loved by God and to be taken care of without having to worry about being beaten or watching others being hurt. He started to back away and Holly knew her time with him was coming to an end.

"Gabriel, if you ever want to talk more about God I am here. If you are ever in trouble you can ask me for help and I will do whatever I can to help you. I will be gone this weekend to Taxco but will be back on Sunday. Bible school is over Thursday but my team and I will be working here in the church painting and making curtains for the next two weeks. I would love to see you during those two weeks if it works out for you. We will also be working with the street people on Friday and then Saturday we leave for Taxco."

Gabriel kept his eyes on Holly as he slowly walked away and replied, "Thanks Holly. Maybe I will see you next week. I can no come tomorrow so I no be able to see you until next week."

"Do not forget we will be working with the street people this Friday," she called out to him as he walked away. He turned and waved and she waved back. She had such a longing to take care of him because he was so sweet and she knew he must have a really hard life. She silently prayed that God would look after him and protect him from whoever was hurting him. A couple of tears slipped down her cheeks as she thought of him being hurt.

She turned, wiped away her tears and went back to the group of children working on their crafts. The rest of the day continued on like the other days. She looked forward to helping the guys next week with the painting and doing something different. She was emotionally drained from her encounter with Gabriel because she knew he was in some kind of trouble and she couldn't help him, at least not yet. But if God showed her a way to help him she determined then and there to do whatever she could to help this little boy who found a place deep within her heart.

CHAPTER 32

Thursday was like the rest of the days and Friday was spent with the street people. Each day they had more people follow them to the vacant lot and Pastor Abraham and Zach took turns sharing the message of the Gospel with the people and the Americans played soccer and fed them. The people seemed to enjoy singing at the end of every message.

Holly would notice that some of the street guys treated the street girls poorly. Some of the young girls had bruises and seemed skittish around those guys. She also noticed that the Mexican guys weren't paying as much attention to Emma or Kylie since Chris and Jackson stayed pretty close to them. She could only imagine what dreadful things they had to put up with given the lives they probably led. Holly's team always left the street people with a sense of heaviness. No one usually spoke for most of the trip back to the church. They seemed to perk up once they were back at the church and removed from the situation. The group devotions were a special blessing because it helped everyone refocus on God and His goodness and mercy even in the midst of difficult circumstances.

Everyone was at the church early Saturday morning to leave for Taxco. Several of their Mexican guides came along with Pastor Abraham and Zach to serve as their tour guides.

The trip took them about four hours and they rode in two vans that were provided by people in the church. Zach drove one and Pastor Abraham drove the other.

Everyone packed an overnight bag with bag lunches prepared by their host families. Holly rode in Zach's van with Jeff, Becca, Chris, Liam and Kylie while Bill, Seth, Jackson and Emma rode in Pastor Abraham's van with the Mexican friends who came along to help show the Americans around Taxco. She couldn't help but notice that Chris was with Kylie and Jackson was with Emma quite often and she smiled because she was with Zach.

Holly loved coming to Taxco because the ride was so beautiful. Mexico City had so many people that there wasn't much green foliage in the city because apartments and houses were everywhere. Most of the housing facilities were built side by side and all that was left was brown dirt and roads. Every now and then you would see a lovely courtyard built inside a fenced or gated area with flowers and shrubs. Rarely would you see grass or any greenery around Mexico City so it was refreshing to see the beautiful scenery as they drove to Taxco.

Driving to Taxco was such a great opportunity to see a different part of Mexico's countryside. If the Americans never had a chance to do this they would have the impression that Mexico was dry, brown and dull. Seeing the mountains on the way to Taxco and the beautiful green hillsides was breath taking. There were luscious fruit orchards along the way and a couple of beautiful waterfalls coming down mountainsides. It was a gorgeous drive!

Women could be seen walking alongside the road with jugs of something balanced on their heads and others had large bowls of fruit balanced on their heads. There were men leading their donkeys along the road and small children were seen every now and again playing ball or running in the fields. It was certainly a different scene than what was seen in Mexico City. There was a clean, fresh smell coming through the windows of the vans while Mexico City smelled mostly like car exhaust and aromas from food being cooked on street corners.

As the vans got closer to Taxco the streets became narrower. Some of the side streets were cobblestones and didn't look big enough for one car to pass through. Holly knew everyone wondered how the buses made it through as the streets were lined with people, cars and buses coming and going. The buses were practically touching each other as they passed one another. Holly was glad they were in vans because at least had a little more space.

The vans started to pull over next to a small, white house with red clay shingles. Zach told them to get their bags out and that they would be walking up to the hotel since the vans couldn't go any further. Their Mexican guides would show them where to go while he and Pastor Abraham parked the vans and would meet them at the hotel. Zach winked at Holly as she was the last one to get out. She grabbed her bag and followed the rest of the people up the hill while the two vans drove off.

Everyone had to walk closely along the side of the cobblestone road. They were practically hugging the buildings as they steadily walked up the hill. Every now and then a small Volkswagon car would toot a horn as it made its way up the hill. They had to be very careful not to get too close to the car. Pedestrians did not have the right of way here either. They hiked up the hill for about 30 minutes when one of their Mexican guides crossed over and headed into an old, rundown building. Everyone followed him with a couple of the other Mexicans following the group.

The inside of the hotel was so different from the outside. There were rooms on two floors overlooking a beautiful courtyard in the middle of the hotel that had a beautiful giant tree growing up the middle which was as tall as the eye could see. Red, yellow and blue tiles were scattered all over the floor and walls and wrought iron chairs and tables placed throughout the courtyard for people to sit and talk. Off to the right of the courtyard were a set of stone stairs that went to the second floor.

Bill went over to register everyone just as Pastor Abraham and Zach walked in. They took a short cut and got to the hotel quickly so they helped everyone register and find their rooms. The girls were rooming together and the guys were split between two rooms. The Mexicans had their own rooms so everyone grabbed their bags and proceeded up the stone staircase to their rooms on the second floor.

The girls' room was decorated with colorful tiles and small twin beds covered with woven blankets and braided rugs on an old wooden floor. The bathroom was done in bright colors with birds painted on the walls and white tiles on the floor and shower. There were large windows without screens that opened onto the cobblestone street and they could hear people coming and going as they made their way along the street.

Becca dropped her bag on one of the beds and Holly took another one. Kylie and Emma decided to share the bunk beds. Becca looked over at Holly lying on her bed and said, "I wonder what the guys' rooms look like. This one is delightful!"

Kylie and Emma squealed in agreement. "I can't wait to see the rest of this area," said Emma.

"Let's go see the guys' rooms," said Becca as she got up from her bed. "I want to see if my husband's room is as cute as our room."

The rest of the girls got up and headed out the door to see the guys. They found their room three doors down from theirs so Becca knocked and Jeff answered.

"We wanted to see what your rooms looked like," she told him as she kissed his cheek.

Jeff waved them into their room as Holly noticed Zach along with Bill and Pastor Abraham. "Jackson, Chris, Seth and Liam are in the next room. Their room looks just like this one only they have two sets of bunk beds," exclaimed Jeff.

Bill looked over at Holly and said, "I told the guys to meet us downstairs in the courtyard in 45 minutes for lunch. Pastor Abraham thought it might be a good time to do some sightseeing and shopping for a couple of hours since the shops close at 5 p.m. Tomorrow we can do a little more shopping after our worship service and devotions since the shops don't open until about 10 a.m. That will give everybody several more hours to shop and then we would like to leave for Mexico City around two, getting us back there by 6 in time for dinner."

"Okay sounds good to me and we'll meet you downstairs. That will give each of us some time to unpack and work on our devotions." Holly looked over at the other girls as they nodded in agreement and filed out the door.

She glanced quickly at Zach as she walked out the door and noticed he was looking right at her as well. Hopefully they would be able to spend some time together while they were here. The girls went to their room and did their own thing for the next 45 minutes while they each secretly looked forward to different aspects of this weekend getaway.

~~~~~~~~~~

Gabriel missed seeing Holly the last couple of days but he couldn't take a chance that Miguel would catch him with her. He had to protect her from Miguel because if Miguel found out about Holly there was no telling what he might do and Gabriel didn't want to see Holly get hurt by Miguel. Gabriel had no doubt Miguel would hurt Holly if he found out she was important to Gabriel.

After Miguel left to collect some bad debts Gabriel went to his bed and lifted up the tattered, thin old mattress which he laid upon every night. He pulled out a slingshot that he purchased after hearing the story of David and Goliath at bible school. He wished he could hide the slingshot in the floorboard but it was too big for the small space. He had found five smooth stones as well and kept them hidden in a small, woven bag he got when he was little. He didn't know where it came from but it meant something to him and he kept it hidden in the floor boards with his other treasures.

Fingering the slingshot Gabriel dreamed of putting a stone in it and shooting it at Miguel. He dreamed of the stone hitting Miguel smack in the middle of his forehead and Miguel dropping over dead. He loved that image and he clung to it. He began to feel a little guilty about it though when he remembered what Holly said about letting God take revenge and not people. He prayed after talking to Holly that God would get rid of Miguel from his life. So far Miguel is still around tormenting and hurting him as well as other people. But Holly said he had to trust God and His timing. He looked forward to seeing Holly again in a few days. He quickly and quietly hid the slingshot and the stones under his mattress because he knew Miguel would never look there since the mattress stunk and was nasty.

~~~~~~~~~

Miguel met with his guys and started putting his plan in action to put an end to the Americanos and the "do gooder" Mexicans coming to his turf. The next time the Americanos worked with the street people his plan was to take the blonde woman and hold her until they promised to keep away from his turf. He decided to wait and see if he had to do anything more drastic than that. He looked forward to getting acquainted with the blonde woman as well as to teach Gabriel a lesson he would never forget. He decided to use the blonde woman to this end since Gabriel seemed to be attracted to her and he would have to put an end to that attachment. He figured he would probably have to dispose of the American woman but he would decide that later. Maybe, just maybe, he would have some fun with her first. His men started laughing as they heard Miguel's plan and looked forward to it as well.

CHAPTER 33

It was now mid-afternoon and all the Americans who were excited to see the sights in Taxco gathered in the courtyard with their Mexican guides as Pastor Abraham led the way. They were going to find a little spot to get something to eat later but for now they were going to walk around and do some shopping.

One of the shops the team went into glittered with lots of sterling silver setting around. The girls started to look at earrings while the guys looked at belt buckles and key chains. Zach enjoyed watching Holly's enthusiasm with the other girls as they shopped. He liked watching Holly as she took her time looking over everything before she decided what she liked best. He watched Jeff and Becca as they looked at watches and finally decided to purchase a sterling silver watch.

Zach walked over to Holly who was by herself while Emma and Kylie looked at bracelets. Holly looked up as Zach approached her.

"This is a beautiful place Zach. It's amazing how much silver they have here!" He loved how her eyes sparkled with awe and excitement!

"Taxco is known around the world for its sterling silver. It used to be a silver mining town and it still gets some from the mines but a lot of it is imported as well."

"I would love to find something special here for my sister-in-law Ellie. She loves sterling silver and I think a pair of earrings would be just the thing. They're so inexpensive too," she exclaimed.

Holly took a pair of dangly earrings and hung them from her ears and said to Zach, "So what do you think?"

"They're really nice Holly."

"I think I will get these for her and I'd like to get her a bracelet as well." She looked shyly up at him and continued as she lifted the bracelet he had previously bought her. "I love my bracelet Zach. It is beautiful. Thank you again."

"You're most welcome. I'm glad you like it."

"I really do!" She moved down to where the bracelets were and Zach followed. She found a nice bangle bracelet that she knew Ellie would enjoy. After paying for her souvenirs she and Zach walked to the entrance and waited for the others to finish with their purchases.

"How do you like Taxco Holly?" Zach asked.

"It's amazing and quite quaint."

"It's one of my favorite places," replied Zach. "I'd love to come back here again someday."

"Me too," Holly responded. She smiled at him and then looked over at the girls. They were having so much fun picking out things for themselves and others.

"Zach, you know the little boy named Gabriel, the one that I have been talking to every once in a while?"

Zach answered, "I have seen you with him but I'm not familiar with him. I don't think I have ever seen him before. Only since you've been here have I noticed him. Why?"

"I really like him and I think he's in some kind of trouble. I don't think he's more than seven or eight and I would like to try to help him if I can."

"So many people are in trouble here and it's so hard to know how to help them most of the time. That's what I love about sharing the Gospel because that would be their biggest help. Even if their circumstances of life don't change their hope and attitude could change. They need the Lord to embrace, endure and sometimes overcome their lifestyles."

"I know you're right but it seems like there should be more that we can do. I like him a lot and I'm scared for him because I know he is afraid of someone but he won't open up to me."

"It's amazing how some of these kids survive living the lifestyles that they have to endure living on the streets. But there is something to be said about the will to live and even with their circumstances there is still that strong desire to make life better."

"I have shared the Gospel with Gabriel and I think he is interested in getting to know more about Jesus and God. Something holds him back though and I don't know what it is. I hope he is around when we meet with the street people next week."

"I would like to meet him so if he is maybe you can introduce me to him," Zach suggested.

"Thanks and I will do that if he is around next week."

Emma and Kylie came up to them at that moment to show them their purchases and how little they had to pay for them. The guys were right behind them as Emma and Kylie helped them find souvenirs for their female family members. They were having fun together but decided it was time to move on to another place.

As they made their way to the middle of the courtyard they noticed a Mexican wedding in progress. The bride was beautifully dressed in a long, flowing lace wedding gown with a veil that covered her face. The groom was impeccably dressed in a black tuxedo and held the hand of his bride as they made their way to the church. They had a large group of people following them that looked like a processional. People stopped, watched and admired the scene unfolding before them while many bystanders cheered and clapped for the beautiful couple.

After watching the wedding processional the group decided to find a restaurant and get something to eat before the evening ended. They needed to get back to the hotel and do their group devotions but they hoped to do a little more shopping on their way to the restaurant. Jeff and Becca were enjoying their time with each other as they made their way to the restaurant. The girls walked with the guys while Pastor Abraham and Bill were deep in conversation, so Zach was glad that he could walk with and talk to Holly for a while longer. Holly was silently grateful as well.

After finding a restaurant they were seated after a short wait. Everyone ordered something different and decided to pass it around for the others to try. They ordered everything from tamales to tacos to frajitas to refried beans to enchiladas. They all loved sampling a little of all these delicious authentic Mexican dishes. As they ate they enjoyed a floor show of Mexican dancers and mariachi players. It was great to hear music playing while they ate and enjoyed their meal. The team found everything in Mexico was colorful and the music was always so lively.

By the time they finished eating it was 9:00 and dark outside. It was time to get back to the hotel and group devotions because they hoped to get to bed by 11:00 so everyone could get an early start in the morning and be rested.

Devotions were wonderful that evening as they talked about God's goodness and mercy. Holly loved to study the attributes of God. When she had questions that she couldn't answer about life situations and choices she went back to the truths of God's Word and His promises. She knew she could trust Him even if she didn't understand the circumstances of life. When she thought of Gabriel she drew comfort in the fact that God knew everything about Gabriel's life. She prayed that God would deliver Gabriel out of anything that was hurting him and take him to a better place.

Holly enjoyed listening to Zach share during their devotions and grew in her appreciation of him and who he was in the Lord. She began praying for him as she knew his desire was to serve God on the mission field. She enjoyed talking with him and spending time with him today and she looked forward to more time with him over the next two weeks before they went back home. It was hard to believe that half their time in Mexico was over and that the next couple of weeks would be filled with lots of physical work rather than bible studies and bible school. They would be able to spend a few more times ministering to the street people and she looked forward to those times.

Later in bed Holly thought about her family in Colorado and sent up a prayer for them. She missed them and hoped she had the opportunity to introduce them to

Zach someday. She prayed that if it was God's will she hoped there might be a place in her future with Zach and hoped he felt the same way about her. She desired God's will for her life because she knew and believed there was nothing better and if God's will was a future with Zach she would be forever grateful.

CHAPTER 34

Zach woke up to a beautiful day with birds singing and a cacophony of sounds outside the window. There were roosters crowing in the distance and he could hear people walking up and down the cobblestone street outside his window. The booths would soon be set up for the day's activity of selling. Zach quietly got out of bed so as not to disturb the other guys and walked over to the window. He leaned out to look at the view of the surrounding buildings. From the second floor of their hotel he could see over the tops of many of the other buildings. People sat on some of the roof tops enjoying the scenery and eating breakfast.

He looked forward to seeing Holly this morning. There was something special about this place and he wanted to share it with her. He lifted up a prayer for her because it seemed like each day he was falling in love more and more with Holly and he hoped she felt the same. Maybe one day they could come back here for their honeymoon. Zach sighed and realized that maybe he was getting a little ahead of himself and of God.

He quickly picked up his clothes and went into the bathroom. He decided to get his morning toiletries out of the way before anyone else woke up and then he planned on taking his bible up to the roof top to read and pray. He wanted to spend time with God before the day got going as well as refocus on what God would have for his life rather than what he wanted.

Later in the morning everyone met up on the top of the roof which was flat with a small wall around it where

Pastor Abraham had breakfast ready. He had orange juice, donuts and some of the Mexican sweet breads that everyone loved so much. He also had hot chocolate with the taste of cinnamon that so many of the Americans enjoyed. Several bought blocks of chocolate laced with cinnamon to take home with them and make their own hot chocolate when they were back in the states. Following a delicious breakfast they all got together in one corner of the roof for a Sunday morning worship service. They sang several praise songs, Bill shared Scripture verses and Zach preached. Holly hadn't realized he was going to preach but was filled with wonder and awe as he shared God's word.

Zach hadn't told anyone about preaching this morning and only Pastor Abraham and Bill knew he had been preparing something for their service. He decided to share about the sacrifice of praise and how pleasing that was to God especially when we go through difficult times and are still able to praise God. God cherishes our sacrifice of praise as we thank Him even in the hardest of times because of our trust in Him and our knowledge of Him. His Scripture text for his message was Hebrews 13:15 which said, *"Through Him then, let us continually offer up a sacrifice of praise to God, that is, the fruit of our lips that give thanks to His name."* He told them that sacrifice means to yield or relinquish whatever is important to us or whatever is troubling us and when we do that we are offering up a gift to God.

Zach said being on a mission trip in a foreign country can produce a lot of anxiety and there are trials that can be experienced as well as the difficulty of seeing the despair in other people's lives. Our sacrifice of praise releases us from fear and anxiety and requires obedience founded upon trust in our God. The sacrifice of praise in difficult situations comes from the desire to obey God and to trust that He knows what He's doing. By offering praise from the fruit of our lips, we are telling God we trust Him no matter what is going on in life. This ability comes from our abiding in Christ and the praise of the lips is cultivated through abiding. We must cultivate an intimate relationship with God every day and live a life that brings honor and glory to Him. The more we know about Him the closer we will walk with Him and abide in Him.

The worship serviced closed with singing praise songs followed by a time of community prayer. The only way Holly could describe the feeling of worshipping together on this roof corresponded to what she hoped and believed it would be like in heaven. In her mind this was a little piece of heaven that she would remember for a very long time.

When they finished everyone took their bibles back to their rooms, got their cameras and money and headed for the market square. They were told to stay in pairs and to return to the market square by 1:00 where Pastor Abraham and Bill would be waiting for them. Then they would return to the hotel, have sandwiches for lunch and then begin their journey back to Mexico City.

Kylie, Emma, Jackson and Chris headed out together while Liam and Seth went in a different direction. Bill and Pastor Abraham didn't really want to shop because they wanted to continue their discussion from the previous night and Bill had already gotten his souvenirs. If anyone needed anything the two men would be positioned in the square in front of the small restaurant where they had dined the previous night. Holly had decided to join Becca and Jeff and Zach came up as they were leaving to ask if he might join them. They all nodded in agreement and Holly was delighted that Zach made the effort to seek her out.

Zach took them to a few special little shops that they discovered through a maze of tiny staircases leading downward. There were many little side cobblestone streets with little open air booths selling colorful pottery, jewelry boxes, leather goods, toys, candy, shoes, blankets, ponchos, straw hats and handcrafted wooden items. There were beautiful water color paintings that Holly couldn't resist. She bought another water color print, this time of Taxco that she would frame when she got home. A couple of times they ran into the college students with the Mexican guides from the church and they were having so much fun bargaining with the shop keepers.

The morning passed too quickly for Holly and Zach and before they realized it, it was time to get back to the market square for lunch and leave for Mexico City. Jeff and Becca were walking ahead of them as Zach and Holly continued to talk.

"This has been wonderful Zach," Holly said. "I'm so glad we've had these last two days together."

"I am too Holly." He squeezed her hand and held it for an extra moment longer. "I hope we will have more times like these together," he said as he stopped and looked directly into her eyes.

"Me too," Holly replied.

"There is so much I want to say to you and so little time. Now is not a good time because we need to get back but I just wanted you to know how much I have grown to care for you in this short period of time and I have been praying about pursuing a relationship with you in the future."

Holly's face became radiant with a beautiful smile that told him she felt the same way. He turned to continue walking, holding her hand for a moment longer and then let go. Right before walking into the hotel Holly quickly said to Zach, "I would like that too Zach." Then she smiled and walked into the hotel. Zach felt wonderful and looked forward to the next two weeks working alongside Holly on the construction projects.

After lunch everyone grabbed their purchases and their backpacks and headed down to the vans. The ride home was quiet as everyone was occupied with his or her own thoughts of the past two weeks and their lovely time in Taxco.

CHAPTER 35

Monday morning came quickly as the team prepared to continue the construction projects that they wanted to finish by the end of the week. The last week would be used tying up any loose ends and preparing for their return home. Everyone looked forward to calling their families in America today with the last calling time being at 2 p.m. It was the second time they had the opportunity to speak with their families since being in Mexico City. Because the cost of phone calls is expensive in Mexico City, Bill decided that everyone would make only two calls home during their trip. Today was the last time they would call home before they left Mexico City and he could feel the anticipation from his team. He looked forward to speaking with his wife and kids too. He knew everyone would be very thankful for the opportunity to reconnect with their loved ones.

The morning started as some of the guys poured cement into the small structures that were made for toilets and sinks. All the plumbing was in place and now the cement would be poured. They were counting on it being dried and hardened by Wednesday so that they could begin setting the toilets and sinks in both structures.

Emma and Holly made good use of their time by painting the kitchen cabinets that had been made within the last two weeks while Becca and Kylie worked on sewing and hanging curtains for the kitchen area. Some of the guys were busy installing windows in the main part of the sanctuary. Pastor Abraham loved watching this American team work. In the beginning he thought there might be too many projects for the Americans to finish in a month but now he believed they might well finish it all before they returned home.

At lunch time everyone finished up what they were doing and got their bagged lunches from their host families. It was nice to take a break together and eat as a group. During the previous two weeks the girls were busy with bible school while the guys worked here and now everyone worked together and it was great feeling of comradery and care.

Zach showed up just as they finished their lunches and Holly waved to him as he walked through the door. He smiled and made his way over to her.

"Hey Holly, how's it going today?" Zach asked. He looked around and marveled at how much the team had accomplished. "It's amazing what you've done. Pastor Abraham and I believe you will finish everything that was given to your team to do."

Holly laughed. "It did seem monumental when you told us all that you hoped we could do while we were here. Some of us had our doubts as well but this is a hard working group. It's fun to see our accomplishments and know that the conditions here will be better for the congregation when they worship God."

Zach nodded in agreement as Bill got everyone together to take a bus ride back to the phone calling station so that they could make their scheduled calls home.

"I can't wait to talk to my family Zach," Holly said with enthusiasm. "I have really missed them. You'll like my family and especially my brother Micah."

Zach smiled. "I'm looking forward to meeting them someday Holly."

Everyone moved toward the door to leave because they had to catch a specific bus to be able to get to the phone station on time. Zach followed Holly out to the front of the building. He was going in a different direction to complete some work he was doing for the street ministry this weekend. They all said goodbye to him as he departed and Holly waved to him as he turned the corner. She turned to follow the rest of the team. She couldn't wait to talk to her mom, Micah, Ellie and Katie. Holly smiled as she thought about her family meeting Zach someday and she knew they would love him as well.

CHAPTER 36

Tuesday saw lots of work accomplished by the team. At lunch time on Wednesday everyone was pretty exhausted because they worked at a quicker speed so they could finish the bathroom structures. Pastor Abraham and some men from the church brought a truck load with two toilets, two sinks, more paint and boards to finish the shelves in the area that would be designated for Sunday school classes. Emma and Holly were finishing the painting in the kitchen and hoped to get started in the sanctuary after lunch when they heard a lot of commotion going on outside. Becca sent a questioning look at Holly as she and Kylie joined them to see what was going on outside. As they stepped out the sanctuary door Pastor Abraham came running toward them.

"Holly, we need to get Liam to the hospital. They were lifting the toilet to set it in place and accidentally dropped it on Liam's foot. I am not sure if it is broken or not so we are going to use the truck to take him to the hospital."

As Pastor Abraham went to get the truck Bill ran over to Holly and said, "I'm going to the hospital with Pastor Abraham. Seth is going as well to help get Liam into the truck. Jeff will stay here to continue getting the toilets set in place with Jackson and Chris. Please keep working with the girls while we're gone. We'll get back as soon as we can. Pastor Abraham said that going to an emergency room here can take a lot of time so if you get finished before we get back go ahead and eat dinner."

216

Holly nodded as the girls looked at Liam limping towards them hanging onto Seth and Jeff. They heard the truck pull up to the entrance door and headed toward the truck. They watched as Pastor Abraham got out and opened the door for Liam. Once Liam was in Seth and Bill jumped into the back of the truck while Pastor Abraham got in the driver's side and left. The team could see that Liam was in a lot of pain and expressed their concern and well wishes to him.

Jeff looked at his team and said, "Hey everyone, why don't we take a few minutes to pray for Liam before we go back to work." They nodded and walked back inside the door into the sanctuary.

The team got into a circle and Jeff prayed, "Father, please be with Liam now and give him courage. Calm his fears and speak peace to his heart. Comfort him now in his pain. We pray, Lord, that his foot won't be broken or deeply injured but we also pray for Your will to be done, not ours. Please give the doctors wisdom as they seek the best treatment for Liam. Be with us now and calm our concerns as we wait for them to return. Continue to help us make good use of our time here and finish what we've started. We thank You for Christ and His work on the cross that gives us access to You. We desire to honor You and give you praise and glory no matter what the circumstances. In Christ's name we pray, Amen."

Throughout the rest of the afternoon everyone continued doing their jobs. They watched the door and prayed that Liam would return soon. As they neared the time to start cleaning up so they could get ready for dinner,

Jeff yelled that Liam, Seth and Bill had returned. The girls dropped everything and ran outside to see them.

Liam was hobbling on crutches with Seth and Bill on either side. He was smiling so that was a good sign. The girls took turns giving Liam hugs and welcoming him back.

"Thanks everyone," Liam said smiling. "The doctor said my foot was severely bruised but not broken. Nothing showed up on the x-ray anyway." They cheered for him and voiced their praised to God.

Bill explained, "I wasn't sure we would make it back for dinner but the x-rays came back pretty quick and the doctor was able to wrap his foot and we left right away. Liam's foot will be painful for a few days so the doctor gave him some pain killers and recommended that he keep his foot elevated the rest of today and stay off it as much as possible for the rest of the week."

Jeff stated, "Bill, we were just cleaning up to get ready for dinner so we are glad you guys got back to join us."

"Thanks Jeff," Bill replied as he turned to Liam. "You can sit and keep your foot elevated while we finish up.

Liam answered, "Sounds good." Liam slowly made his way over to the table while Seth pulled a chair out for him. Liam sat down and Seth pulled another chair out so Liam could rest his foot on it. Liam didn't like not helping his team but his foot was throbbing and he thought it was a good idea to keep his foot elevated as he waited for the team to finish.

Everyone got busy cleaning up so they could eat and visit with Liam. They were all curious as to what happened at the hospital. Never having been to a foreign hospital they wondered how different it was from American hospitals.

After the last paint brush was cleaned everyone sat down to eat and Liam filled them in on the experience of being treated at a foreign hospital. Everyone was relieved and thankful that Liam's foot wasn't broken and that he could to finish the trip with them. They all saw God's faithfulness to them in the midst of a trial. Holly knew she would never forget God's answered prayer in protecting Liam from anything more serious than a badly bruised foot.

CHAPTER 37

Miguel looked forward to today because this was the day that he planned on kidnapping the blonde American woman to get all the "do-gooders" off his streets. His men had been watching the Americans all week and when they reported to him that one of the guys got hurt he was really pleased. That would mean one less person to interfere with his plans.

Miguel kept Gabriel busy all week so that he had no time to go to the church and visit the American woman. He would let Gabriel know at the right time, after his plan was accomplished, what he had done which would teach Gabriel a lesson he would never forget. Miguel knew that Gabriel had a soft spot for the blonde woman and he was going to put an end to that this weekend.

Miguel smiled as he continued thinking about what he was going to do with the America woman. He had the perfect place picked out for keeping her prisoner until he was finished with her. Miguel knew there would be a lot of fuss made because she would be a missing American, but he would wait that out and then send word to the man they called Zach to stop coming to his streets or he would kill the woman. He hadn't decided whether he would kill her or just rough her up some and then let her return to her people. Miguel was pretty arrogant and felt that no one would ever be able to catch him so he never considered that anyone would come after him in retaliation. He counted on the fact that the Mexican police didn't bother with drug runners even though occasionally they liked to flex their muscles, but he wasn't worried.

To his way of thinking Miguel was on top of his game and nothing could or would knock him off his pedestal. There was nothing that Gabriel could do either because Miguel would have him right where he wanted him. Gabriel would know without a doubt that Miguel was king of his life and the streets. Miguel didn't know that Gabriel had changed a lot in recent days or he would not have been so arrogant.

~~~~~~~~~

On Friday, the Americans met Zach at the church before heading to the streets. It was decided that Liam would stay back with Jeff and Becca while they did some cleaning at the church after the week's projects. Yesterday when Liam tried to help with some of the construction he realized his foot would not let him do anything. After Jeff and Becca finished the cleaning Pastor Abraham would pick them up and take them on a tour of the heart of Mexico City. Liam would be able to keep his foot elevated in the car and they also would be able to do something else rather than wait at the church until the team returned.

Saying goodbye to Jeff, Becca and Liam the team which was headed by Zach left to catch the bus. Chris and Kylie talked as they walked while Seth, Jackson and Emma followed. Bill talked with Zach while Holly was the last to follow. She enjoyed these few minutes so that she could reflect on all that they got finished at the church this week.

The girls finished painting the cabinets and the walls in the kitchen. They also finished the curtains and had them hung. The guys got the toilets and sinks set and the plumbing would be hooked up on Monday. The only thing left to do the following week other than the plumbing was to paint the bathroom stalls and the sanctuary. With everyone working together on the painting it should be completed by Wednesday.

Holly loved thinking about all that they had accomplished in the past three weeks. It was such a wonderful trip so far even though Liam got hurt. She thought about Gabriel who she hadn't seen all week and prayed several times throughout the week that he was safe. Little did she know what was being planned and how she would be involved.

The bus pulled up on time and everyone got on board. At the drop off spot Bill took the lead talking to Chris and Kylie with Zach and Holly at the end with the others between them. Zach enjoyed these moments with Holly even when she was quiet as was the case at this moment. It was just nice to have her by his side.

In a few moments Holly realized she was not alone and looked up to see Zach smiling at her.

"I have enjoyed watching you in deep thought Holly." He saw a quick flash of a smile as she looked over at him.

"I was just thinking about all that we've done since we've been here. It's really exciting to be a part of something like this." She paused a minute and then continued, "I was also thinking about Gabriel who I haven't seen all week. I've been praying that he's okay. I really hope I can see him next week before we go back home."

She glanced at Zach for a moment and he saw deep concern in her eyes for this one little boy that apparently captured her heart.

"I'll be praying that you see him again soon Holly. He seems to have made an impression on you and from the way I saw him looking at you last week I would say he seems taken with you as well." Zach smiled.

"Thanks Zach." He caught her hand and gently squeezed. Then Zach moved up to the front of the group as they started making their way down the streets. Some of the street people had already begun to follow them.

Fortunately, the day went really well with the street ministry. They had a great game of soccer in the store parking lot and none of the men acted up. For some reason everyone seemed to be on their best behavior so Holly thought that they were anxious to eat today because they knew it was some of their favorite food.

Miguel and his men were watching from a distance and waiting for the blonde American girl to go into the store. That's when they would grab her and take her out the back entrance. Miguel noticed Gabriel watching Holly from a different position and became very angry. Gabriel probably thought he went unnoticed which made Miguel even angrier and more resentful. Gabriel was in for a big surprise and Miguel couldn't wait to see his reaction!

Holly saw Gabriel standing near a tree across the street from the parking lot. She told Kylie that she was going over to visit with him for a few minutes. As she started walking over to him Holly noticed the fear on Gabriel's face. She prayed he wouldn't run away until she could talk to him. She could tell he was thinking about running away but, thankfully, he stayed until she was close enough to say hello to him.

"Gabriel,' she said quietly and cautiously. "It's really good to see you again. I missed seeing you this past week."

"You did. Why?" he questioned her almost in awe.

"Because I like you and wanted to spend some more time with you before I go back to America. We leave at the end of next week." Holly saw his face drop and his shoulders droop in sadness at her statement.

"I was busy last week and had no time to come to the church." He shrugged his shoulders and kicked dirt with his foot.

Holly sat down on the curb at Gabriel's feet and looked up at him. "Have you thought anymore about the bible stories you heard at bible school?' she asked him.

"Not too much. I have thought about David though. I still like how he got rid of the awful giant man Goliath."

"Yeah, me too. I like that story because it fills me with a sense of strength. Not my own strength, Gabriel, but God's strength. That's the only way that David was able to defeat Goliath because God was with him and gave him the ability to do it. When things are so overwhelming for me, like too big for me to take care of, I like to remember what God did in David's life and that gives me the courage to deal with whatever my situation is at the time."

She noticed Gabriel nodding in agreement. "Holly, do you think God would give me that strength if I needed it too?"

"I know He will, Gabriel. God will never leave His people and He is always there to help when needed. Many times the Bible says the only thing God's people have to do is to ask for His help and He will hear them and help them. Throughout the Bible, God is called the Deliverer, Helper, Redeemer, Friend, Rock, Fortress and many other names. He also tells us that it is by His strength and power, not ours that we will endure. So yes Gabriel, I believe without a doubt that God will give you the strength you need whenever you need it if you just ask Him."

Holly watched Gabriel closely because he seemed to be struggling inside to share something with her but was still not able to. She saw something shut down in his eyes and knew he wouldn't share anymore.

"Okay, thanks again, Holly." He was backing up as if to leave. "I hope I will get to see you again soon." He started walking away and then turned back to say one more thing to Holly. He was so serious that it sent a shiver up Holly's spine. "Please, Holly, be very careful. Whatever you do don't go anywhere by yourself. Okay?"

Holly nodded and Gabriel took off running. She felt fear and didn't know why. She turned to go back to her team and a shiver rolled down her back. It felt as if someone were watching her and it was an unnerving feeling. She looked around as she walked back to Zach and the others but didn't see anyone unusual. She felt safe being around her team which was strange because at no time on this trip had she felt unsafe. Not until this moment!

Gabriel stopped a safe distance from where he had left Holly so that he could keep an eye on her. She had gone into the store with one of the girls so he knew she wouldn't see him again that day.

~~~~~~~

Miguel watched the interchange between Gabriel and Holly as his anger built up moment by moment. Even his men noticed his intense gaze on those two and they knew better than to say anything. One of the men elbowed the other when he noticed Holly and one of the girls going inside the store. They got Miguel's attention and quickly hurried down the slope and into the back of the store. Now was the time they had been waiting for as they prepared to kidnap the American woman.

Miguel and his men kept looking down the aisles for Holly so they could follow her and determine the best time to snatch her. They found Holly and one of the young girls picking up paper plates and napkins. Miguel's men wondered if they should take that girl with them too but Miguel quickly said no to that idea. They only needed the older one and they had to get her alone to take her.

Emma wandered around to the next aisle to see if they had any plastic forks. They ran out of some of the items they used to feed the kids and Laura had forgotten to stock up the van with these products. Emma told Holly she would be right back. Holly looked at a few things while Emma walked around the corner. Miguel decided now was the time so he and his men moved very quietly and closer to Holly.

Holly picked up a magazine that was in English to glance at it. She experienced a funny feeling as if someone was watching her so she looked around and felt goose bumps on her arms. She didn't see anyone so she continued to look at the magazine. The feeling didn't leave her though as Miguel's men were making their way closer to her. They saw her turn around as they stopped behind an aisle so that she wouldn't see them. When she turned around again they started down the aisle and were almost close enough to grab her when Emma jumped around the corner. Emma saw three men quickly turn around and go the other way. Holly turned to look but they were already gone.

"Did you see those three men Holly?" asked Emma. "They looked like they were coming up to talk to you."

"No, I was just glancing at this magazine that was in English and didn't see anyone." She didn't tell Emma about the feeling of being watched. In that second she remembered Gabriel's warning to be careful.

Interrupting Holly's thoughts Emma continued, "Well, they didn't look too reputable if you know what I mean. Let's pay for this stuff and get back to the rest of the team." Emma was frightened by these men so Holly put the magazine away and headed to the front of the store with Emma.

Miguel was cussing and cursing at this missed opportunity as he and his men made their way outside to the back of the store. His men knew better than to defend themselves or to say anything at all. They let him carry on and hoped it would soon stop before he got violent. Miguel knew he needed to relax and calm down so that he could plan for another attempt tomorrow. That would be their last chance so he glared at his men. They better not mess it up! His look said it all and if they knew what was good for them they would get it done. He turned and they followed him out of the store realizing that they better get the American girl tomorrow or their lives would be worth nothing.

CHAPTER 38

Gabriel saw Holly and the younger girl walk out of the store and over to their friends. He knew he needed to get back and finish his collections for the day or Miguel would be mad. Holly looked up and surprise registered on her face when she saw him further away than before. Gabriel smiled, waved and turned to go home. She waved back and prayed a silent pray that she would see him again before they left for the States.

Holly and the team packed the remaining food and supplies into the van. Laura left in the van while the team headed back to the bus stop to return to the church and their host families. Liam, Becca and Jeff would meet them there so they could finish out the evening.

Once they returned to the church the team had their group devotions and left for their host homes. Many of them would be going out with their host families that night and the families looked forward to spending this extra time with the team. They usually went out for dinner and some went to the movies with English subtitles, some went bowling, some went down into the center of Mexico City to visit a lot of little market shops and others went to parks. There were lots of things to see in Mexico City and the Americans enjoyed this time with their host families because it was an opportunity to strengthen relationships with each other.

~~~~~~~~~~

Everyone met at church on Saturday morning to participate in the children's bible club program. This had been a favorite time for the Americans because each Saturday morning more Mexican children showed up than the previous Saturday. Today they were expecting about 100 children and Pastor Abraham was thrilled to see how many children came out each week. Some of the parents came as well and it gave him and some of his elders a chance to talk with them and share the Gospel.

The American team helped in different classes from the previous time so Holly enjoyed hanging with Jackson and Emma in the first and second grade classes. It was such a joy to watch them interact with the kids. Holly saw a couple of little girls climb up on Emma's lap to listen to the bible story and Jackson had several little boys hanging all over him.

Becca, Kylie and Seth helped with the pre-school/kindergarten class while Jeff and Bill helped with the middle school kids. Chris and Liam worked with the third, fourth and fifth grade kids since Liam's foot was doing much better and he enjoyed playing with them now that he could. Each of them enjoyed helping with crafts and answering questions from the children after the bible lesson.

Holly looked forward to the group lesson because Zach was going to teach today and she loved hearing him present God's word. He would be teaching in Spanish but Laura was going to interpret during the large session so that the Americans could follow along with the lesson.

The bell rang signifying that small classes were over and that it was time for a snack before the large session began. Bill, Zach and Jeff had gone to the grocery store last night after their evening with their host families to buy food for today. The snack was going to be bologna sandwiches with ketchup and mayo along with apples and cookies. The Mexican children loved bologna sandwiches. It was gratifying for the American team to see the children enjoy their food as they remembered that this could be their only meal that day so they made sure to get plenty of food for extras to be taken home by the kids. The children loved taking home the extra food for their family members who weren't able to come and participate in this Saturday morning bible club. They packed up the extra food in plastic bags to hand out at the end of the morning.

After cleaning up and getting the children ready for the large session the Americans sat scattered among the children to keep them quiet as Zach taught. His lesson today was about Nehemiah's desire to rebuild the walls in Jerusalem. Much of the book of Nehemiah was about the importance of prayer. Zach first read in Nehemiah 1:4 when Nehemiah heard about the distress of God's people because of the broken walls in Jerusalem. When Nehemiah heard them cry out he wept and mourned for days. He fasted and prayed before God.

Zach read verses 5-6 to everyone. "Nehemiah said to God, *'I ask You, God of heaven, the great and awesome God who preserves the covenant and lovingkindness for those who love Him and keep His commandments, let Your ear now be attentive and Your eyes open to hear the prayer of Your servant, Nehemiah, which I am praying before You now, day and night, on behalf of the sons of Israel Your servants, confessing the sins of the sons of Israel which we have sinned against You, I and my father's house have sinned.'"* Zach stopped for a moment to elaborate on how Nehemiah approached God.

"Nehemiah approached God with reverence and respect and focused on who he knew God was and what He had promised. He knew God made a promise with His people because of His love for them. That is what we need to remember as well. We can always go to God in prayer remembering who He is. Let me continue reading the rest of Nehemiah's first prayer to God."

He paused before reading and looked at everyone as they smiled and focused on what he read from the Bible. He was glad the Americans were mixed in with the children and kept everyone under control. He noticed Holly looking out the window and he glanced over to see what she was staring at. Gabriel, the little boy that she had gotten to know, was standing outside the window listening. He saw her wink at him as he nodded back. He gathered his thoughts to continue what he was saying about Nehemiah.

"Nehemiah continues in verse 7 and says *'We have acted wrongly against You and have not kept the commandments or statutes, nor the ordinances which You commanded Your servant Moses.'"* Zach stopped for a moment to share a few thoughts on this verse.

"Nehemiah was confessing his sins for himself and the Israelites. All God asks of us is that we come before Him in prayer and confess our sins. He asked the children, "How many of you pray to God?" Several hands went up.

"How many of you tell God when you have been bad and done something wrong?" Fewer hands went up that time.

"It is important for us to pray to God because that is how we communicate with Him. It is really important that we tell Him we are sorry for the bad things we have done. He will always forgive us and will always love us no matter what we have done. Do you understand that?" He looked out over the group of kids seeing heads nodding yes.

"I will finish reading this prayer of Nehemiah's by continuing in verses 10 and 11. *'The Israelites are Your servants and Your people whom You redeemed and saved by Your great power and by Your strong hand. Father, I ask You hear the prayer of Your servant, Nehemiah and the prayer of Your servants who delight to respect Your name and make Your servant successful today.'"*

Zach closed his Bible and looked at the children with thoughtfulness. "God is the only One who saves us when we confess our sins and ask Jesus into our lives because of His great love for us and His great power. We become His children and this is called salvation. He will hear your prayers and forgive your sins. All you have to do is ask Him. Throughout the book of Nehemiah you will see how God answered Nehemiah's prayers and helped him rebuild the walls of Jerusalem. There were difficulties that Nehemiah had to deal with and he even was fearful at times but God was faithful in answering the prayers of Nehemiah by accomplishing His plan. As children of God we can always count on Him. He will never let us down because He loves us with a love that is unconditional and everlasting no matter what. Pastor Abraham will close us in prayer."

Pastor Abraham came up front and led the group in prayer. When he finished he noticed that several of the parents had come into the group and had listened to what Zach shared. He silently prayed that God would touch their hearts with knowledge of Himself and that he would see them back for Sunday morning worship.

Holly made her way over to the window where Gabriel stood but before she got there Gabriel turned and ran away. She was hoping to talk with him before he left so she silently prayed for him instead. Holly was filled with an overwhelming sense of sadness for Gabriel and wished she knew how she could help him. She had very little time left here and really knew very little about him. Zach came up to her as she stared longingly out the window.

"I saw him, too, Holly. He seems like such a sad little boy." She nodded without looking at him. Zach noticed the tears in her eyes and was touched by her love for this little boy even though she hardly knew him. He put his hand on her shoulder and gently squeezed communicating his compassion and understanding to her over this little guy. He turned and went to say goodbye to the people leaving. Holly wiped the wetness off her cheeks and turned to do the same. They still had one more opportunity with the street kids later this afternoon and she prayed she would see Gabriel then.

~~~~~~~~~~

Gabriel hated to leave when he saw Holly coming to talk with him but he needed to get back to Miguel. He had already been gone too long but secretly he was glad he decided to stop by the little church this morning. He loved hearing stories about people in the Bible. It was somehow comforting to him to know that these people struggled with fear and unhappiness and yet God answered their prayers and blessed them despite their misbehavior. He would never let Miguel know that he actually prayed to God and he always felt better after talking with God. His life was a mess and he hoped God would change it soon because he wanted to get away from Miguel and live a better life, maybe a life for God.

His last thought before turning down the street to his house was that maybe God would answer his prayers and get him away from Miguel in the near future. He kicked a pebble down the street with a smile on his face.

CHAPTER 39

They were just about finished playing the soccer game with the street people when Laura came up to Holly and asked her to run into the store and buy some tortillas. They had a larger number of street people today and she didn't think she had enough tortillas. Holly nodded, took the money and walked into the store by herself to buy the tortillas. She was sad because she hadn't seen Gabriel yet and felt like she might not see him again before she left for the States. Unbeknownst to Holly, Gabriel was watching from a distance trying to decide whether he might be able to sneak down and see her for a few minutes. He watched her walk inside the grocery store so he decided he would wait until she came out and then run down to say hello one last time.

A movement out of the corner of his eye caught his attention and he turned to see Miguel and his men moving toward the grocery store. With fear in his heart he started moving toward the store as well to be sure that Holly was safe.

Once inside the store Gabriel followed a safe distance behind Miguel and his men praying that they would not see Holly. He saw her ahead and realized that Miguel was moving in her direction. Fear welled up inside him as he watched Miguel and his men get closer to her. There was no one else around and he didn't know how to warn her. All his instincts from the streets were telling him she was in danger and he didn't know how to prevent it or help her. He thought about running out to get one of her friends but he was afraid he would not see what Miguel was going to do so he decided to wait and watch.

Miguel's men quickly snuck up behind Holly and just as she was getting ready to turn around one of the men quickly grabbed her and put a cloth up to her nose. Holly tried to get away but he was too strong for her. She felt herself losing consciousness and prayed that God would help her as everything went dark.

Gabriel watched in horror as Miguel picked her up and the men followed him to the back of the store and out the back door. Gabriel followed so he could see where they were taking her. He was shaking with fear because he knows that Miguel is a very dangerous man and would stop at nothing to get his way. He whispered, "Please God, help me know how to help Holly. Please protect her." Silently he followed Miguel out the back door and down the back alley as he constantly prayed. He couldn't understand how God could let this happen but he remembered something that he heard at bible school the day they talked about Noah. Even though Noah didn't understand what God was doing or why He was asking Noah to build this huge ark, Noah chose to trust God and follow His instructions. Gabriel decided right then to trust God even though he didn't understand why He let Miguel take Holly. He was going to trust God to help him help Holly somehow. He just had to be careful, pray and listen to God.

Gabriel followed Miguel and his men for several miles as they came to an abandoned shed outside of Miguel's territory. Gabriel had been here before when he witnessed Miguel killing a man who had tried to usurp his authority and take over his territory. Gabriel had hoped that he would never have to come back to this place again but now he found there was nothing he could do but watch them take Holly inside the shed.

Gabriel silently watched as they opened the door of the shed and put Holly on an empty cot. She was still sleeping and Gabriel figured they drugged her so she was still unconscious from that drug. "Please keep her safe," he silently prayed. He watched Miguel and most of his men leave and knew he needed to get back before Miguel returned. One of Miguel's men stayed behind to guard the shed for a few hours just to be sure no one had followed them, then he would report back to Miguel. As long as Miguel was not here with Holly she would be safe because none of the men would do anything without Miguel's orders. He would try to get back this evening to help her.

~~~~~~~~~~

When the soccer game was over the street people lined up at the van to get their food and drink, Laura realized Holly hadn't come back from inside the store yet with the rest of the tortillas and just figured she was held up in line. She got finished serving half the people when she ran out of tortillas and realized Holly had still not returned.

Laura noticed the Americans helping some of the women with their children as they ate but she didn't see Holly anywhere. The guys talked with some of the Mexicans and she didn't notice Holly there either. She looked to Zach who was talking with Bill. When Zach

238

finally looked up she signaled for him to come over with a nod of her head. Zach said something to the guys and began to make his way over to her.

"Hi Laura, did you need something?" he asked.

"Hey Zach, yes. I knew I would need some more tortillas today so earlier I asked Holly to go in to the store and get some but she hasn't come back yet. Have you seen her in the last couple of minutes?"

Zach looked around with concerned mirrored in his eyes and said, "No, I haven't. How long ago did she go to buy the tortillas?"

"Probably about twenty minutes ago. I didn't realize how much time went by because I was getting ready to serve."

"Did anyone go with her?"

"I don't know," replied Laura. "I gave her the money and turned back to the van to prepare for lunch."

Zach looked for each of the Americans to see if anyone else was missing. He noticed Kylie and Emma helping a couple of children eat; Becca was with a mom and her kids; Seth, Liam and Jackson were talking with some guys and Chris was kicking the soccer ball with a little boy. He knew that Bill and Jeff were here because he was just talking with them. He started getting anxious when they were all accounted for except for Holly.

Zach walked over to Bill and Jeff, pulled them aside and told them the situation. They wondered why Holly would go inside the store alone and not get someone to go with her. Zach told Chris to keep an eye on everyone else while he, Bill and Jeff went inside the store to look for Holly. Chris didn't let on to anyone else and continued kicking the soccer ball with the little boys all the while watching for the men to come out of the store.

Zach asked one of the cashiers at the front of the store if they saw a young, blonde American woman come into the store. Bill and Jeff scanned the store with their eyes as they awaited her response. She acknowledged seeing Holly come in because she remembered thinking what beautiful blonde hair she had. Zach looked at the other men and they decided to separate and look throughout the store. They decided to meet back at this same spot in ten minutes.

They scoured the aisles, looked in the bathrooms, out the side doors, but none of them spotted Holly or anything suspicious. When they met without Holly fear was coursing through each of them. They went back outside to see the street people off and talk with the rest of their team.

Chris watched them come out of the store without Holly. He picked up the soccer ball and got the rest of the Americans together. They were all saying goodbye to the street people as Bill, Zach and Jeff walked over to them. Laura slammed the back of the van down and walked over to their group.

"Holly's not anywhere in the store," stated Bill. "We need to get some help to find her. Did anyone see her go into the store?" Everyone nodded no.

"Where is she Bill?" Kylie asked.

"Laura asked her to run in and buy some tortillas because she didn't think she had enough. Apparently, Holly ran in by herself and never came out."

Becca snuggled closer to Jeff and hung onto his arm. Chris was next to Kylie with his arm around her shoulder. The rest of the team talked at the same time. Finally Zach interrupted everyone and asked them to calm down.

"Laura, can you call Jose Luis and tell him what's happened? Ask him to meet us here as soon as possible." Laura nodded and got in her van to retrieve her cell phone. She walked away from the group as she made the phone call.

Looking at the group Zach continued, "It's not a good idea for all of us to be here waiting when Jose comes. When it gets dark it's very difficult and dangerous to be riding the buses back to the church. Jose is a good police officer in our church and a wonderful, godly man and I know he will help us. He will also know what other policemen we can trust to help since many policemen in Mexico City are corrupt and only seek money. We will have to trust Jose to help us and to get others that we can trust as well."

Laura came back after her phone call and said that Jose was on his way. She also called Pastor Abraham and he would be here too. She needed to leave so she asked Zach to keep her informed. He nodded as she got in her van and left. Bill made a decision that he would stay but that Jeff and the guys would get the girls back to the church. There was nothing they could to help at the moment and it was best to get them off the streets now. Jeff and the guys felt confident that they could get the right bus and get back to the church so they gathered together to pray before leaving. The girls were trembling with fear and huddled close to the guys. They put their arms around each other as Bill prayed. "Father, please be with Holly wherever she is. Please protect her and keep her safe. Give us wisdom and guide those looking for her so that they will know best what to do next. Please calm our spirits and help us remember that You are always with us and that you never leave us nor forsake us. We know that You know right where Holly is and that You are with her. Give her peace and give us peace. In Christ's Name we pray, Amen." Everyone said amen in unison.

The guys took the girls and headed to the bus stop while Bill and Zach waited for Jose Luis and Pastor Abraham. There wasn't really much to say to each other as they were deep in thought. Zach was scared for Holly and he kept silently praying for her. Bill knew that he would have to call Holly's family if they couldn't find her to let them know and he dreaded that call. He prayed that call wouldn't be necessary. Pastor Abraham arrived and prayed with Bill and Zach while they waited for Jose, asking God to deliver Holly safely back to her team and that this would not affect them or others in wanting to come back to Mexico City in the future.

A short time later Jose Luis pulled up in his car. He was off duty so he wasn't wearing a uniform. The men walked over to him and Pastor Abraham introduced each of them. They all walked into the grocery store without saying anything more. Jose Luis did the talking as he questioned several employees. A couple remembered seeing her come in but no one saw her leave.

Zach noticed a short, older woman cowering in the background saying nothing. He walked over to her quietly and asked her if she remembered seeing Holly leave the store. Supposedly she spoke very good English but she looked so fearful without saying a word that Zach wasn't sure that she actually did speak English. He called Jose Luis over to question her further.

Then to Zach's surprise, in English she spoke, "I saw this, uh, lovely young woooman, um, pppick up tortortillas ad begin wwwalking up to the fffront. Um, ah, ttthree men came up bbbehind her, ah, ah, pppput a cloth over her mmmouth and she wwwent to sleep. Um, ah they pppicked her up and tttook her out the bbback door of the ssstore." She was so nervous she stuttered through her statement, licking her lips, twisting her hands in front of her and looking all around her as if someone was watching her.

"Why didn't you tell someone?' asked Jose Luis calmly.

"Bbbecause the mmmen were dddangerous and I dddid nnnot think it wwwas ssafe," answered the woman clearly agitated and scared.

Jose Luis continued calmly questioning her. "Do you know who the men were?"

"Yyyes but I dddo nnnot ttthink I sssshould say. I ttthink he wwwould hhhurt me if I tttell you hhhis name." She started backing away from Jose but Zach stood right behind her and in the way. He gently turned her around to look at him and she could tell by the look in his eyes that he would not let her go until she gave them a name.

Zach whispered quietly even though he was filled with anxiety for Holly. "Please tell us his name. She is an American and she was here helping your people. She needs your help now. Please."

The lady stared at Zach for a moment indecision filling her eyes. Then she turned to Jose and said, "Hhhis name is MMMiguel. I do not know hhhis last name. He is the kkking of these sssstreets." Tears ran down her cheeks as she told his name knowing and fearing that he would come after her.

Jose took her hand and thanked her for this information. She quickly ran out of the store leaving her employee vest behind. Jose Luis figured she probably wouldn't be back.

He turned to Bill, Zach and Pastor Abraham with a look in his eyes that they could tell didn't bode well for Holly. "Miguel is the street kingpin here. There have been many killings that we know he committed but have never been able to arrest him for them. No one will testify against him. Everyone is scared to death of him. He runs drugs here and has a protection unit that requires every business to pay extortion or suffer the consequences. If Holly is with him we need to find her fast."

The guys looked at each other and somehow knew they were each silently praying for God's protection over Holly. While they walked out of the store Jose told them that he would take them back to the church and then call some of his police friends to help look for her. They got into the car and started driving away.

"I will need to call Holly's family," Bill said solemnly. "I will call her brother Micah first since Holly's dad died several years ago. I don't think her mom Abigail could take it so Micah needs to tell her in person. When we get back to the church that's the first thing I need to do."

244

Looking at Zach he continued, "Please gather our team together and let them know what we've found out so far."

Pastor Abraham interrupted Bill and said, "When the host families come to get your team, I'd like to have a time of corporate prayer for Holly, if it is okay with you Bill. We need to keep this quiet but I believe the more saints we have praying for Holly the better." Bill nodded his approval.

Pastor Abraham and Bill looked compassionately at Zach and could feel his fear for Holly because they felt it, too. They both knew how he felt about her so they each prayed quietly to themselves that God would grant him peace and that He would grant them blessing and favor in finding Holly quickly. They all knew that time was of the essence.

~~~~~~~~~

Micah heard the phone ringing and wondered who would be calling this late on a Saturday. Ellie had just gone up to bed. The kids hadn't felt well today so she had a long day with them and was pretty tired. His mom came over to help Ellie because he had to get some horses ready to transport to their new owners and they had some new cows to brand so it was a pretty busy day for him, too.

He quickly grabbed the phone so that it wouldn't disturb the kids or Ellie. "Hello."

"Hi Micah, this is Bill Nash calling."

"Hi Bill, this is a surprise. What can I do for you?" Micah thought it was curious that Bill would be calling this late. They were due to come home next week and he was looking forward to seeing Holly. They all missed her while she was in Mexico. A small sliver of apprehension crept up his spine.

"Micah, I'm not sure how to tell you this but Holly is missing." Bill heard Micah's sudden intake of breath.

"What do you mean missing Bill? How can she be missing?" Micah was visibly upset now and Bill heard it in his voice.

"We were finishing up with the street ministry today when Holly went into the store to get some extra tortillas to feed the street people and she never came out. Everyone was supposed to go in pairs at all times so I'm not sure why she didn't this time. Anyway we have a local policeman from the church investigating and looking for Holly. When he went in to talk to some of the employees there was a lady who told us that she saw Holly being drugged and taken out the back door by three men. She gave us the name of the man she saw and so this policeman is getting some of his police friends together to look for her. They can't do anything more until tomorrow though. I'm so sorry Micah. We are all praying for her."

Greatly shaken, Micah said, "Thanks for calling Bill. I will tell my family and I will be on the first plane out of here tomorrow. As soon as I get a reservation I will call to let you know what time I will be arriving in Mexico City. Can you arrange for someone to pick me up at the airport when I arrive?"

"That will be no problem Micah. I thought maybe you would come down. I will ask Zach Benson to pick you up when you let me know the time. He is an American intern that is working with the church here and with us. I know he will be glad to get you. You can reach me at 0015675554324 once you've made your reservations and know your arrival time. Micah, we're all praying for Holly's safety."

"Thanks Bill." Micah hung up not sure what to do first. He needed to tell his mom but he should first tell Ellie and then head to his mom's house to inform her. He would have Ellie make a plane reservation for him while he was talking with his mom. Telling her wouldn't be easy so he quickly prayed that God would keep Holly safe and that they would find her soon. "Please God, give my mom the strength to deal with this," he whispered as he ran up the stairs to tell Ellie.

CHAPTER 40

Holly rolled over on the cot, disoriented and wiped her eyes. Everything was blurry and she couldn't make out where she was. Her head hurt and the light that penetrated her eyes as they opened hurt her head even more. She shut them quickly trying to remember how she got to this place. She tried again to slowly open her eyes as she adjusted to the light coming through the window. She realized it must be a street light since it was dark outside. She slowly sat upright on the cot surveying her surroundings. She was scared and couldn't imagine where she was.

"Please, God, help me. I'm really scared and don't know where I am or how I got here." As she sat on the edge of the cot she noticed that it looked like she was in a wooden building somewhere. The walls were wooden planks with one window on the opposite side of the door. It looked like there was a pile of junk in the room because it was badly cluttered. She couldn't tell much else because she only had the street light coming through the window and it didn't reveal much inside the room.

As she stood up, she felt dizzy and swayed a little, but determination made her walk over to the door and check to see if it would open. She found it was locked and there was no way for her to get out. She made her way to the window and realized that there were bars on the outside of it so breaking it and climbing through was not an option. From the little bit that she could see it looked pretty isolated outside the building so that even if she screamed she didn't think anyone would hear her. Tears started flowing down her cheeks. She couldn't think of a reason why anyone would bring her to a place like this. The last thing she could remember was being inside the store to buy tortillas and then she woke up here. She tried to feel her way around the small building to see if there might possibly be another opening, but she only stumbled over boxes and metal objects. With all the junk everywhere she couldn't go far except back to the cot. She silently prayed again as she sat back down on the cot. She remembered one of her memory scriptures from Hebrews 13:5b-6 and she said it aloud personalizing it to herself. *"I will never leave you nor will I ever forsake you, Holly, so that you can confidently say, The Lord is my Helper, I will not be afraid, what can man do to me!"* At that moment Holly felt God's presence with her in this dark, scary building. She reminded herself that God was in control and He knew right where she was. Holly also knew she was in the palm of God's hand no matter what happened to her.

Holly rested on the cot trusting God to protect her and rescue her even though she didn't know what tomorrow would bring. As she drifted off to sleep she continued to silently pray asking God to deliver her out of this situation. Tears coursed down her cheeks as she prayed asking God to forgive her for being fearful and distressed. He reminded her of the verse again which spoke peace to her heart. She tossed and turned all night as she dreamed of Zach, Gabriel and her family. Holly wrestled all night long with conflicting feelings of fear, terror and peace.

~~~~~~~~~~

Gabriel was in his own bed struggling with his own terror when he heard Miguel come in the door. He pretended to be asleep as he heard Miguel's men talking and wanted to see if he could learn what the plan was for Holly. He listened carefully as he heard Miguel talk.

"Tomorrow I will visit the girl while you two get a message to the one they call Zach. I will write the note tonight and then you can come by at 5 in the morning to pick it up and deliver it. I will take Gabriel with me so that he can see what happens to people who get in my way."

"What are you going to do with the girl, Miguel?" one of his men asked.

"I am not sure yet but it will depend on what answer I get from the note." With a gleam in his eye he continued, "I might like to get to know her a little first." The men knew that didn't bode well for the girl but given who they were they laughed in acknowledgement of what Miguel said.

Miguel interrupted and said, "I want to teach Gabriel a lesson he will never forget so I may just kill her when I get finished with her." The men laughed again.

Gabriel covered his mouth with his hands so that he would not blurt out his fear for Holly. He was trembling so violently he was sure that Miguel would hear him. He knew he needed to do something but he just didn't know what. "Please God, help us both," he whispered.

Gabriel heard the men leave and Miguel in the kitchen. All Gabriel could do was to get some rest and pray that God would figure out some way to protect Holly. He knew that he would not be able to do it by himself. Then he remembered the story of David and Goliath and thought about the sling shot he had hidden beneath the floor boards. Mostly he remembered David's courage in the face of a very difficult and seemingly insurmountable situation. David's faith was in God who delivered the giant into his hands that day. Would God deliver Miguel into Gabriel's hand? Would God deliver Holly out of Miguel's hand? Gabriel shook with fear at the thought of what Miguel could do to Holly and he passionately and silently pleaded with God to get them out of this mess. As tears rolled down his cheeks, he thought about Holly by herself inside that building knowing she was probably just as scared as he was at that moment. He turned over and pulled the blanket closer to his neck for warmth and trembled all night thinking about tomorrow.

Gabriel woke a while later and all was quiet in the house. He decided at that moment to go see Holly even if he couldn't get her out. He wanted to let her know that she was not alone so he quietly got out of his bed, picked up his shoes and walked softly into the outer room. He was glad he didn't get undressed last night before going to bed. He would have wasted needless time getting dressed now. He heard Miguel snoring in the other room so he quietly walked to the door, gently opened it and let himself out. He put on his shoes and began running to the place where Miguel left Holly. He had to get back before Miguel woke up and found him gone. He figured it would take him about thirty minutes to get to the building and thirty minutes to get back. It was still dark outside and he had to be careful not to run into any of Miguel's men. He prayed as he ran that God would keep Miguel asleep until he returned.

~~~~~~~~~~

Holly imagined she was dreaming and someone knocked softly at the door, but as she came out of the blackness of sleep she realized that someone was actually knocking at the door. She jumped up quickly, hurried to the door and listened intently as she held her breath. "Holly, are you okay?" She heard the whispered voice talking to her.

"Yes, I am. Who are you?"

"It is me, Gabriel."

Shocked Holly whispered back. "Gabriel, what are you doing here?"

"I saw Miguel and some of his men take you from the store and I followed them as they brought you here. I could not get here before now but I wanted to let you know that you were not alone."

She breathed a sigh of relief and a thank you to God with tears in her eyes. "I am okay Gabriel, but who is Miguel and why would he bring me here?"

"Miguel is the man I live with and he is not a very nice man. He has brought you here to stop Zach and the others from ever coming back to the streets to share about Jesus. He runs those streets. He sells drugs and makes stores pay him money. I guess you could say he is a king here."

She tentatively asked him, "Gabriel, is he the one who hurts you?"

There was silence and she thought Gabriel had left. "Gabriel," she said urgently with fear in her voice.

"I am still here Holly. Yes, he is." Gabriel talked so softly that Holly could barely hear him. She did hear the fear and hurt in his voice though.

"Can you get me out of here Gabriel?" Holly asked.

"I cannot, not yet. But I am going to try Holly. Miguel is bringing me here to see you in the morning. He came after you because of me. He hurts anything that I get close to because he wants me to be like him one day. That is why I never wanted him to know about you. I do not know how he found out about you but I am scared for you Holly. I do not know what to do or how to help you."

Holly sat down on the floor next to the door and could hear the tears in Gabriel's voice. It took everything she had not to let him hear her fear and her tears.

"Gabriel, maybe you could get a note to Zach to let him know where Miguel has taken me. Could you do that?"

"Maybe. I know Miguel is sending a note to Zach tomorrow about taking you. How can I get in touch with Zach?"

"I can give you a phone number so that you could call him. Will you do that Gabriel?"

"I can try. I do not have anything to write the number on but I will try to remember it."

Holly was almost breathless thinking that this could be her way out of here. She slowly repeated the church's phone number to Gabriel, praying all the time that he would remember it.

Gabriel found a stick and wrote the phone number in the dirt as Holly said it. He was not sure that he would remember it but he had to try. It was the only way that he would be able to help her.

"I wrote it in the dirt Holly. I will not be able to call until tomorrow though. I have to get back before Miguel wakes up and finds me gone. I will be back tomorrow."

"I will be okay Gabriel. I want you to be very careful though. Do not do anything that will get you in trouble with Miguel. God is with me and will protect me. Do not forget that. Remember the bible stories you heard during bible school. Remember those men and how God took care of them and helped them in the different situations. I want you to remember them and find your courage and strength in God just as I am going to do. God is always with us Gabriel. He will never leave us nor forsake us."

Gabriel whispered as he leaned his forehead on the door. "I remember Holly and I have been praying ever since Miguel and his men took you from the store. I am scared but I am going to keep praying that God will help me find a way to call Zach. I do not care what Miguel does to me Holly, but I do not want him hurting you and I want God to protect you."

"He will, Gabriel. I believe that with all my heart." She realized at that moment that she really did believe that and trusted God no matter what. "You better go now. I will see you soon." She felt tears flowing down her cheeks. She wanted Gabriel to be gone before he heard her cry. She put her hand on the door as if she were touching his hand.

Gabriel put his hand to the door. He didn't realize it but Holly was doing the same thing on the other side of the door to feel closer to him. He left with tears in his eyes.

Holly sat down on the cot when she couldn't hear his footsteps any longer and cried. She was more afraid for Gabriel than she was for herself. She prayed that God would keep him safe and deliver him out of Miguel's hands.

~~~~~~~~~~

Gabriel crept back into the house quietly and heard Miguel snoring as he made his way into his bed. He thanked God for keeping Miguel asleep and for letting him talk to Holly. He asked God to let him be successful tomorrow in getting in touch with Zach. As he drifted off to sleep Gabriel thought of Noah and David and all they accomplished through the power of God. A smile slowly came over his face as he fell asleep.

CHAPTER 41

Micah got back to his house after spending an hour or so with his mom. She was pretty distraught when he told her about Holly but she was a strong woman with a strong faith in God. She had survived many difficult times in her life with the help of God and she would survive this one as well. She knew Holly was in God's hands which was the best place for her to be. Before Micah left they got on their knees to pray for Holly's rescue and safe return.

Ellie was waiting for Micah when he got back. She could tell by the look on his face that he was having a difficult time as he worried about Holly. She walked over to him, hugged him tight and they prayed together for Holly again. Ellie was thankful the kids slept through everything which gave her time to make Micah's reservation with American Airlines. She told him he would be flying out at 6:30 in the morning and would arrive in Mexico City about one in the afternoon.

Since he had to get up very early in the morning, they made their way upstairs to bed with their arms tightly around each other with both of them deep in thought over Holly. It would be a very short night for them and probably not very restful. They knew God was looking out for Holly, but they stilled prayed silently for her to be safe. Micah was restless all night long as he was anxious to get to Mexico City to look for his sister.

Micah got up earlier than needed and after kissing his sleeping kids goodbye, gave Ellie a kiss and wiped the tears off her face. They prayed together and then he left.

Ellie knew he needed to be on the road even if he had to wait longer than necessary at the airport. It was better for him to be doing something than to be sitting at home. She knew Abigail would be over later so they could go to church together and ask the congregation to pray for Holly and also to put her on the church prayer list.

~~~~~~~~~~

Zach woke up Sunday morning to a knock on his door. He quickly got up, opened the door and found no on there. He looked down the hall of the small apartment building where he stayed for the summer but saw no one there. He felt something at his feet and looked down to find a note with his name on the outside. He picked it up and opened it. He read it with fear as he found out why Holly had been taken. He had to let Bill and everyone else know so that maybe Jose Luis would know where to being looking for her. Then he remembered it was Sunday morning and he had to help with the church service. He would let Pastor Abraham know of this development so that he could be freed to help look for Holly. He closed his door, dressed quickly and headed over to Pastor Abraham's house so they could get in touch with Jose Luis and Bill.

Once at Pastor Abraham's house Zach showed him the note. Pastor Abraham said he would take over Zach's responsibilities for the church service today so that he could go with Jose Luis. Zach got in touch with Jose Luis and made plans to meet him at the grocery store where

Holly was taken. When Zach called Bill to let him know of the plans and to tell him about the note, Bill told him that Holly's brother Micah would be arriving in Mexico City at 1 pm. Bill was hoping Zach would be able to pick Micah up at the airport after church. Zach said he would and that he would bring Micah to the grocery story to help with the search.

Bill knew that he couldn't go with Zach to help look for Holly because he had to be with his team. They were meeting at 10 am at the church for the Sunday services and then they would talk about the plans for the day. No one was going to be interested in sightseeing with Holly missing. He knew it would be best for them to keep busy plus they needed to finish their work in the next couple of days before they returned home. Maybe they could work on their plans and then talk about their return home. Jeff had devotions today for their group and Bill knew that Jeff was planning a time of prayer for Holly. That would be comforting for everyone in the midst of their concern and fear. Even thinking of returning home was difficult for Bill as the thought of not knowing if they would be returning with the same number of team members that they came with continually came to his mind. He silently prayed for Holly's protection and that they would get her back soon.

Zach didn't like the idea of having to leave the search in order to pick up Holly's brother but he knew that it if were his brother in this situation he would want to be in on the search too. After showing Jose Luis the note they discussed what the best plan of action would be. Jose knew who Miguel was because they had been trying to get him for several years but could never get anyone to testify against him. He either paid the witness to be silent or he had them killed, but nothing against him could ever be proven. Jose was very concerned for this young American woman who was in Miguel's possession. He prayed, like everyone else, for her protection and safe return to her friends and family. Jose brought a couple of his police friends with him to help search. Zach told Jose he would have to leave at noon to pick up Holly's brother at the airport because he wanted to be a part of the search and rescue team. Jose affirmatively nodded because he fully understood.

Jose pulled out a map of the area in an effort to determine where Miguel might be holding Holly. They decided to spread out over a certain section of the area for the next couple of hours and regroup back at the store at noon. That way Zach could leave and the men could start their search over another section of the area. They each left in a different direction praying for success in locating Holly.

~~~~~~~~~~

Miguel woke with excitement because he had the girl well-hidden and the Americano "do gooders" right where he wanted them. He looked forward to seeing the girl today and couldn't wait to see the look on Gabriel's face when he realized that Miguel was holding her. That would be sweet!

Gabriel woke up with anticipation and confidence that God would help them out of this terrible and dangerous situation. Maybe God would use Gabriel to get rid of Miguel like He used David to kill Goliath. Gabriel liked that thought a lot! He quietly pulled up the floor board and retrieved his sling shot and the stones that he had been hiding. He put the stones inside his shoe and the slingshot down the inside of his pants along his back. Gabriel couldn't help but shiver at the thought of what might happen today. He couldn't think too far ahead because it was enough for him to anticipate seeing Miguel this morning, knowing that he would have to go with him to see Holly as he had overheard Miguel's conversation with his men the night before.

When Gabriel walked into the kitchen Miguel sat at the table with a cup of coffee and a hardened look on his face.

"I want you to come with me today Gabriel."

"Where to Miguel?" Gabriel asked as he slightly trembling because he already knew the answer but didn't want to let Miguel know that he knew. He was finally a step ahead of Miguel for the first time in his short life.

"I have something in my possession that means a lot to you. I want you to tell me what I should do with it." Miguel snickered as he talked. This was going to be such a blow to Gabriel that he would do whatever Miguel wanted from now on. He thought that he might just keep the girl around for good so that he could keep Gabriel on a short leash and enjoy the pleasures of the girl as well. A devious smile came over Miguel's face that made Gabriel cringe when he saw it. Please God give me Your strength to endure what is to come Gabriel silently prayed once again.

"Okay, let us go so we can get it over with," Gabriel said pathetically to throw Miguel off track.

Miguel threw his coffee in the trash, grabbed his coat and left with Gabriel following him. It was somewhat comforting to Gabriel that Miguel's men wouldn't be with them. Miguel rarely went anywhere without them but he did today.

~~~~~~~~~~

Holly woke from a fitful night's rest. She knew that Miguel and Gabriel would be coming soon and she needed every bit of courage and strength that she could get from God. She didn't know what was ahead of her but she wanted to trust that God did. She got on her knees by the side of the cot and prayed. "Please God, please give me strength and courage to endure what's to come. I want to trust You but I am struggling because of my fear. I feel like the man in Mark who said I believe but help my unbelief. I trust You Father, but help me as I am struggling to believe. Please protect Gabriel from Miguel. I would rather Miguel hurt me than hurt Gabriel any more than he has in the past. Help me be brave for Gabriel no matter what happens. I am yours, Father, and nothing can change that. Please forgive me of my sins and help me keep my eyes focused on You. And if it's alright to ask, please protect me through this and get me back to Zach. I sure

would like to have a life with him, if that's okay with You."
She felt the tears, wiped them off quickly determining to be
a witness for God and His love for her.

CHAPTER 42

As Micah traveled to Mexico City, Jose Luis, his men and Zach searched for Holly. Miguel and Gabriel made their way to Holly while the Americans and Hispanics prayed diligently in church for her safety.

Since Jose, the police officers and Zach had not found Holly they returned to the grocery store to get something for lunch while Zach left to pick up Micah.

~~~~~~~~~~

When Miguel and Gabriel arrived at the shed, Miguel took the key out of his pocket to open the door. Gabriel knew he would never be able to get the key away from Miguel. He would have to watch very carefully to see if Miguel ever took it out at home and put it somewhere other than his pants. Gabriel was breathing deeply because he knew who he would see when the door opened. Miguel, on the other hand, greatly anticipated seeing this American beauty up close and personal.

Holly heard the door open and stood up ready for whatever happened. She took deep breaths to calm her trembling and nervousness before seeing Miguel. When he walked into the light of the window she was amazed at what she saw. Miguel was a very attractive man, muscular but not overly tall. She had a hard time equating this guy with a killer who was mean and cruel. She looked over and saw Gabriel with an astonished look on his face. He was such a beautiful boy and she needed to get him away from this man as soon as possible. The first words out of Miguel's mouth validated his reputation as an animal despite what he looked like.

"Well, woman, looks like I have you all to myself to do whatever I want." Looking at Gabriel with a sly smile Miguel said, "Do you see who I have here Gabriel?" Gabriel nodded with fear etched on his small face. "Why do you think I have her here Gabriel?" Gabriel looked baffled and shrugged his shoulders. "I want to teach you a lesson about caring about anything or anybody without my permission." Miguel continued. "I know you have been meeting her because I have been watching you and I had you watched. I told you before that there was nothing you should care about unless you have my permission, did I not?" Miguel walked closer to Gabriel with a menacing look on his face. "I am tired of having to teach you this same lesson over and over again. Maybe this time will be the last time you have to learn it Gabriel." Gabriel backed up as far as he could before Miguel reached for him and shoved him in front of Holly.

Holly grabbed Gabriel's shoulders as she experienced fear like never before. She was at the mercy of this man just like Gabriel. She backed away pulling Gabriel behind her as Miguel inched his way closer to her. He reached out and ran his hand along her cheek. Holly jerked her face away and moved as far back as she could when she felt Gabriel hit the wall and they could go no further. Again, Miguel slowly and menacingly approached her and took a piece of her hair in his hand, fingering it.

Gabriel jumped in front of Holly and tried to push him away from her.

Miguel laughed at them both. "I think we will leave now Gabriel and I will come back alone later." He looked pointedly at Holly so she knew exactly what he meant. He grabbed Gabriel by the shirt and pushed him out of the shed in front of him. Holly pleaded with Miguel to let her out and to leave Gabriel alone. All she heard was Miguel's sinister laugh. Gabriel never uttered a word but knew deep in his heart he had to find Zach and get him here before Miguel hurt Holly. His resolved deepened at that moment and nothing would stand in his way. He would save Holly.

After Miguel locked the door and left with Gabriel the tears flowed down Holly's face and she started shaking uncontrollably. Please help me God she silently prayed. Please protect Gabriel and me today. With that last thought she curled up on the cot and waited.

~~~~~~~~~~~

Making their way back to the house, Gabriel knew he had to slip away from Miguel to call the number Holly had given him last night. "God help me find out how to get away from Miguel long enough to make a phone call," he prayed. At that moment Miguel looked at Gabriel and wondered what was going through his mind. He believed he had sufficiently scared Gabriel this time so his confidence took over and he made a fatal mistake. "Gabriel, I want you to go to Louisa's to collect the money she owes me from her work last night. Do not mess around. I want you back within thirty minutes or I will come looking for you and you do not want that to happen, do you?" Gabriel shook his head in fear. "No, I do not Miguel. Please do not hurt Holly." He wanted Miguel to believe that he would do anything he said as long as Holly was safe. He also realized that the likelihood of Miguel not hurting Holly was slim.

Miguel laughed loudly and pushed him away saying, "I have not decided what I am going to do with your beautiful American friend. A lot will depend on your behavior. Understand?" Gabriel nodded and ran knowing that this was his opportunity to make that call. Thank you, God, for making a way so quickly, he silently whispered.

CHAPTER 43

Zach was standing at the arrival gate waiting for Micah. He didn't know what Micah looked like so he had made a sign with Micah's name on it. As he scanned the crowd a large, dark haired man came up to him and addressed him by name.

"Micah Brady?" Zach questioned tentatively.

Micah held out his hand to shake Zach's and answered, "Yes I am. I take it your Zach Benson."

Shaking Micah's hand he replied, "I am. It's good to meet you Micah. Holly's spoken to me about you and your family."

Not wanting to waste too much time on pleasantries, Micah started questioning Zach. "Have you any idea yet where Holly is?"

"Not exactly. I got a note this morning that said Holly was being held until we stop ministering to the street people. A man named Miguel has her and he is considered the king of the area where we are working. He deals in drugs, extortion and many other criminal activities. Right now several men are searching for her with several police officers as well. We will be meeting them at a local grocery store."

As they walked to Zach's car he glanced at Micah and saw fierce determination on his face. He knew with every fiber of his being that Micah was not a man to mess with. If Micah had his way he would deal severely with anyone who hurt his sister. Even with Zach's height of 6'2", Micah was a few inches taller.

There was silence in the car as they drove to the grocery store and there was obvious tension due to the stress of the situation. While stopped at a light, Zach looked at Micah and said, "I want you to know that since Holly's been here I have fallen in love with her. I pray that I will have the opportunity to ask her to marry me in the future." Micah just looked at him. Zach continued, "I know you don't know me yet but I give you my word, Micah, I love Holly with all of my heart. I will take care of her to the best of my ability and I will always encourage her to make her relationship with our Lord her highest priority."

Micah continued to look at him and then smiled. "Zach, Holly wrote to us recently that she feels the same way about you. She told us all about you and your love for God and her."

The light changed and Zach continued to drive, feeling relief at Micah's statement. "Thanks Micah, I'm not sure what God has in store for me, but I want to share every moment of it with your sister."

Micah nodded with a slight smile. Micah knew within his heart that this was a man worthy of his sister. He silently thanked God for him and offered another prayer of protection for his sister.

Pulling into the grocery store an hour later, Zach saw Jose waiting for him by the front entrance. They parked and walked straight to him. Jose saw them and was sorry that he still didn't have anything to report. Zach introduced Micah to Jose and then they started to discuss what plan of action they needed to take now. As they talked a gentleman came running forward yelling Zach's name. By the time he reached the men he was out of breath and Zach told him to take a few deep breaths and then talk.

"Zach, we got a phone call at the church a while ago from a young boy who gave us a location where Holly might be held."

Jose got the location and left to round up the police officers so they could go to this location. Micah and Zach waited for them to return and then they would follow them in Zach's car.

~~~~~~~~~~

With Gabriel occupied for thirty minutes Miguel decided to go back and visit Holly and have some fun with her. Even if Gabriel returned home he would not think anything of the fact that Miguel was not there. He underestimated Gabriel.

After making the phone call, Gabriel decided to go back and keep an eye on Holly. He would do it from a distance so that if Miguel or any of his men returned he would not be seen. He would also know when Zach arrived. He wasn't going to worry about getting Louisa's money because he didn't want to waste time. He knew a short cut in returning to the warehouse so he ran quickly in that direction.

CHAPTER 44

Gabriel stationed himself behind some bushes as he kept watch over the shed. His stomach growled because he missed lunch. He prayed that Zach would get here before Miguel and his men came back.

All of a sudden the hairs on the back of Gabriel's neck stood up and he knew something was wrong. He felt it in the core of his being. He squinted trying to get a closer view of the shed and saw Miguel returning. Fear mounted up inside Gabriel as Miguel made his way closer to the shed. God help me he cried out silently.

Holly heard the lock being opened again and cried out to God for protection. The door opened and Holly moved to the back of the shed. She saw Miguel and every nerve in her body became tense as she froze with fear, hoping to find a way to defend herself.

Miguel stared at her. With not much light coming into the shed it was not easy to see her while she stood against the wall.

"Come over here Holly. I came back to have some fun. You knew I was coming back." As he moved closer to her Holly cringed knowing that she would fight with all her might, even if it meant her death.

He grabbed for her and she screamed. "There is no reason to scream Holly. No one will hear you. I can do anything I want to you and there is nothing you can do and there is no one to help you."

"You are wrong Miguel." Gabriel walked through the door quietly and quickly. "I will help her and I will not let you hurt her."

Miguel could see that Gabriel was serious but laughed sarcastically at him. "I can do anything I want with her and you too Gabriel." At that moment he slapped Holly across the face and she fell to the side beside the wall, landing hard on the floor. Gabriel jumped on Miguel hitting him on the back. Miguel through Gabriel off and he landed on the floor as well. Miguel kicked him in the ribs and Gabriel groaned. Holly jumped up and started pulling Miguel away from Gabriel using her fists on his back.

Gabriel struggled on the floor as he tried to catch his breath from the blow to his ribs. He needed to get up and help Holly. In the distance he thought he heard a police siren. He prayed that they were coming to rescue Holly.

Miguel punched Holly in the jaw and threw her across the floor. Holly landed on her ankle and heard it crack. She screamed in pain as Gabriel tried to get up. Miguel was walking toward Holly and Gabriel knew he somehow needed to help her. Miguel grabbed Holly just as he heard the police siren stop nearby. He knew he needed to get out of there but he could not leave Holly alive. He would deal with Gabriel later.

He turned and grabbed Gabriel off the floor and told him to stand at the door. Gabriel would not obey Miguel. He knew Miguel meant to kill Holly and he could not let that happen.

Miguel pulled his gun and pointed it at Holly. She couldn't move because her ankle was broken so she looked

271

at Miguel with resignation, knowing she would be with God in a few moments. She experienced a peace like none before and she looked over at Gabriel with love and compassion shining from her eyes.

"Remember Gabriel, God loves you and nothing can separate you from that love."

"Shut up," yelled Miguel.

Everything that happened next was surreal to Holly as Gabriel jumped on Miguel's back and then thrown against the wall. Miguel cocked the gun and Gabriel got up and jumped in front of Holly as Miguel pulled the trigger. The bullet caught Gabriel in the middle of the chest and threw him several feet back into Holly's lap as she reached out to catch him. At the same moment the police broke through the door, grabbed Miguel and took the gun away from him. Zach and Micah rushed in behind them with fear in their eyes. The first thing they saw was this little boy lying in Holly's lap with blood everywhere. Tears ran down her face as she looked up at them.

Holly looked down into Gabriel's eyes and rubbed his cheek with her hand. "Gabriel, why did you jump in front of Miguel's gun?" she asked him quietly.

It took everything Gabriel had to answer her as his breathing was labored. His eyelids fluttered up and down. He answered her softly in almost a whisper. "I could not let him hurt you, Holly. You are my friend. Miguel has hurt everything I ever cared about and I could not let him do that to you." He struggled to breathe.

"Please Gabriel, stay with me," Holly whispered to him with tears streaming down her face.

Softly with great difficulty he replied, "No Holly, I do not want to. I want to go and be with Jesus. I think it will be much better for me to be with Him than here with Miguel. Do you not think so? Other than being with you I would rather be with Jesus."

"Yes Gabriel, but I don't want you to go yet."

With every bit of effort Gabriel took his hand and wiped tears off Holly's cheek. His breathing was sporadic now and Holly could feel him slipping away. "Do not cry for me Holly. I am very happy to go be with Jesus. Am I not doing what He did for us? Did He not die for us so that we could live forever with Him? That is what I needed to do for you."

Crying harder now Holly replied, "Yes, He did do that for us Gabriel. He did just that and so did you."

"Do you think He will think I am like Him just a little bit? That my heart is like His and like yours?"

"Yes, I am sure He will think that Gabriel. You have the heart of Jesus. I love you Gabriel."

As Gabriel smiled and struggled while laboring to take some more breaths he pulled his hand out of his pocket and put his hand on Holly's and said one last thing to her. "I love you Holly. Thank you for telling me about Jesus. I think being with Him will be wonderful. In my hand is a coin that I have always carried with me. My mother gave it to me before she died and I want you to have it so you will think of me. I will look forward to seeing you one day in heaven. Okay?"

Quietly sobbing Holly nodded her head and took the coin out of his hand. "Thank you Gabriel." She kissed his cheek. "I will treasure this coin and I will think of you often." Through her tears she saw his sweet smile and love shining through his eyes. Then Gabriel gently closed his eyes and she knew that at that moment he was with Jesus and finally at peace. She bowed her head over him and cried.

After witnessing all of this Zach came over to her, bent down and gently put his arms around her. He wanted to be sure the bullet had not struck Holly even though he saw no evidence that it had. She looked up and saw tears in his eyes and continued to cry in his arms. He cradled her as she cradled Gabriel in her arms softly sobbing her heart out and asked her if she had been shot. Through the tears she assured him she had not been shot but that she thought her ankle had been broken.

Micah stood back watching with tears in his eyes as he silently thanked God for protecting his sister's life and for this little boy who displayed the perfect heart of Jesus Christ in loving his sister and dying for her. He knew she would be forever changed because of the love she had for this little boy and his love for her.

After the police escorted Miguel out of the warehouse a policeman came over to her and said they needed to take Gabriel out. Zach stood up because he knew Holly was reluctant to let the little boy leave her lap and her embrace so he helped the policeman gently remove Gabriel from her lap and put him on a stretcher that had been brought to the shed. She looked up and saw Micah with tears streaming down her face. She was surprised to see him but very glad he was here.

"Please Micah, will you find out where they will be taking him? I want to give him a proper burial before we leave here." He nodded and came over to her, bent down, hugged her and kissed the top of her head. As she moved to hug him back, she groaned in pain because of her ankle. Micah stood up and noticed the bruise on her jaw and experienced anger like never before. Zach also noticed the injuries to her face and Micah could see the fury on his face.

"Miguel hit me and I landed on my ankle and heard it crack, so I am pretty certain it is broken, but don't worry, the ankle and the bruises will heal."

Instantly Micah reached down to pick her up at the same time Zach started to gently pick her up. Micah and Zach's eyes locked for a moment and an understanding passed between the two of them as Micah backed up to let Zach take care of Holly. Zach tenderly lifted Holly realizing that it would be painful for her no matter how gentle he was. Holly cried out in pain as Micah watched Zach kiss her forehead and carry her out the door. She was in the hands of the man who loved her and he was thankful.

As he followed them out of the shed Micah said, "I'll go ask where the little boy is being taken while Zach gets you to the ambulance and then I will follow the ambulance to the hospital in Zach's car." Zach then said he would ride with Holly. The men with them who had been searching for Holly said they would let the others at the church know what had happened.

Zach carried her to the ambulance. He gently cradled her in his arms like a priceless treasure as if he would never let go. Micah watched from a distance as he observed how gentle Zach treated Holly as he put her on the stretcher and helped get her into the ambulance. Micah silently thanked God again for protecting Holly and got in to Zach's car to follow the ambulance to the hospital.

Holly rested her head on Zach's shoulders still crying because the pain in her ankle was excruciating. She silently thanked God for His protection and that Gabriel was with Him now and no longer had to suffer here on earth. Gabriel saved her life and she would never forget him, confident she would always remember that he was a reflection of Jesus who died to save those He loved.

CHAPTER 45

It took the ambulance about 45 minutes to get Holly to the hospital. Micah followed closely behind in Zach's car which was challenging given the traffic and the way people drove. He wasn't about to lose them because he had no idea where the hospital was located.

Micah followed the ambulance to the emergency entrance and parked the car as Holly was taken into the emergency room. It took several hours for her to be seen by a doctor but after having x-rays taken she was admitted with a broken ankle. During that time Micah called Bill to let him know what was happening. He told Bill he would meet them at the church around 9 in the morning and fill them in on all the details. He told Bill that the doctor would do surgery in the morning to set and cast Holly's ankle. She would have to be in the hospital through tomorrow and hopefully then she could leave.

Once Holly got to her hospital room the doctor ordered a sedative and pain killer to help her sleep for the rest of the evening. Zach wanted to stay with Holly so Micah decided to leave and make arrangements for her to stay at the hotel with him when she was released from the hospital.

After the nurse left Micah walked to the side of the bed. Holly was already beginning to drift off to sleep. He gently wiped the hair off of her forehead and bent over to kiss her cheek. "I will be back in the morning Holly," he whispered. "If you need anything Zach will stay with you tonight." She nodded and closed her eyes. "I love you Holly."

She quietly replied, "I love you too Micah." He looked at Zach and mouthed with his lips for Zach to take care of her. Zach nodded and Micah left the room.

Holly whispered, "Zach".

"I'm here Holly."

"Good." She smiled and drifted off to sleep.

Zach pulled up a chair, grabbed a blanket out of the closet and sat down. With a giant sigh of relief, the first since Holly was kidnapped; he prayed a prayer of thanksgiving. God had delivered Holly out of the hands of the enemy. He would be forever grateful for the little boy named Gabriel. A smile came to his lips as his eyes rested on Holly.

~~~~~~~~~~

When Micah returned to the hotel after seeing Holly in the hospital he called his mom and Ellie to let them know Holly was safe. After talking to them he said a silent prayer thanking God for protecting Holly and for the special little boy that saved her.

CHAPTER 46

Holly had surgery early the next morning. Micah had been waiting with Zach during the surgery and when the doctor came out he told them that the ankle had been repaired and that over time she should fully recover with physical therapy. They both thanked him. Micah left to talk with Bill and the American team while Zach waited in Holly's hospital room for her to get out of recovery.

When Micah got to the church Bill and the others were finishing their group devotions with a time of prayer. Bill saw Micah as they finished, got up and greeted him with a hug. The rest of the team jumped up and had a lot of questions for Micah. Finally Jeff and Becca got everyone quiet so that Micah could give them a report on Holly's situation.

"Holly was kidnapped by a man named Miguel who was the kingpin of the streets in the area where the team was ministering. Miguel thought if he took Holly that would make Zach and anyone else stop coming there and sharing about Jesus because the Gospel offered hope and the last thing he wanted was for the people on the street to have hope in anything other than what he offered. There was a little boy named Gabriel whom Holly apparently met shortly after arriving here. He lived with and worked for Miguel. Gabriel came to know Jesus as His Lord and Savior while attending bible school here in the last couple of weeks. He died saving Holly by taking a bullet meant for her." As Micah wiped away a tear from his cheek he noticed the girls had tears streaming down their faces. The guys just sat quietly.

Micah continued, "Holly just had surgery on her ankle which broke when Miguel hit her. Zach stayed at the hospital to wait until she comes out of recovery. I'm thankful to say she should fully recover with physical therapy."

"Can we visit Holly today?" Kylie asked.

"I don't see why not Kylie. Holly should be awake later this afternoon and I think she would like that."

"Holly wants to give Gabriel a proper burial before she leaves Mexico so I am going to be making plans for that this afternoon."

Looking at Bill, Emma asked, "Can we attend the funeral?"

Bill glanced at Micah and Micah nodded yes. "As long as it can be done within the next day or so I think that's a fine idea Emma. We leave in three days."

"I hope to get the burial scheduled for Wednesday," Micah replied. "That will give Holly tomorrow to recuperate. Hopefully on Wednesday we can have the funeral, say goodbye to your host families and then leave Thursday." Looking at Bill he asked, "Does that work for you?"

"Yes, that will work fine," responded Bill. "I can let Pastor Abraham know the plan and then they can work on their farewell party for Wednesday evening."

Micah was anxious to get back to the hospital so he left shortly after talking to the team. He told them that he would let Holly know they were coming to see her later today.

Zach waited for Holly to wake up from the surgery. He knew she was sleeping peacefully at the moment but realized that she would be in pain once the medicines wore off. He loved looking at her and knew her beauty was not just outward but inward as well. He couldn't stop thanking God for her and for keeping her safe and he couldn't wait to ask her to marry him.

Holly's eyes fluttered and she mumbled. Zach put down the magazine he was reading and walked over to the side of her bed. He gently caressed her cheek and called her name.

Holly responded slowly, "Zach, is that you?" She looked at him with her eyes half opened.

"Yeah, it's me Holly." He bent over and kissed her cheek. "How are you feeling?"

"Not bad right now. How's my ankle?"

"The doctor said with some physical therapy you should make a complete recovery," Zach replied.

"Good. Is Micah here?" Holly asked.

"No, not yet. He was here while you were in surgery and once he knew you were out and doing fine he went to meet with Bill and the others to give them an update. I'm sure he'll be here soon."

Holly started recalling the events of last night and sadness washed over her again. There was something that she was struggling to remember that was really important but she couldn't quite grasp it. Zach took her hand, opened it and gently laid the coin in her palm. Relief swept over her because that was what she couldn't grasp. She couldn't remember what had happened to the coin Gabriel gave her.

"You gave it to me when you went in for x-rays. I knew you would want it as soon as you woke up."

"Thanks Zach." Tears felled down her cheeks. "I want to make a pendant out of it and wear it around my neck. I told Gabriel I would keep it close to my heart."

Zach wiped away her tears. There were no words to be said.

Micah walked in shortly afterward and by that time Holly was wide awake. When she saw him come through the door she reached for him. He came over to her and hugged her tightly.

"I'm so glad to see that you're feeling better Holly." He gently lifted her chin and looked at the bruise on her jaw. She saw the muscles twitch alongside his face.

She put her hand over his. "It's alright Micah. It will go away in time. I'm feeling much better and I am safe now." He squeezed her hand and she saw him visibly relax because she was safe and that's all mattered to him at the moment.

"I did want to ask you about the burial arrangements. Have you done anything about it yet?" Holly questioned.

"As a matter of fact I just got finished making the arrangements. It will be Wednesday at 11:00 at the church and Pastor Abraham will officiate for the service. Gabriel will be buried at the church's cemetery. Bill and the others will be there as well."

Quietly Holly said, "Thank you."

Micah nodded. "Bill and the team are coming by to see you later today. They are all anxious to see for themselves that you're okay. Hopefully, later this evening, we can take you back to the hotel to recuperate until Wednesday. The church families want to have a farewell party for everyone Wednesday night before we leave Thursday."

"That's fine," Holly said.

Zach looked at Micah and then at Holly. "Do you think you will feel up to all of this? It's a lot in just a couple of days given all you've been through as well as your injuries." Zach inquired.

Looking at Micah, Holly said, "I can rest all day tomorrow at the hotel and also when I get home. I really want to do this and with both of you helping me, I'm sure I'll be fine."

Zach and Micah looked at each other nodding affirmatively. "Okay then. It's settled," replied Micah.

Later that day the Americans visited Holly in the hospital. There was a lot of hugging and kissing going on. Holly was exhausted by the time they left but she felt good. She kept clutching Gabriel's coin in her hand as she thought about him.

After dinner Holly was released from the hospital. Zach drove Micah and Holly to the hotel where he helped Micah get Holly settled into her room. Zach needed to talk with Pastor Abraham since he hadn't seen him since Holly had been found. Micah gave them some privacy as Zach got ready to leave.

"Holly, I'm going to miss you tonight. I'm glad Micah is here to take care of you and now I need to speak with Pastor Abraham for a while."

"I know Zach. I'll miss you as well. Thanks for staying with me. I know you have a lot of things to finish up before we leave Thursday."

"I want to talk to you soon about our relationship but now isn't the time." He was stroking her cheek as she gazed at him with eyes of love.

"I know Zach, and I'll look forward to the time when we can talk alone." He gently kissed her lips.

"The next couple of days will be long and hard so please rest tomorrow as much as you can and I'll stop by to see you later in the day," replied Zach.

"I will." Micah came back into Holly's room as Zach walked out. "See you tomorrow Micah."

"Bye Zach." Zach left the hotel suite.

Micah walked over to the side of Holly's bed and sat down with care so as not to jog her leg.

"Zach seems like a good man and I know he really loves you," Micah said. Holly nodded, blushed and smiled.

"I know and I feel so special when I am with him." She said softly, "Micah, I love him too." These were such intimate feelings to be sharing with someone but Micah would be the first one with whom she would share such feelings.

Micah smiled. "I know. I can tell. He's God's blessing to you and you are to him as well." She hugged her big brother again and thanked God for him.

"Can I get you anything?' Micah asked.

"No I'm fine but thanks for being here Micah. I'm sorry you had to go through this. Oh, did you call mom and Ellie?"

"I called them both after you were admitted to the hospital just to let them know how you were doing."

Anxiously Holly questioned, "Are they okay? I'm sure mom must have been really worried."

"She was, but you know mom, she was praying a lot. So did Ellie. They wanted me to give you their love and to tell you they can't wait for you to be home so they can take care of you."

Holly started softly crying and Micah gently wrapped his arms around her and held her tightly while she sobbed. He knew she would have some sad times ahead when she thought about everything that happened here and especially when she thought about Gabriel. So he kept holding on tightly as she cried.

She finally lifted her head from his shoulders and he wiped her tears with his handkerchief.

"I'm sorry, Micah, I got your shirt all wet. The pain is unbearable sometimes, both emotionally and physically and then I remember Gabriel's joy in going to be with the Lord and that makes me feel better."

"I know. I'm grateful for what Gabriel did for you Holly. I couldn't bear the thought of losing you and I'm so glad you're safe. I have to admit that I'm anxious to get you away from this place and back on the ranch where I know you will be safe."

"Thanks, I am too." Holly's eyes started to droop and Micah knew she was ready to get some rest. "Can you do one more thing for me Micah, and then I think I would like to get some sleep?"

"Sure. What?"

She pulled her hand from under the covers and reached out to him. He reached his hand out to hers and she gave him the gold coin.

"Gabriel gave this to me just before he died. Tomorrow could you possibly get this put on a gold chain so I can wear it to the burial service? It was the only thing he had from his mother."

Micah took the gold coin in his hand knowing she would always cherish it. "Sure. I will try to get it done. When Zach comes over I will go out because I don't want you left alone."

"Thanks Micah." He wrapped the covers around her and gave her a kiss on the top of her head as she drifted off to sleep.

"Sleep well Holly. If you need anything just call. I'll be in the other room." She nodded as he walked to the door.

God willing she would get a good night's sleep. She had two long days ahead of her and she would need all of her strength. He knew the pain pills would help and he prayed that God would bless her with a restful night. He turned out the light and left the door slightly cracked in case she called for him. He prayed God would give him a good night's rest as well. He had been very stressed since he learned of her disappearance and this was the first time he could relax now that she was with him and safe.

CHAPTER 47

Holly woke the next morning after a good night's rest and was thankful that the pain medicine and sleep sedative did the trick. Her ankle was really painful now though since the medicine had worn off. She called for Micah so she could get some more and tried to wiggle herself to the side of the bed. Micah came through the door just as she lowered her foot to the floor. He had shaving cream all over his face and was still in his pajamas. She grabbed for the crutches as he came over to her.

"Good morning Micah. I'm sorry, but I couldn't wait. I don't mean to be a bother, but I need to get some more medicine. My ankle is killing me." She looked up at him and he could see the pain in her eyes.

"Just a minute and I'll get it." He walked back to the bathroom to get her medicine as she hobbled on her crutches into the sitting room to wait for him and the pills. She sat on a chair and lifted her leg onto the ottoman. She didn't remember being in this room but she must have come through here to get to her bedroom. The chair she sat in was soft brown leather and was quite comfortable. There was a leather loveseat of the same color in the corner with a small coffee table in front of it. The burgundy flowered drapes on a beige background along with the carpet in this room matching the color of the flowers made it a very comfortable room. Micah's bedroom was next to the bathroom. She would have to compliment Micah on his choice of hotels because this was a great suite. Micah came over and gave her a glass of water with her medicine.

Holly noticed he had wiped off the shaving cream from his face.

"Holly, Zach will be here in about an hour. I asked him to have breakfast with us. After we finish I am going out to see about getting your gold coin put onto a gold chain. He will stay with you until I get back." Walking back into his bedroom he continued, "I really want you to rest today. Tomorrow is going to be a busy day and an emotionally draining day. Then we leave on Thursday which will be physically exhausting so today is the only day you will be able to rest."

"I know and I will rest. I'm looking forward to spending some time with Zach." She laid her head back on the chair as the medicines started taking effect. "It was nice to see everyone at the hospital yesterday though I can only remember bits and pieces of their visit." Her words started slurring and she had soon fallen asleep. Micah walked quietly over to her, lifted her up and carried her back into her bedroom. He was glad she could sleep for a while before breakfast.

Micah was going to make a few calls to some jewelers so he didn't waste a lot of time going from one to another trying to find one who could make a pendant of the gold coin. He wanted to have it done today so that Holly could wear it to the funeral. He bent down and kissed her forehead, moved some of her hair off her face and then pulled the covers up over her body. He loved his little sister a lot and thanked God once against for protecting her.

When Holly woke up Zach was sitting next to her. She looked a little disoriented and for a moment didn't seem to remember where she was. As she looked around her bedroom she noticed the wallpaper had blue and yellow flowers on a white background. She loved those colors but didn't particularly like the drapes because they were a deep yellow, almost gold. She thought a blue drape would have looked better but, all in all, it was an attractive and cozy room. Then all the things that had happened within the last 24 hours came flooding back to her memory. Zach looked up at that moment and realized she was awake.

"Hey sleepy head, how are you feeling?" he said with great tenderness. Zach couldn't take his eyes off her because even with the bruises on her face, she was still beautiful. He ran his hand through her hair to move it off her shoulders.

"I feel better than I did earlier. My ankle throbs a lot but I don't think I want to take much more of that medicine. It knocks me out quickly and then I feel really disoriented when I wake up. I want to be alert and wide awake for the funeral tomorrow."

Zach got serious all of a sudden and remarked, "Holly, I thought I might have lost you." He got up and moved closer to the side of her bed and sat down on it. He took her hand in his and said, "Just when I found you I thought you were gone. I prayed more fervently in the last couple of days than I ever have prayed. I knew God had you in His care but I wasn't ready to lose you."

Tears fell down his face and Holly reached up and gently wiped his cheek. She let her hand rest on his cheek as Zach turned and kissed it. "I love you Zach. I was really scared I wouldn't see you again or have the chance to share life with you." Her voice was raspy as she shared her feelings with him. "I knew God was with me and I trusted

Him to take care of me even if that meant I was to go and be with Him."

She smiled slightly and looked Zach straight in the eyes and said, "But I'm really glad He didn't because I want to spend my life getting to know you, love you, have kids with you, minister with you and whatever else God might have us do together."

Zach leaned over and kissed Holly gently but thoroughly. He left no doubt as to how he felt about her.

"I love you too. You're going to be leaving on Thursday and I can't leave for another two weeks. Once I get everything finished here I'm going to fly out to Colorado and spend a couple of weeks with you before I have to get back to seminary for my last semester."

Holly held his hand tightly and caressed it, glorying in the fact that this man loved her. "I'll miss you Zach but it's going to take me awhile to get back on my feet. I am going to be working really hard at physical therapy which I can't even start for about six weeks. The doctor told Micah my cast can't come off before then."

"That's okay Holly. When I get to your home we'll just spend more time sitting and talking. I called my parents today and told them what happened. I had already told them about you before and they are looking forward to meeting you in the very near future."

"I look forward to meeting them as well," Holly replied.

Holly and Zach started talking about the team and how they were putting the finishing touches to the last of the projects. Zach told her that Pastor Abraham was extremely pleased with how much the team accomplished in the past month and how the church had been blessed by all their hard work.

Holly and Zach both looked toward the door as they heard the outside hotel room door open. Micah came walking into her room looking first at her and then Zach.

"Hey guys, just me." Looking at Holly he continued, "It's a really nice day outside. How are you feeling?"

"Better since I woke up, but I told Zach I want to try not to use as much of the pain medicine now because it makes me groggy and disoriented. I want to be totally aware of everything tomorrow even if my ankle kills me. Okay Micah?"

"Whatever you want Holly, but if you need some relief please take some of the medicine, maybe even just a partial dose." She nodded in agreement.

Micah walked over to her and pulled a box out of his pocket. Opening the box he pulled out a beautiful gold chain with Gabriel's gold coin threaded through it. Tears flowed from Holly's eyes and she said, "It's absolutely perfect Micah! How were you able to get it done so quickly?" He handed it to her and she clutched it close to her heart and closed her eyes.

"The jeweler was really accommodating. Here, let me put it on for you."

Holly handed him the necklace and lifted her hair so Micah could fasten it behind her neck. It was the perfect length. She marveled at how beautiful it was and couldn't stop running it through her fingers.

"Thank you Micah. It's gorgeous!"

"Good. I'm glad you like it."

"I do Micah. It's perfect! Thank you again."

Looking at both of the men she felt a need to be by herself for a while so she said, "I would like to get some rest now as I'm feeling really tired."

Zach got up from the chair and said, "I'm going to head out for a while so I can get some work done. I will be back for dinner." He walked over and gave Holly a kiss on the cheek. He said goodbye to Micah and Micah left the room as well.

Once they were both gone, Holly cried softly to herself as she kept her hand around the coin. Her thoughts were of Gabriel and how much she missed him. She asked God for the strength to get through tomorrow and she also thanked Him for bringing Gabriel into her life. Mostly she thanked God for saving Gabriel because she knew she would see him again one day. With that thought in mind she drifted off to sleep.

Holly slept through the evening while Zach and Micah had dinner. They knew she needed as much rest as possible and they enjoyed getting to know each other better. Zach shared his plans with Micah and asked his blessing to marry Holly in the near future. Micah couldn't be happier with God's choice for his sister and he looked forward to having a brother.

Later, Zach left after checking in on Holly who was sleeping at the time. She slept through the night..

CHAPTER 48

Wednesday morning arrived quickly for Holly after a good night of sleep. She had slept straight through the night and was thankful. She missed seeing Zach but knew she needed the rest and would see him today. Micah came in to see if she needed some help. She told him she would like some toast and coffee and then wanted to get into the bathroom. Holly asked him to help her wash her hair since she couldn't shower easily and would just take a sponge bath.

After finishing her toast and coffee with Micah she got her crutches and went into the bathroom. When she was finished with everything but her hair she called to Micah. He came in and washed her hair as she stood tottering on one foot over the sink. Afterward he put a towel on her head and then helped her over to the counter where the hair dryer was located. As she held onto the counter's edge Micah blew her hair dry. Fortunately she would just braid it for the day.

Zach came to pick them up around 10:30. He had a wheel chair that he had borrowed from the church with him so they wheeled Holly to the elevator and then to the lobby. Zach's car was parked out front and he helped her into the car.

When they got to the cemetery Holly noticed Bill and the other team members had already arrived. Zach got the wheel chair out of the trunk while Micah helped Holly out of the car and then into the wheel chair. Zach wheeled her over to the grave site with Micah following close behind. Everyone walked over to greet her with hugs and kisses. Pastor Abraham came over as well and greeted them.

When he was sure everyone who would be there had arrived, Pastor Abraham started the funeral service with a prayer. He said a few words about Gabriel's faith and how he exhibited it by dying for Holly and how this reflected Christ's love for His saints. He then quoted Jesus from John 15:13 saying *"greater love has no one than this that one lay down his life for his friends."* Zach's hands were on Holly's shoulders as he stood behind her. Emma, Kylie and Becca had tears running down their cheeks. Just seeing Holly in a wheel chair and thinking about this little boy dying for her touched their hearts deeply. Jeff put his arm around Becca to comfort her and Holly kept her fingers around the gold coin as Pastor Abraham spoke.

When he finished speaking one of the church members in attendance brought roses and discreetly passed one to each of the people in attendance giving Holly two. After the final prayer each of the people placed their rose on the top of the coffin. Holly with the assistance of Zach was the last to do that but kept one for herself as a remembrance of Gabriel and what he did for her.

Pastor Abraham came over to tell Holly how sorry he was for all of this but also how grateful he was to Gabriel for saving her. Holly thanked him for performing the service and for getting the coffin. They were going to head back to the church where the church people had prepared a small meal for them. Holly, Zach and Micah were the last to leave the funeral. Holly asked if she could have a few moments alone beside Gabriel's coffin before they left so Micah and Zach walked over to the car to wait for her.

As Holly looked at the coffin tears welled up in her eyes. She put her hand on it saying, "Gabriel, I don't know if you can hear me, but I will miss you. You were one brave little boy and I still can't believe all of this has happened." As she fingered her gold coin pendant she continued, "I will never forget you and I'm so glad God let me know you even for just a little while. You are very special to me and when I wear this gold coin I will remember what you did for me. Thank you for loving me enough to die for me. I'm so glad you are safe now and at peace. It would have been difficult for me to go back to the states if you were still here living with Miguel. I'm glad you're with our Lord and Savior now and that one day I will see you again. I love you Gabriel." Just then a soft wind blew over her and Holly experienced peace like a river flowing over her. She whispered a thank you to God, wiped the tears away, and waved to Micah and Zach that she was ready to leave.

Zach walked over to get her and as he wheeled her away she looked over her shoulder back at the grave and blew a kiss. Then she put her hand over Zach's as they made their way to the car. Because of Gabriel's sacrifice she had a future with Zach and she whispered a silent thank you to Gabriel and God once again.

~~~~~~~~~~

After the meal at the church the Americans got together for their last group devotion. Holly was tired and her ankle throbbed but she didn't want to miss this last devotion. Zach and Micah sat in as well while Bill led the devotion starting with Psalm 18:30-32. *"As for God, His way is blameless; the word of the Lord tried; He is a shield to all who take refuge in Him. For who is God but the Lord and who is a rock, except our God who girds me with strength and makes my way blameless."* Bill continued to share his thoughts. "During this difficult time I kept thinking about God as our Rock. He is a shield to all who trust Him and take refuge in Him. I believe Gabriel did that when he stepped in front of the bullet meant for Holly. His strength was from God." He continued by reading Psalm 9:1-2. *"I will give thanks to the Lord with all my heart; I will tell of all Your wonders. I will be glad and exult in You; I will sing praise to Your name, O Most High."* He also read Psalm 8:1. *"O Lord, our Lord, how majestic is Your name in all the earth, who have displayed Your splendor above the heavens!"* Bill reminded them that they could and should praise God for who He is even in the midst of difficult circumstances. He said, "God's hand is in everything and He is blameless. Praising God turns sadness into glory and worshipping Him brings joy and peace. I want you to remember all that happened on this trip and that God is due glory, honor and praise. Please remember that Gabriel knew this in his new found faith and by his heroic actions he was praising and worshipping God as he sacrificed his life for Holly's. God was his stronghold when he needed Him to be and God was faithful to him. Now Gabriel is enjoying intimate fellowship with our Lord and Savior. That's what we look forward to one day as well." Bill closed in prayer.

After devotions the team waited for the Mexicans to come and start their farewell party. Holly rested in one of the chairs in the courtyard with Emma and Kylie. They couldn't wait to talk to Holly alone. Holly learned that Kylie and Chris were going to pursue their friendship on a more intimate basis when they returned home. Emma told Holly that she secretly prayed that she could get to know Jackson a little better once they got home as well. Holly smiled at them both as they shared their hopes and dreams with her.

Becca came up to her after the girls left and wanted to know how Holly was doing. She shared how this whole trip impacted her and Jeff and that they were praying about what God wanted them to do with the rest of their lives. After seeing how Gabriel came to know God through bible school they started praying about going into full time mission work. Holly hugged Becca and told her how happy she was to hear that and also told Becca about some of her conversations with Zach. She told Becca they loved each other and Becca responded with a hug. She told her not to hesitate contacting her if Holly needed any help when they were back in Colorado.

Soon the Mexicans arrived with food and the celebration began. Zach came to get Holly and he wheeled her into the courtyard where the festivities were beginning. He knew she was tired and needed to get back to the hotel soon. Micah kept a close eye on her as well. They weren't going to let her stay much longer, especially since they had a long airplane flight home tomorrow. They knew the

Mexicans would understand even though they also knew Holly would want to stay for a little while out of appreciation for all they had done for her and the team. Pastor Abraham opened their time of celebration with prayer. He thanked the Americans for all they had accomplished in the last month. He offered a special prayer of thanksgiving for delivering Holly out of a dangerous situation and for Gabriel. Many people uttered quiet thank yous and amens. Holly held Micah's hand on one side and Zach's hand on the other.

The evening ended with the Mexican people giving each of the team members a gift as their way of saying thank you. The gift was a lovely ten piece nativity scene carved and painted by different people in the church. It was a gift that every team member would cherish and they said so as they left the church with their host families one last time.

Holly was grateful for this experience and it was one she would never forget. She thought about her time in Mexico long after the celebration ended and she slept peacefully for the first time in days as she held Gabriel's gold coin pendant with her fingers.

CHAPTER 49

Thursday morning came with a whirlwind of activity for the team. Micah packed his clothes and had his luggage by the front door waiting for Zach to pick them up. He then went to check to see if Holly was awake. She was already sitting up on the side of her bed with most of her belongings already packed. When Zach had brought her things to the hotel from her host family she didn't use much of it, so she had unpacked very little.

"Good morning, Micah," Holly said. "What's for breakfast? I am starving." She smiled.

Micah was glad to see her smile and that she seemed more like her old self. He replied, "Since we are on a tight schedule I'm going to order room service this morning. So what would you like to eat?"

"An English muffin with jelly and a cup of tea sounds good as well as a banana if they have any." She hobbled across the room to get to the bathroom as Micah nodded and headed to the telephone.

Holly got inside the bathroom and laid her crutches next to the sink. She found getting her toiletries completed more challenging than she would have imagined. As she washed her face she thought about the funeral, Gabriel and all the things she experienced in Mexico City. She hoped to return in the future to see Gabriel's tombstone that would be placed at the head of his grave in about three weeks by the church. She lost her balance once and leaned up against the wall. She was anxious to get to the church and see everyone as they gathered to head home. Being with everyone gave her a sense of normalcy and she couldn't wait to get home and see her mom, Ellie and the kids. She decided to let her hair hang loose today and not braid it like she usually did.

Holly changed her shirt but kept on the same jeans since she didn't want to ask Micah for help and it would take a lot more time which they didn't have. Holly got the rest of her belongings packed with Micah's help before their breakfast arrived. They decided to eat first and then Micah would take her luggage to the car when Zach arrived. They enjoyed sitting together as they ate breakfast and Holly realized she missed that more than she realized. Once Micah got married she rarely saw him for breakfast.

"You're not saying much Holly," Micah commented. He was enjoying a Belgian waffle with mounds of whip cream and strawberries. He savored the flavor of the last bite as it melted in his mouth.

"Just thinking."

Micah noted, "When we get to the church there will be a lot of commotion with the host families saying goodbye to your team."

"I know and I'm looking forward to seeing the Sandovals. I feel bad because I couldn't spend the last few days with them."

"Holly, I have no doubt they understood why I wanted you here with me."

"Yeah, I know. They visited me once at the hospital but I was pretty much out of it. It will be nice to see them once more before we leave." Finishing the last bite of her English muffin she continued with her thought.

"Will we be on the van with the others?" Holly asked Micah.

"No, Zach will drive us to the airport in his car and we will be right behind the van. We decided it would be a lot easier on you. I hope you don't mind us making that decision for you."

"No not at all. Thank you. I was hoping we would be doing that anyway."

Micah finished his coffee and licked his fingers. "Boy was that ever good. I'll have to get Ellie to make Belgian waffles a little more often at home. It was great with whip cream and strawberries!"

Holly made her way into the bathroom to brush her teeth while Micah took her bags to the front door of their suite. She gave him her toothbrush and toothpaste so he could place them in one of her bags. When Zach got there Micah told her to wait while he took her bags to the car and then check out. He would meet her downstairs and Zach would be up to help wheel her down so Holly sat down for the few moments and waited.

When Zach came up he brought the wheel chair over to her and gave her a long, lingering kiss. He asked, "How are you this morning?"

Holly relied, "Better now that you're here."

Zach smiled, "I'm glad. I'm also glad we still have this wheel chair. It will be a lot easier getting you downstairs rather than you trying to maneuver with your crutches. You ready?"

"Yep, let's go." She got into the wheel chair and put her crutches in her lap. Zach gave her another quick kiss before he rolled her out to the elevator and then once they were at the lobby he rolled her out the front door to the car meeting Micah. Twenty minutes later they arrived at the church and everyone was excited to see Holly. The Sandovals came over and hugged Holly and pulled over some chairs so they could visit with her while there was time. Micah headed over to talk with Bill.

"Micah, how's Holly doing?" Bill asked.

"I think she's okay. She slept pretty well last night and she's only taking half a dose of the pain medication. She hates being disoriented so she's fighting through the pain." Micah looked over at Holly to be sure she was doing okay.

"How do you think she will do traveling today? I've been concerned about that."

"We've decided to use an airport wheel chair to get her on and off the airplanes and hopefully we can get her an aisle seat, too. I think she'll be okay, but will probably experience some pain at times. I don't see any way around her being uncomfortable while we're traveling."

"Yeah, I know. The van should be here in a few minutes. I'd like to get everyone loaded up quickly so you have plenty of time at the airport with Holly."

"Thanks Bill. I appreciate all you've done for Holly and this team. Frankly, I'm grateful that we're able to fly back with everyone and that Holly only has a broken ankle. I shudder to think of other alternatives that could be our reality now."

Bill nodded in agreement as Zach walked into the church announcing that the van was here. Everyone started hugging the host families and then grabbed their luggage to get on the van. The Sandovals gave Holly a couple of gifts and when Micah came over to help her get to the car he talked with them for a minute and then started wheeling Holly out to the car. Becca and Jeff were gathering up the last of the college students and their belongings before making their way to the van as Zach helped Holly get into the car.

After arriving at the airport Micah got the wheel chair out for Holly while Zach got their belongings out of the car, leaving it by the curb. The van was unloading right in front of the car and Zach knew he didn't have much time with Holly because people who were not traveling weren't allowed beyond the terminal gate. He walked over to Holly's side, opened the door and bent down to speak with her before Micah came with the chair.

Zach took Holly's hand and kissed it. "I want to tell you that I'm going to miss you and that I love you with all my heart." She looked into his eyes and saw all the love he had for her shining through them.

"I'll miss you too Zach."

"I will call you tonight after you get home." He turned to see if anyone was looking and softly kissed her. She cupped his face in both of her hands and kissed him soundly. When she was finished he smiled.

"They all know how we feel about each other," she said tenderly. "I couldn't leave without really feeling your lips on mine. I love you Zach."

"Be careful Holly. Rest while you're home and don't do too much. I'll get there as soon as I can and in the meantime we'll burn up the phone lines."

Holly nodded with a tear running down her cheek while her fingers held on to the bracelet Zach gave her.

303

Zach gently wiped the tear away with his thumb as Micah rolled the wheel chair to Holly. Zach helped Holly out of the car and into the chair. The rest of the team was already in the airport and Micah rolled Holly into the airport while Zach brought the luggage. Once Micah got their tickets he could take Holly directly to their gate given her lack of mobility. There they would wait for the rest of their team to arrive.

As Zach waited with Holly while Micah got their tickets he pulled a small box out of his pocket and handed it to Holly. "Open this when you're on the plane. It will remind you of how much I love you." Micah held out his hand to Zach and Zach shook it with a nod of understanding between the two men that only a brother and a future brother-in-law could recognize.

"We'll look forward to seeing you in a couple of weeks Zach. Thanks for everything." Micah said.

"I'll be there in two weeks Micah. I know you'll take good care of Holly until I get there." He talked to Micah but looked at Holly.

"You can count on that Zach."

Zach gave Holly another kiss and squeezed her hand one last time as she and Micah headed to their gate. Holly looked at Zach as she was being wheeled away and blew him a kiss. Zach smiled and blew her a kiss too.

After Holly and Micah made their way through security they rode the shuttle to the terminal where their gate was located and Micah went to get them coffee from Starbucks. Holly loved the café au lait and Micah liked their lattes. Holly was glad to be resting now and waiting for her team to arrive at their gate. While she waited Holly

304

took out the box Zach gave her because she couldn't stand to wait until she was on the plane. She opened it and lifted a beautiful sterling silver bracelet with a heart that had an inscription engraved on to it. The inscription said Zach loves Holly. Holly put it on next to the sterling silver chain bracelet he gave her earlier in the trip. They looked beautiful together and she smiled. Holly realized God blessed her on this trip with difficult and wonderful things and she was very thankful for both.

Holly put the small box in her backpack and leaned back to rest while she waited for Micah to get back with their coffees. The last several days were exhausting physically and emotionally and before she knew it she fell asleep with her hand covering her bracelets.

As the rest of the team arrived after getting food and drink they tried to be quiet enough to let Holly rest, but being in an airport made anything other than short naps virtually impossible. Holly woke up and was glad to see everyone there, especially Micah sitting with her café au lait. The café au lait hit the spot for Holly especially while talking with Kylie, Emma and Becca. She was able to catch up on things she missed over the last several days when she was abducted, in the hospital and then recuperating at the hotel. They were happy being with her and knowing that she was alive and well, heading home with them.

Micah took a few minutes to watch his sister talk to the girls and thanked God she was alive and traveling home with them all. As he watched her, he marveled at her outward beauty but knew it didn't compare to the inward beauty she displayed to those around her. He looked forward to getting her home so she could rest and recuperate fully. He also looked forward to seeing his family as well. He really missed Ellie and his kids and after this experience not a day passed that didn't remind him of how much his family meant to him, not to mention how almost losing Holly impressed that even more on his heart. Peace settled over Micah now that he had the last couple of days behind him, fully assured that Holly was recovering and safely on her way home. He whispered a silent thank you to Gabriel for giving his sister back to him and knew he would always be grateful to God and to that little boy for protecting and saving her.

CHAPTER 50

Two weeks later Zach drove up to the Brady ranch and it was just as Holly described. A beautiful white house with a wraparound porch nestled in a lovely landscaped area of colorful flowers and green shrubbery everywhere. It was a peaceful setting with gorgeous mountains in the background with horses and wildlife roaming around the area.

Zach saw Micah sitting on the porch with two women. Zach assumed one was his wife, Ellie, from Micah's description of her while they were in Mexico and the other must be his mother. He took his hand off the steering wheel, reached into his pocket and pulled out a ring box. He smiled and set it on the seat as he waited for the moment he would put that ring on Holly's finger.

As he pulled up in front of the house Micah walked down the porch steps and the women followed. Zach put the ring box back in his coat pocket and got out of the car.

"Hey, Zach, it's good to see you!" Micah said as he approached Zach before giving him a bear hug. "No more handshakes between family members." Zach smiled and nodded.

"Zach, let me introduce you to my wife, Ellie." Ellie stepped forward and gave Zach a hug. "It's good to meet you Zach. I've heard so much about you from Micah and Holly, but especially Holly."

"It's good to meet you as well Ellie. When we were in Mexico Micah talked about you and the kids a lot."

Smiling at Micah he continued. "He missed you all a great deal."

"Thanks Zach."

Micah continued with introductions. "Zach, this is my mother Abigail Brady."

Abigail walked over to Zach, gazed into his eyes with tears in her own and hugged him. "Thank you for taking care of Holly in Mexico. I am so grateful to God for you and what you did for her." Wiping the tears away from her eyes she smiled and whispered into his ears, only for him to hear. "Welcome to our family!" Then she winked at him.

Micah said, "Our kids are resting so you can meet them later."

Zach nodded and then asked, "Where's Holly? Is she expecting me today?"

Micah responded. "No I didn't say anything. The last she knew was what you told her a few days ago that you would be here soon."

"Good. Can I see her now?"

Abigail jumped in to respond. "You sure can. She's sitting in the sunroom at the back of the house. She was resting after lunch and we decided to come out here so she could have some time for herself. Go in through the door," Abigail pointed, "and follow the hallway to the kitchen. Through the kitchen you'll see the sunroom."

"Thanks." He moved toward the steps looking back with a smile on his face.'

After he went through the door Abigail looked at Micah and Ellie and made a comment on what a handsome man Zach was. Ellie agreed, took Micah's arm and they headed toward the porch, each silently praying that this would be a very special moment for Holly and Zach. It had been a difficult time for Holly since she'd been home. Recuperating was taking a little longer than she anticipated and she still occasionally woke up sometimes at night with nightmares about all that happened in Mexico. She had yet to take off the gold coin pendant that Gabriel gave her. Micah, Ellie and Abigail were engrossed in their own private thoughts about Zach's arrival. They prayed that Zach's presence would help Holly begin to feel like herself and help her move on with her life again.

~~~~~~~~~~

Zach found Holly resting on the couch and just looked at her which took his breath away. He turned to look out the window that she must have looked at a million times and marveled at the beautiful, peaceful scene that was before him. The majesty of the mountains touched his soul when thinking of God the Creator. He didn't want to wake her up but instinctively Holly felt someone in the room and began to wake up. Zach walked over and knelt beside the couch as she woke up.

Zach gently rubbed his knuckles alongside her cheek. Holly turned to look at him and her eyes lit up. "Zach," she said breathlessly.

"Hey Holly, I'm here."

Holly reached up to him and they hugged each other like they never wanted to let go. She clung tightly to him and said, "I have missed you so much." Tears welled up in her eyes. "I can't believe you're really here."

He pulled back to see her wiping away her tears. "I have missed you as well." He leaned over and gave her a long, passionate kiss.

After their kiss Holly touched her lips with her fingers as if awestruck. Then she reached over and ran her hand over his hair. It had been such a long two weeks without Zach and she could hardly believe he was with her now.

"Holly, will you marry me?" Zach blurted out while he still knelt beside her. "I had a plan how I would do this, but seeing you now I just don't want to wait another minute."

Without hesitation she answered him. "Yes, Zach, I would love to marry you as long as we don't have to wait too long. I want to be your wife as soon as possible."

"I'm all for that!" he said with excitement and joy. Then Zach kissed her again and reached into his pocket for the ring box. Holly was so excited as Zach handed her the box. She slowly opened the box. There nestled in the black velvet box was a beautiful oval shaped diamond with two smaller round diamonds on either side of the larger diamond. The diamonds rested on a gold tiffany setting and to Holly was the most beautiful ring she had ever seen. She handed the ring to Zach.

"Would you please put it on my finger Zach?" she asked with tears again.

Zach nodded with tears in his eyes as well. He took the ring and gently put it on her left ring finger at the same time noticing that she was wearing the bracelets he gave her in Mexico. Once the ring was on her finger, he kissed her finger and then dropped a feather kiss on her lips leaving Holly breathless again.

"You know Holly, when Gabriel was lying on your lap after he was shot you told him he had a heart like Jesus. I've thought about that over the last two weeks and I just want you to know that in you I have found someone who has a heart like Jesus. I thank God every day that He brought you into my life and that we will be one because of Him."

"Thank you Zach. I've actually thought the same about you. And I too thank God every day for you." She smiled.

"Can you help me up so we can go tell my family?"

Shyly Zach said, "We can but they won't be surprised. I asked Micah in Mexico for his permission to marry you. He knew I was coming today but I didn't want him to tell you so I could surprise you."

He got her crutches, helped her up, gave her one last hug and then they made their way out to the porch. Zach followed Holly as she made her way on the crutches. Oh how he loved that woman! He sent a silent pray and plea up to the Lord to help him be the best husband he could be to Holly. Zach gave God all the glory, honor and praise for blessing him with Holly and for the future they would have together.

EPILOGUE

Two years later Holly and Zach were in Mexico City visiting Pastor Abraham. It took the church those two years to complete the remodeling with the help of many additional mission teams. He invited them to attend the dedication of their new sanctuary since their team had started the remodeling process. After the dedication there was a reception which Holly and Zach attended and where they saw many of their friends. Those who knew them congratulated them on their marriage, saying how happy they were for them.

Pastor Abraham pulled Zach and Holly aside. He thought they might want to know the outcome of Miguel's trial. With some trepidation they told him they would like to know. So Pastor Abraham shared the outcome with them.

"As you know life here is very different than in American in many ways. Miguel was convicted of kidnapping and murder and was sentenced to 20 years in prison. He would not name any of his men however they seemed to have moved on so those streets are a lot safer due to Gabriel. As far as justice goes, Mexican prisons are very hard places to survive and men who harm little boys are often targeted. But, having said that, and I realize you already know this even Miguel is not beyond the reach of God's grace. Would it not be something if one day, because of Gabriel, Miguel would be saved and join Gabriel in heaven."

While hard to accept, Zach and Holly nodded in agreement. They knew Pastor Abraham had spoken the truth.

Later during the reception they decided to walk over to the church cemetery to see Gabriel's tombstone. Holly had picked up some flowers earlier. When they arrived she kneeled and laid the flowers near the stone. The inscription on the stone read "Gabriel, he reflected the heart and love of Jesus."

Holly looked at Zach and asked, "How did Pastor Abraham know to put that on Gabriel's tombstone?"

"I told him that would be what you would want."

Holly stood up and hugged Zach. "Thank you. It's perfect."

"You're welcome." Zach kissed her gently.

Holly rubbed her hand over the tombstone and then over her rounded stomach. Zach came up behind her and put his arms around her and over her pregnant belly.

Holly said, "Gabriel, we are having a little boy in a couple of months and we wanted you to know that we are going to name him Gabriel Micah Benson after you. You will always be a part of our lives and one day we will all be together in heaven. Thank you for giving me my life and because of you I am giving life in a few months."

Holly brought her hand to her lips and then laid her hand on the tombstone. "Until later Gabriel."

Holly and Zach walked back to the church very thankful that they could visit Gabriel's grave to share their wonderful news with him. Never did Holly imagine the pain and blessings that would come from the amazing mission trip she took two years ago or the impact one special little boy would forever have on her life!

Made in United States
Troutdale, OR
11/23/2024

25216574R00176